I0687044

PROTECTOR
OF MY
SOUL

J.K Rose

PROTECTOR OF MY SOUL

Copyright © 2022 by J.K Rose. All rights reserved.

No part of this publication may be reproduced, stored in a retrieval system or transmitted in any way by any means, electronic, mechanical, photocopy, recording or otherwise without the prior permission of the author except as provided by USA copyright law.

CHAPTER 1

"Demons are so simple-minded, it makes it too easy to track them. There's no fun in it anymore," I grumble to myself as I sit on top of a building across from a nightclub.

I can smell maybe thirty demons inside, but unfortunately, I can't just go in there and kill them all like I want to. When fear rolls off humans, it feeds the demons—almost like when you smell fresh coffee brewing in the morning, and just the smell alone can give you energy. Smelling fear for demons is like that but a hundred times more effective. You can even see the drool dripping down their chins.

Apparently, the fear makes their meat taste better too. Demons need to eat humans to stay powerful. I'm not sure if there is a demon out there that doesn't need to eat humans, but I highly doubt it… they are selfish beings. And the more fear-infused meat they eat, the stronger they are. So, they tend to eat humans alive and torture them before they either pass out from the pain or die from the loss of blood. I have never seen it happen nor could I just sit by and let it happen.

I shiver at the thought of being eaten alive and being as powerless as a human.

My phone starts to vibrate in my pocket, I know who it is without looking. "What are you doing up so late, Eric?"

"I could ask you the same thing, Alexandra." He knows I hate my full name. "Doesn't the church know you have school tomorrow?"

I roll my eyes. *Of course, they do... it's Wednesday,* I think to myself.

He goes off on one of his lectures, and I stop listening to him. Eric is my only true friend. People don't like me much—they know that there is something wrong with me, so they stay clear. I don't mind it anymore, I like my space. Eric has the power of God's Knowledge, so he knows everything—past, present, and sometimes the future. Only the strong K.G can see the future. Eric is the youngest to see the future but he can't really control it, he can only see it once in a while.

Eric is the only one in the school who knows I am an Angel Saviour. It's the worst-kept secret though since everyone knows what I do for the church. It helps build the fear for the other students... my gift is so powerful that I am able to be an Angel Saviour at seventeen.

Angel Saviours are a group of warriors that hunt down demons and rid this world of them. We are almost like a larger group of Van Helsings, but there are no other creatures we hunt. We are also like doorways for demons to leave this world. They have to pass through us and get sent to wherever they belong.

Eric is still blabbering on about how I need sleep and something about watching my back or needing backup, I'm not really sure.

Sighing, "Eric, you know I don't need as much sleep as most people, so I might as well be doing something useful."

"Yeah, you can be doing your mountain of homework, and it's just the beginning of the school year."

My face wrinkles up in disgust—I hate doing homework.

"Or you can be training for the Ultram."

I let out a groan. *I can't wait for this stupid thing to be over.* "To be fair, I am training and I still have until the end of the month before it starts."

He went off on me again.

The Ultram is only for the children who have the gift of God's Right Hand, which, unfortunately, I have. I have a great deal of power and responsibilities… blah, blah, blah. I have a huge amount of strength, speed, and I can look into people's minds and erase or change things in their minds if I have to, and I can do some spells. I can also read movements before they do them, so that helps me a lot while I'm fighting, but it's not that strong yet and doesn't work all the time. I can look into people's hearts to see if they have a crystal heart or a black one. I can also use some shields to defend the mind or the body.

If I win the Ultram, I'll get more gifts, but if I lose, I'll lose all of my gifts besides the basics like my wings and some strength. Losers become what we call God's Angels, which is the lowest man on the totem pole. There are some demi-angels that are just born God's Angels. They might be the lowest on the totem but they are free to do whatever they want, like get real human jobs. I don't know if I envy them or pity them.

A crow swoops in and starts to squawk at me. I glare at her and flip her the bird. The crow is my God's Creature and she has the ability to shapeshift into all of God's Creatures. Her name is Anna and she is a huge pain in my butt; she is a few years older than I am and always trying to boss me around. Normally, an Angel Saviour can choose their own G.C, but we both didn't have a choice in the matter. She is more like an older sister though and we fight like siblings.

With Anna and Eric squealing at me, I almost miss my target. His smell drifts up to me as he's throwing a skinny girl into the back of a cab.

"Not much to eat," I mumble to myself. "Hey, Eric, I have to go, I'll see you in class." I hang up before he says anything.

I stretch out my legs as I watch them tumble into the cab. Anna keeps pestering me, pulling on strands of my hair. I wave my hand at her, really hoping to hit her, but she dodges it. She's like an annoying little bug.

The cab takes off and I follow along the rooftops with Anna flapping her little wings fast to keep up with me. The cab keeps heading to the bad side of town where there are more abandoned buildings than anything—most of the windows are smashed or boarded up. The cab stops in front of an old apartment building. There is a huge condemned sign on the front door. The demon practically drags the girl out, she can't even stand on her own anymore. The cab driver doesn't say anything… just takes the money and drives off.

If only I could kill humans too. I snarl at the cab driver.

Once the cab disappears around the corner, the demon throws the girl over his shoulder and jumps up to the third balcony. I can smell about five of them in the apartment and four humans.

I let out a groan. *This job just got a lot harder than I wanted it to. Well, I haven't had a challenge in a while. Maybe I should call for some backup? Is this what Eric was talking about?* I laugh at myself. *I can still take them.*

I don't take my eyes off the building but I can hear Anna shifting to her human form. It almost sounds like paper ripping when she shifts.

"We should get backup," Anna whispers, coming up beside me.

"Go ahead and get backup I will wait here for them."

I can feel her glaring at me, "Do you think I am stupid? I know you won't wait… you'll wait for me to be far enough away that I can't hear you."

"Look, Anna, I don't need you anymore. You brought me to my target so I'll take the rest from here. You can go back to the school."

"Whatever." She screeches in my ear before leaving, "Want me to stay for backup?"

I shrug, "Doesn't matter." I look at her sideways, "Don't you have a breakfast date tomorrow? You should get some beauty sleep." I smirk.

She sighs, "Yeah, I should. The guy is too cute for me to stand him up. Call me if you need me to come back, okay?"

She takes off before I can answer her.

With barely thinking of it, my wings explode from my back. They are black, and when the moonlight hits them just right, there are flecks of purple. I am the only demi-angel with black wings, everyone else has white—another reason people stay away—but I love my wings nonetheless. They are larger and stronger than most demi-angels in my school, they almost drag on the ground if I'm not too careful.

Flying over to the apartment building and gracefully landing on the fourth floor, I slide open the window slowly, making sure none of them can hear me. The apartment looks like the people didn't even have time to pack before they were kicked out. There are pictures still hanging on the wall and the smell of moldy food and the stale room air is so bad, I need to sneeze.

I can hear the demons speaking in a low murmur, but then a girl lets loose a high-pitched scream. I feel my ears to make sure there's no blood coming out of them. The demons laugh as they are feeding off the fear that is rolling from her. Most angels can't stand the smell—the first time they ever smell it, they throw up. The smell of fear doesn't really bother me, if anything, it feeds me, too, but not in the same way. It feeds me to kill the demons. I'm not always hungry for it or addicted to it like they are.

The girl screams again and the fear that is waving off her almost knocks me down. I slam my fist into the floor as I come crashing into the apartment below me. All five demons freeze as the dust settles. I can't help but smile at them as their eyes pop out of their heads.

They are the mice to my cat game. I'm also a little disappointed that I didn't land on one. Only four girls are awake and screaming their heads off. I hate doing this, but I need to put a knockout spell on them. It will be more difficult to erase their minds later. For me to be able to do that, I just need to touch them. But the demons are in the way.

If I win the Ultram, I won't need to touch them... I will be able to do it from across the room. Just the idea of wanting them to be asleep would be enough. That would be a nice gift to have.

The demons are hissing at me, I unleash the God's Blades from my back, they are just regular swords but a Father from the church blesses it.

"Why couldn't we smell you coming, demi-angel?" the one I've been tracking asks.

To human eyes, they are beautiful men or women. They can shapeshift into whatever you desire sexually. They can get into your mind and find out what your greatest desires are and become them— it even works on us demi-angels, but to me, they are just black ash shaped like a man, with red eyes. I can see their sharp wolf-like teeth and their fingernails that look like daggers growing out of them (they are like really long cat claws), and that is all that I can see.

Father Jack says they are like this for me because I don't think there is a perfect match out there for me, which I have to agree with a hundred percent. The only way I can get my target is if my God's Creature is able to get something that the demons touch or own and I can track them down like a bloodhound.

They might look like puffs of black smoke, but they are as solid as a mountain, and if they get their claws in you, it hurts like hell.

I smile at him, "I think I would have to have a soul for you to smell me."

(I'll tell you later why I am soulless—I'm a little busy right now.)

"The soulless bitch," one whispers.

I love the names they come up with for me, but my favourite one has to be—

The leader hisses, "Hell among the angels."

My smile darkens, "It's so great to hear that you guys know me. I worked really hard to be this famous!" I squeal like a little schoolgirl as if this is all a game.

Since we have the ability to see everyone's hearts, even demons, we have the capability to save them and they can go to Heaven. That has not happened to me yet.

"So, who wants to be saved so they can go to Heaven?" I have to ask that or I get in a lot of shit and the church always knows when I don't.

They answer me with a growl. Demons don't need weapons, they have their claws, teeth, and strength.

I gave them a fair warning, now it's time to play!

I move faster than they were expecting. I'm able to disable two of them before they even blink. They lay unconscious on the dirty ground. Running behind the girls and sweeping my fingers along the line of girls, and their heads went limp and relaxed, and a few of them even began snoring.

You can feel the fear slipping from the room—a normal demi-angel would be able to breathe better. I react the same way as the demons do... I slow down and get a weird tingling in the back of my throat, but demons are hungry for it and crave it. Thankfully, I don't—yet.

I smile at them. "Do you find it's a bit crowded in here?" I ask. "Because I do."

I dash to where one of them is standing by the door and kick him through it. Watching him fly through the walls like a cartoon is very amusing, but I didn't hear one of them sneaking up and grabbing one of my wings. I let out a scream as he digs his claws into my beautiful wings. Trying to wiggle out of it, I attempt to sink my teeth in his arm (the angrier I get, the longer and sharper my teeth become—they almost look like a demon) but I can't reach him. He's using my wing as a leash and whips me onto the ground. My face kisses the floor, and losing my breath, the demon presses his knee into my back right between my wings. I go to hide my wings but he pulls on them and orders the other demon to hold my other one.

"You are going to regret this," I grunt out.

I can feel him laugh as he says, "This is going to hurt."

He takes his other hand and digs his claws into my back, and he's right… it hurts like hell. I spit out blood; it's the only colour in the room. I can hear the blood gushing out between his claws as he goes in deeper.

He laughs, "Call the Lord and tell him we have her," he orders the other demon, who's plucking feathers out of my wings.

The demon listens and gets up to make the call. The demon on top of me flips me over so fast that I didn't realize it until the back of my head is smashing into the floor. My wings are awkwardly twisted behind me, it almost feels like when your arm is twisted behind your back.

Idiot! I think to myself. *I know better than to leave my wings out!*

The demon on top of me runs one of his nails down my face. It's like an annoying cat scratch and I can feel the blood running down my cheek.

"You better hope that heals nicely," I warn him.

His tongue flicks out of his mouth, it's black and too long and pointy to be anything close to a human's. He bends down and runs his tongue along the cut. I don't think having ten showers will wash away how gross it has made me feel.

He stays by my ear and lets out a moan. I head-butt him from the side, which I am sure hurts me more than him, but it gets him away from me. He lifts his fist to get one shot before his buddy grabs his arm.

"The Lord ordered that we don't hurt her," he sneers at me.

The leader rips his arm away, "She started it." He leans down again.

As he's moving down, I hack a loogie right into his face, causing him to jerk far enough back that he doesn't notice something he did that is so very wrong. A smirk twitches at the edge of my mouth. Before he can even wipe the spit from his eyes, I wrap my legs around his throat and throw him to the ground. I can hear and feel his skull shattering to pieces. Just as I get up, the other demon jumps onto my back. I flip him over and run to get one of the God's Blades. The demon is able to grab a fist full of my hair, wrenching me back.

Lifting my blade over my head, I drive it into his throat, twisting the blade and making his head pop off like a dandelion. He falls backwards and hits the ground.

Moving quickly, I go through the hole in the wall to find the fifth demon. I begin digging around, moving a large piece of wall, and the demon grabs my foot and digs his claws into my ankle, making me drop to a knee.

"I'm getting really sick of your claws," I hiss at him. I take my blade and slice through his fingers as if they're butter.

His roar is so loud, it's shaking the building.

"I'm going to take my time with you," I threaten.

The demon looks at me—I can't tell if he's scared or pissed. "Don't you know mercy?"

Most angels kill the demons as quickly as they can so the demons don't have to suffer any longer than they have to, but I don't think like that... I think they should suffer as much as possible. Sometimes I can get information out of them, like where more of them are. If I can finish the job quickly, I move on to more demons. The church doesn't approve of me doing this because they are scared I'll wear myself out or get hurt. I think they don't like me doing this because I'm almost too valuable to lose.

Before I can start slicing him, I can hear one of the other demons waking up.

Grabbing the demon by the shoulder, I say, "It's your lucky day." And drive the God's Blade into his chest.

I throw the demon over my shoulder and rush to where the other demons are.

To get rid of a demon is simple, but not as simple as them turning into ash—that would be too easy. Tossing all the demons into a pile and carving a circle around them with my blade, and where the two ends meet, I drive my blade into the floor. I kneel in front of it with both of my hands on the hilt.

I bow my head and say a simple prayer, "Dear Lord, for I have found you more lost souls that need a door to the next world. Please use me as that door." My voice sounds different when I say this prayer; it's deeper and almost sounds like there is an echo to it.

A bright white light goes around the circle, and once it reaches the end, it travels up the blade, up to my arms, and the light gathers around my chest. It's so bright that you can't see anything. I tilt my head back, making my chest wide open as if I am welcoming the demons.

I can feel them entering through the door, but I can also feel all their pain, suffering, guilt, and the small amount of joy. Having five demons pass through me is a lot harder than just having one. The one that is waking up is being difficult and not following the light, but once you are in the circle, you can only leave through me.

It doesn't take him too long to pass through me, and once he does, I slump down with the light leaving me. I'm breathing heavily and sweat is soaking the back of my neck and back. I look at the circle and all that's left is five black crystal hearts for me to take. They are my trophies, which I take with pride.

CHAPTER 2

As I pick up the last heart, the girls are starting to wake up. The girl I followed here lives alone, so I call a cab to pick all five of them up to take them back to the girl's place. I'm able to erase all of their minds and replace their memories with ones that they all met at a hidden bar in the warehouse part of town, and that the bar keeps moving around so they will never find it again. They all thought it would be a great idea to go back to their new friend's place and crash.

I also gave them a lecture about not going to dirty clubs anymore and not trusting anyone, especially hot guys. Even though I don't like most humans, I still feel like I need to protect them because they are so weak and fragile. Demons are the nasty bullies and I'm the hero. I stay in the shadows of the apartment building and keep an eye on the girls.

They all stumble into the cab, laughing and joking around, except for one of the girls. She has a small smile and her blue eyes are wide. Her blonde curly hair is almost making me jealous of its perfection. Even though she just went out, she doesn't have a lot of makeup on. She is in dark jeans and a nice shirt, unlike the other girls who are in short, tight clothing. She doesn't look like she should be in with these types of girls.

She gets into the cab last—I swear she glances over at me for a split second. It's confusing, she's awake and yet there is no fear rolling off of her.

I know I should follow her, especially if she remembers me. I move to take a step but my whole body is screaming no.

I should just sleep here tonight. I should be healed enough by daybreak to walk back to the school.

"I think I saw a flea-ridden, mouldy mattress just down the hall. Well, I just grossed myself out, the slow shuffle back to the school; I'll have to deal with that girl later," I mumble myself out of sleeping here.

I'm just going to have to limp back to the school.

The school is just for the children with God's Gifts. There are seven main gifts:

1: God's Daughter (D.G): She is the chosen one to give humans hope. She is able to move things with her mind, great at healing, she can make a black heart pure again with just a simple touch.

2: God's Right Hand (G.R.H): He has some magic, the strength of a God's Guard. And amazing stamina, can heal and change people's hearts, but not as great as the G.D.

3: God's Guard (G.G): They are like the hulk, they are able to grow massive, have incredible strength, but instead of turning green, they turn yellow/gold. They also have very short tempers, almost like steroid junkies.

4: God's Knowledge (G.K): They are able to see the past, present, and sometimes the future. They get tired when they do so but they are very smart. The nerds of the world.

5: Voice of God (V.G): They can control you with their voice. They usually have to sing as a group to activate it. Their voices are beautiful to listen to when they are singing by themselves.

6: God's Creatures (G.C): They are able to shapeshift into anything God has created. They are normally more animal than angel.

7: God's Angels (G.A): They just have some strength and angel wings. They are at the bottom of the gift chart.

I'm sticking to the shadows, for if a human sees me, they will freak out… or any sane human should. I can feel chunks of drywall tangling in my short black hair, which is just long enough to fit into a ponytail. My lips taste disgusting, all I can taste is dirt and a bit of my blood. I don't even want to know what the rest of my face looks like.

And my poor clothes! I have to wrap my arms around my chest so tight to make sure my shirt stays on, and my jeans are all torn up and most of it is stained with blood. If I was going to start a new fashion, it would be called the homeless line.

If that doesn't scare the humans, my eyes sure will… they are so dark, they look all black. There is something unholy about them and my death glare makes people piss themselves. I love it when I wear makeup as it makes my eyes look a lot scarier.

Unfortunately, the school is half an hour outside of the city by car and, of course, I am on the far side of the city. If I didn't wreck my wings so badly, I could be home within minutes, but since it hurt so much just to move them, let alone flap them, I'm going to have to walk.

As I limp on, a car slows down to a crawl. "Why didn't you call for backup?" Anna's voice calls.

I sigh in relief—I could probably take on a human right now, but I'd rather not.

I drop into the passenger seat of her yellow sunfire.

"I was able to handle all five of them just fine," I mumble.

"Ha! I can smell the blood dripping from inside the car, that's why I was able to follow you here. You could have at least called for a ride!" she hisses.

I pull my phone out of my pocket and it's almost bent in half, with the screen cracked so badly that glass is falling out.

"I couldn't. Can you get me another tomorrow?" I ask.

15

"Another one! That's the second one this month!"

I moan, "So? It's my money, I can get as many as I want. Are you going to get me one or not?"

"Ugh! Yes!"

I look over to her, "Thank you, and thank you for picking me up."

She sighs, "You know I have your back."

Anna and I don't say anything to each other for the rest of the trip.

By the time we can see the school, the sun is starting to light up the sky, turning the sky a dark blue with sea green and cotton candy pink. The school grounds are fairly large, and a huge stonewall surrounds it. The only part that doesn't have a wall is the backside, and that's because it's on the cliff of a riverbank.

Inside of this is the school, which is three stories—the first floor is kindergarten to grade five, the second floor is six to nine, and the third floor is ten to twelve. On both sides of the school are the dorm rooms—one is for girls and the other one is for boys. Behind the girls' dorm is the teachers' dorm, and behind the guys' dorm is a building where guests stay.

The church is in the dead middle of the grounds. It's big enough to hold over five hundred people. My favourite thing about the church is all of the stained-glass windows.

Right beside the church is a large garden, and when everyone is still sleeping, I like to go in there and weed. It's peaceful and helps clear my head when I don't want to work out. There are two large gyms on the school grounds, but one is all mine—I built it with the money I get from killing demons. And then the fighting dome, which is right behind the school's gym, and there is a large underground garage. There are also lots of fields.

If Anna didn't come to rescue me, the way I would've had to sneak into the school without anyone seeing me, I would need to go through this maze of tunnels that are under the school and its grounds.

When I was younger, I thought I was old enough to go through it alone. I got lost, and as punishment, I was left down there. It took me three days to find my way out, and trust me, no one can hear you scream. I tried a lot. They have never told me if they were ever planning to come and find me. I know… dicks, right? They might be hard on me, but most of the time, I deserve it. Thanks to being stuck in these tunnels for so long, I know all of them like the back of my hand.

There are only four entrances on the school grounds—one in the church, one in the school, and there is one in each of the dorms. But there are only two entrances outside of the school grounds—one on the east and one on the west. On the east side, you have to fly in, so that would have been out of the question for tonight. On the west side, it's a small cave and you have to move three large rocks to get in.

When most kids have at least one of their parents to go back to, they stay in the dorms and I stay in the school's attic. It's not as bad as it sounds… it's almost like a small apartment and I don't have to share with anyone and it's quiet and perfect for me. And the best part is that I have a fireplace in it, so I have a big comfy chair, and if I get some time alone, I curl up and watch a movie on my large screen TV with surround sound.

Anna pulls into the parking garage, then gets out and helps me up to my room. Unfortunately, we have a lot of steps to climb.

"This would be so much easier if you could just carry me and fly up to my room," I hiss out as she pulls me up another flight of stairs.

She groans, "Well, I'm sorry that I'm not as strong as you."

"Shapeshift into a horse or something! Or what about an ass!"

She gasps and drops me, "Walk the rest of the way yourself!"

She shifts into her red hawk and flies away. She only got me up one floor, so I have three more to go!

"Bitch!" I grunt, pushing myself off the floor.

So, the reason I am soulless is because my own father sold my soul to the Lord of Hell himself before I was even born. My father apparently thought he could save my mother. Some angels get really sick when they are down here, but there are so few that get sick. So, a lot of them are worried about it. I think my mother was the tenth to have ever gotten sick, and once they get sick, there is no coming back from it. So, my father tried making a deal, to give Lucifer my soul so my father could keep his angel.

Once my mother found out what was going on, she was furious, apparently. So, on the night I was born (which was three am… Devil's hour—how ironic), my mother put my soul in a little doll and gave it to the church before Lucifer could get his hands on it. My mother died shortly after that and my father is nowhere to be found. The only thing that sucks about it is that I don't even know what he looks like, so I can't go and hunt his ass down.

As I unlock the door to the stairwell to the attic, I can hear people in my room.

I let out a groan, knowing who it is this early in the morning. I want to turn around and leave, but as badly as I'm torn up, I can't really get that far and I know they already heard this door open.

I take a deep breath before opening the door. "Hello, Father Jack and Anna. To what do I owe this pleasure of having you two in my room so early in the morning?" I ask, glaring at Father Jack.

Father Jack is rather tall, built like a pencil—his head looks like it's too small for his body. His eyes are too small for his head too; they are dark green with some brown in them. When he wears his glasses, it makes it look better but not a whole lot. He has short red hair, that's the eraser part. When I was little, I would always make fun of him, but now his look is more annoying to me for some reason.

Anna and Father Jack are related, I think Anna is his niece. Father Jack has a twin brother who was in the Angel Saviours. His brother passed away three years ago, so Father Jack is taking care of both of us and that is also the reason why we didn't get to choose to be together.

He turns around to look at me and his eyes shoot up in surprise. "Looks like you had some trouble last night. You should have called for backup. You are only qualified to hunt one or two demons at a time, not five."

Anna is sitting in my chair as if she owns the place. She fidgets a little, looking guilty.

I shrug, "Obviously I handled it without anyone, so you can leave now."

Demons sometimes hunt alone, but most of them hunt in a pack—it's safer that way. They are that scared of us demi-angels, so most Angel Saviours hunt together, too.

I set my black hearts on a shelf, which is the only thing that separates my bedroom from the rest of the place. If I had no hearts on the shelf, you could see my bed and right out the large window. I watch the sunset almost every night that I'm in here. To this day, it still takes my breath away. But with over five hundred hearts on my shelf, you can barely see what colour my sheets are.

My shoulders drop, wanting them out of here, "So, why are you here?"

"Am I not allowed to come and check up on you? Anna informed me that you were breaking the rules again."

I shoot a glare at her; she usually throws me under the bus. I'm used to it, she's the goody-good and she pays me back later.

I bark a laugh, "Since when do you care if I come back or not?"

I know he cares about me, I'm just not in the mood to deal with him.

He narrows his eyes at me. "I promised your mother I would take care of you. And I also came up here to see if you need anything and to give you your months' pay." He drops a wad of cash on the table.

I pick it up and count it. I have to give thirty percent of all my earnings to Anna. I get paid less than normal Angel Saviours warriors because I have to pay for school and the entire extra cost, but I kill more than most of them in a month so it doesn't bother me.

"Why is it less than last month? I killed more this time around," I ask, counting it again.

"Because we've had to replace the gym twice this month," he simply answers.

Oh, right. I smirk at the thought of wrecking my gym.

"I also came to tell you that one of the God's Right Hand is here, he showed up last night while you were out and I would like you to show him around."

My nostrils flare. "What! Why is he here so early? And I refuse… get someone else to do it! Get Jennifer to do it! It seems more suitable for the God's Daughter to do it. Or even Anna, she can hit on him and keep him distracted. She hasn't had a boyfriend in a week, so she's probably lonely."

The black hearts start to cling together like they are encouraging my behaviour.

Anna stands up, "How dare you talk to me like that! I will never tempt a G.R.H!"

Yeah, right! You're just saying that because Father Jack is here, I think to myself.

We both glare at each other.

Father Jack groans, "That's enough, you two, it's too early to be dealing with this right now and, Alexandra, I wasn't asking. I was telling you, and if you don't do this, I won't let you go out of the school grounds for a month," he says as he calmly gets up and walks to the door. "I'll get one of the Sisters to come up and bring you more clothes."

"Don't bother," I say, snarling at him.

He lets out a sigh. "This isn't a punishment, Alexandra. Come to my office after school. I do care about you, don't forget that," he says as he leaves.

Anna is waiting for Father Jack to be out of earshot. "I'm sorry you have to deal with a G.R.H., they probably aren't going to be nice to you. And if I could distract them, I would, but I am already on a short leash from my last fling. And if I got caught with a God's Right Hand…"

We both know what will happen if she and a G.R.H get caught. We both shiver at the thought of getting our wings cut off.

I smile at her, "I know and I appreciate it anyway."

"But if you need anything else, just let me know. I'll be looking for another target for you today, but loner demons are getting harder to find. They are getting smarter and staying in parties." She places a hand on my shoulder, "You have to team up soon."

I can't help but think of what happened to me in the past when I was training to become an Angel Saviour. I had to go into a team. No one wanted me as they thought they would have to babysit me, and asking a worrier to babysit is like asking a fish to breathe on land. They are just not equipped with the equipment to do it.

They didn't want to have me with them, so they thought they could scare me and told me to storm into a nest of demons. They, of course, told me that they would be right behind me, but as I ran in, I never felt so alone. I was young and stupid and didn't know better that I shouldn't trust anyone. As I stormed the nest, ten demons were coming at me. I remember the room smelt of fear and death. By the time the other A.Ss came in, I already disabled two of them but more demons were rushing in all different directions. The A.Ss didn't come and help me right away, they just stood by the door in shock that I was still standing and fighting. I was badly wounded, I could feel my energy draining and I was becoming worried about the Sister who had my doll. If I was this close to passing out, the Sister must be almost out of soul

Once the other Angel Saviours snapped out of it and finally started to help, my will to keep fighting dropped, I knew they wouldn't let me die after this. I passed out and woke up in the hospital.

To this day, I don't understand how I was able to fight them all off, then I almost get my wings ripped off when I just fight five. Ever since that day, I didn't trust anyone with the A.S. Father Jack only made me work with them a few more jobs, then figured I could take care of myself, even though I told him that countless times.

Anna notices the darkness flash through my eyes. She sighs and leaves, saying she has to get some beauty sleep.

Anna and I fight a lot, but it's more like sisterly fighting, she's the closest thing I have to one. I just wish she wouldn't think of me as a little sister. She's only two years older than me.

"Don't forget to get me another phone!" I yell at her as she leaves.

She just waves her hand.

CHAPTER 3

I shut the door behind her and look over to the clock. It's twenty minutes to six. I let out a groan, I don't need a lot of sleep but I do need some… I don't see me having any tonight though.

I call Eric on my landline (yes, I have one! I break my cell phone too much not to have one) and ask him to come up—he's the only student who has ever been to my place. Eric gives a soft knock on the door and just walks in.

He has brown curly hair that almost hangs in his eyes. His eyes are milky from being blind. He always says that God lets him see more than eyes would have ever let him see. He also has really bad acne and is a little on the chubby side, but he's gotten thinner as he's gotten older. When we were younger, he would get picked on all the time for it—it didn't help that he's shorter than me too.

I saw him getting bullied one day when I was skipping class and I tried to ignore them, but when they knocked him down, Eric looked over to me. I knew he couldn't actually see me but I had a feeling he was staring at me for help, and ever since then, he hasn't left my side. I don't mind him as much as everyone else; I need him as much as he needs me. I just hope he never realizes that he's better off not being my friend. I am a very selfish person.

He sniffs the air, and by the look on his face, regrets it instantly. "Dear Lord, you smell horrible," then he glares at me. "You didn't listen to me, did you? You went in and fought those demons on your own." There is no question behind it.

I flinch, even though he can't see me.

I then give him a fake chuckle. "I need you to sew me up, please," I say, taking off my shirt and turning my back to him.

You would think I would be uncomfortable with a boy touching my skin with my shirt off, but I am not worried about Eric... I'm not his type in the slightest. It also helps that he can't see me. Normally, I would still have my sports bra on, but where the demon's claws went in, they shredded my bra too, so I need to take that off. I am sitting in my kitchen exposing my chest to the chilly room.

He comes over slowly and slides his hand over my back, I can barely feel him, "Oh, my! Alex, why did you let them get the jump on you?"

"Hey, I didn't let it happen! Can you fix it, or do I have to go to the nurse?"

He lets out a grunt, "Of course I can, it's already healing."

"I know, but I can feel it bleeding still and I can't go to class with it doing that."

He's starting to poke around it.

I let out a gasp, "Do you think you can be nicer about it?" I hiss through my teeth.

He whispers, "Sorry," and starts to sew my back up.

"What about my wings? Do you think I can fly tonight?"

"I don't recommend you flying tonight. Maybe in a few nights. You have some feathers missing and it will take longer for them to grow back."

I groan, "A flightless angel."

Eric laughs. "Maybe the church will let you have a night off!"

"Ha, I doubt it, there's nothing wrong with my legs and arms. They also want the streets to be as clean as possible before the Ultram."

He clicks his tongue, "There is more than one Angel Saviour warrior and I don't see anyone working as hard as you! Also, if the demons are smart at all, they would stay clear because there will be so many more demi-angels in this area in the next few months."

He begins pulling my skin and I can't help but flinch a little.

"Why do you think I called you last night? I saw you pinned by two demons. I even told you that, but you weren't listening to me yet again."

This time, I flinch at the harshness of his voice—he rarely talks to me like that.

"I am sorry. I will listen to you from now on," I promise.

He chuckles, "Lying is a sin." He pauses for a second, "Did Father Jack tell you that there is a G.R.H here?"

"Ugh, yeah. Father said I had to show him around this morning. Did you see him?"

"I could hear the girls swarm him like annoying flies and the guys were complaining about not getting any dates for a while."

Ugh, I bet he's an arrogant prick, I think to myself.

He finishes the last knot, "Go and have a shower, then I'll put gauze over it."

My body is already starting to stiffen up, "I'd rather not meet another G.R.H when I feel like this." I go into the bathroom.

I don't bother looking in the mirror; I slowly take my jeans off and turn on the water. The water stings my back, but I am getting used to the pain and watch the water turn a reddish brown. There's more dirt and ash on me than I thought. There are some pieces of rubble in my hair that are really tangled; I almost gave up getting them out. I stay in the shower until the water runs clear and the smell of bacon is calling my name.

Wiping off the mirror as best as I can, the steam is still hanging in the air even with the water off. I have a huge bruise on my cheek with a long cut along my cheekbone, and it's really red from me scrubbing at it in the shower. I can still feel the demon's tongue on it, but it's already starting to scab.

I leave my hair down to hide it the best I can and get dressed in the school's uniform. I refuse to dress in the females' uniform, so I get to wear the males'. Which is just a pair of black dress pants with a white long-sleeve shirt and the collar is gold. We have to have it tucked in but I never do. I don't like how it feels. The uniform also comes with a gold tie but it looks more like piss-yellow. I always wear it loose. I get in shit for it every day but I still wear it how I like it. Our church's crest is stitched over the heart. It's a gold God cross with two swords in an X behind it stitched in red. I'm surprised that it hasn't burned into my skin yet.

As I walk into the main room, I see that I only have an hour before my dreaded day starts.

Eric feels my mood and shakes his head, "I don't understand how they can treat you so badly, you're the youngest Angel Saviour and you have more black hearts than most of them, and you just took on five demons by yourself!" I watch his nostrils flare.

I can't help but smile, "Hey, if I had help last night, I would have had to share my hearts with them."

"Greed is a sin, Alex, and that greed could have gotten you killed!" Eric says through his teeth.

I shake my head, "For someone who is so smart and knows everything about me, you should realize I can't die."

He turns towards me, "I know your body can't die, and I know where your soul is. I just don't like sewing you up every other morning. I can't do anything to help you, besides your homework!" He pulls a roll of paper from his back pocket and hands it to me.

It's my homework all finished. "I can't believe there is so much homework already. It hasn't even been two weeks since school started, and you're more than just here to do my homework, Eric. You're the only smart one here to become my friend. I'm sure if I didn't have you to talk to, I would go crazy and have to unleash my gifts upon the school. So, really, you're saving everyone here and they don't even know it." I put my arm around him, "You're braver than anyone here."

He gives me a smile, "You're so full of shit."

I point my finger at him, "Oh, you swore!"

That makes him laugh, but as soon as I forget how crappy my life really is, my phone rings and Father Jack wants to see me before classes start.

We clean up breakfast and head down. I still have to take the stairs slowly but my body isn't screaming as loud. As we enter the school hallways, no one is in them yet—still too early. Eric's first class is in the opposite direction of Father Jack's office, so we say bye and go our separate ways.

I am really grateful that his office is on the third floor. I don't even knock as I walk in. His office is rather plain. On one side, there is a full-wall bookcase; on the other side is a very old, very comfy couch that I've spent more time on than anywhere else. And behind his big dark wood desk is a stained window of an angel with her face hidden behind her long black hair, standing over a demon with the God's Blades over her head. When I was a kid and even now, there was something rather creepy and eerie about it. I've never liked it, yet I can't help but stare at it because of how beautiful it is.

I don't pay any attention to Father Jack; I just go straight to the couch and sink onto it.

God, I love this couch.

Without opening my eyes, I ask, "What do you want?"

Clearing his throat, he says, "I wanted you to meet Jayden Lantion, and I wanted you to do it before school starts."

Opening my eyes slightly, I see broad shoulders and golden ruffled hair. As he stands and faces me, he is well above six feet tall, with crystal blues eyes and nice tan skin. His shirt almost looks too small for him—I'm sure if he flexes, it will rip. He looks like a surfer boy.

Looking him up and down, I say, "Well, you're a perfect specimen, aren't you?"

He smiles. "You must be Alex. Father Jack has told me so much about you and I've heard about you since I was a little kid."

I give him a blank look before turning my icy glare on Father, "I didn't have much of a break before you called me down here to fucking lead him around." I can feel my canines growing.

"Alexandra!"

I stand up and start to walk toward the door, "Just add it to the rest of the Hail Marys."

I can hear Jayden whispering, "Sorry," before taking off after me. We are only silent for a few seconds before he starts speaking.

I can feel him eyeing me, "So, you're the soulless bitch, hell among us angels, I thought you would be ugly or maybe taller."

I don't look at him, but I smile to show him my fangs. I'm hoping it'll shut him up but it seems to make him more fascinated.

"How many black hearts do you have? Do they call you soulless because you are or do you just act like it?"

Oh, God, please help me!

"Look, I don't want to be your friend, you will be my competition at the end of the month. So, stop being creepy."

His eyes twinkle as if this is all a game, "Do you really think that you can win the Ultram?" he asks, giving me a grin.

He goes to move my hair but I grip his hand and fling him over my shoulder, jumping onto his chest and shoving my knee into his throat.

Snarling at him and at the pain in my back, I say, "Listen here, you little prick, I will crush you and anyone who thinks they can stand in my way."

"Alex!" my name rings in the hallway. I look up to see Jennifer standing in the middle of the hall. Before I can even move off Jayden, I'm flying against the lockers and stay there like a fly on a sticky paper.

Jennifer has the power to move objects with her mind, it is one of the only defensive powers a God's Daughter has. Jennifer has long, wavy black hair that flows past her butt (yes, I'm jealous of her hair…

I can't grow my hair or it will just be a leash for the demons), her eyes are crystal blue and her dark skin makes them stand out even more. The only thing bad I have to say about her is that she has thin lips and a flat ass—besides that, she is absolutely beautiful.

When we were younger, we were close friends. Her father is a very important man… always busy, I forget what he actually does, but I know it's important. So, Jennifer would stay at the school most of the time. The first time we met was in the library and we wanted to read the same book, but we had to share, and after that, we became inseparable for a few years. Once I turned ten, Father Jack put me into my training and Jennifer in hers, so we drifted apart but we were still pleasant to each other for a few more years. And now we don't even say hello to each other, not even the casual head nod in the hallway.

"Okay, Jennifer, I'm off of him, you can release me now," I grunt.

She ignores me and goes straight for Jayden, "Are you okay? Alex can be real harsh at times."

"Hey, Jennifer! How have you been?" Jayden asks.

She smiles at him, "Oh, I've been good! Nice to see you again."

They have the conversation like I'm not even here!

"Oh, before I forget!" Jayden drops to one knee, puts his fist over his heart, and bows his head.

"I pledge myself to thee Jennifer to win this Ultram for her. So I can protect her and her gifts as she heals these lands."

Jennifer giggles, "Rise, God's Right Hand, and I pray thee fights bravely and truthfully in the Ultram."

I roll my eyes at them.

We have to pledge ourselves to Jennifer if we want to be part of the Ultram. I did mine so long ago, I hardly remember it—once I found out I was going to be my friend's bodyguard, I ran straight to her and bent to one knee and said the same words Jayden just said. Jennifer laughed and called me silly and said she'd pick me but I doubt that now, no matter how gifted I am.

She's still ignoring me and helps Jayden onto his feet. "I expect you to do well in the Ultram." She smiles.

He makes himself look all bashful, "Jennifer, I was wondering if you wouldn't mind showing me around the school? Alex was doing it before she jumped me."

She's beaming, "I would be happy to."

They start to walk away.

"Would you mind showing me the library? I asked Alex but she said it was just for girls and G.Ks," Jayden says, acting all innocent.

Jennifer looks back at me and I can see it in her eyes that she knows he is lying and is sorry for putting me through this. I just shrug the best I can with being still pinned against the lockers. Once they round the corner, she releases me, almost bashing my knee into the ground. I stand up and turn towards my first class. The hallway is already filling up, I can feel their eyes on me… it's easier to ignore them as I get older. I'm sure I'm so used to it that if people weren't gawking at me I would notice.

As I walk into class, Mr. Daniel is writing on the board. He is my English teacher and trainer. I also have a schoolgirl crush on him, he has chocolate brown hair just long enough to run my fingers through, dark blue eyes with flecks of brown in them, and has just enough scruff on his face to make him look rugged but not sloppy. He's about a head taller than me, and with all the training we do, he's in really great shape. It's hard not to drool on him, especially when he is really close and I can smell his cologne. I know I am not the only girl here who thinks the same thoughts.

His muscles are moving under his shirt. I can stand here all day and watch them work. When he takes off his shirt when we are training, I have to fight so hard to keep my mind on the task and not on the idea of licking the sweat off his bare chest.

I give my head a shake, trying to get the image out of my head.

"I think this is the earliest you've ever been to my class," he says, keeping his back to me. "So that means the church had you out all night and you haven't gone to sleep."

"Yet," I finish for him. "And it wasn't as bad as you think."

He turns around; his eyes narrow at my cheek, "Wasn't that bad? When are you going to start trusting the Angle Saviours? They are supposed to be your brothers and sisters. And I can smell the fresh wounds on you halfway down the hall."

"Well, thank God I had a shower then. And the Angel Saviours are going to stab me in the back before the demons do. The demons at least want me to live."

He shakes his head, "You shouldn't be alone."

"Why should I work in a party? I am not a good little white sheep that follows the leader." I'm trying to keep calm, but my temper is spiking and my canines are poking my bottom lip.

Amusement dances in his eyes, "Well, we don't need any more white sheep, we need more black wolves, but even wolves run in packs, Alex."

"Okay, fine, next time I fight five demons, I'll give you a call."

"You fought five of them! Alone! Why did Anna leave you alone?"

I flinch. *Damn it. I really need to learn to keep my mouth shut.* "Look, I'm sorry but it's just easier for me to be alone. And it's not like I can die anyway, and if Anna stayed around, I would just be worried about her."

He lets out a sigh, "I know that, Alex."

I give him a smile. "So, there is nothing to worry about."

He moves to the front of his desk and sits on it. "I think we need to set you up with your own party. I think that will be a new challenge for you."

I raise my eyebrow, "You want me to lead my own party?"

He nods. "Yes. That way, you'll have your own sheep."

I bend over and laugh at the idea of that happening.

As he is wiping his face in frustration, I see the chain around his neck. I move so fast that he doesn't know what's happening until I rip it off and it hurts me like hell to do so. Not just because I'm still healing, but because I jerk 'IT' too hard and that pain is worse than any other pain I can get.

He jerks back, "What the hell!"

I glare at him, "Why do you have this 'Thing'?"

Rolling his eyes, "You know that we all have to take turns with it, Alex, and I am more than happy to do it."

Taking a closer look at him, he has dark circles under his eyes, and his hair is a little more messy than normal, I'm sure I can't even run my fingers through it. He looks like he is worn right out like he's the one that's been up all night fighting, and it's my entire fault.

"No, you will not. You will tell me when it's your turn and give it to me. I definitely don't want you to have 'it' when I go out. You know that when I get hurt, it makes things worse for whoever is holding it." I look down at it, "I don't need you hating me too."

Before he can say anything, the bell rings and students start to pour in. I just turn to my desk and sit down.

CHAPTER 4

I look down at the thing in my hand, it's such an ugly doll and, unfortunately, my soul is in it. The doll can fit perfectly in my hand, and its eyes are two different size buttons—the smaller one is white and the larger one is black. Its smile looks like someone has sewn the mouth shut. It doesn't have any clothes or anything, just a black heart on it; the colour of the heart has gotten darker over the years, it used to be red. This doll has to be older than seventeen years; so the fact that it's holding up this well, I am surprised. The only thing we have added to it is a chain that was sewn into its back.

That's the worst pain I have ever felt in my life. Father Jack didn't know I would feel anything, let alone that severe. I was in the first grade, and it was during class. Out of nowhere, I dropped out of the desk, screaming bloody murder. I kept clawing at my back, trying to make it stop. It felt like someone was stabbing me in the back over and over again, and like someone was pulling barbwire through each hole. I could feel the blood running down my back and soaking my shirt. That's the first time I ever cried… and the last.

I remember my classmates looking at me like I was getting possessed; my teacher was freaking out, she pushed her hand on my back to try to stop the bleeding but that made the pain worse. She didn't know what to do with me. Daniel, who was on the elementary side doing volunteer work, heard me scream and he scooped me up and ran to the nurses. Apparently, I passed out halfway there.

When I woke up, that was the first time I saw Father Jack look horrified. He apologized and promised me that he didn't know it would cause me so much pain. I didn't move from my bed for weeks, it felt like I was paralyzed. On my back, I have the matching stitching pattern to the one on the doll, where the needle went into it. It is one of my tiniest scars but definitely the most painful.

Once in a while, it will start bleeding randomly. No one knows that it does that, maybe Eric knows but it's not from me telling him. I think it's a sign of weakness and it also shows how much the stupid doll affects me.

I don't know if it's possible to hate your own soul, but I'm sure I do. If I ever get to see my mother, I would ask her two questions—number one would be, "What did you see in my father?" And number two would be, "Why did you pick this ugly thing to put my soul in?"

She already knew what your soul was going to look like, that asshole inside of me said.

My soul needs to be near another full human (a normal person with a soul in their body) or I will start to get sick then die. There is a whole lot more to it, I'm just not going to get into it. If the person holds onto it for more than a week, the doll will have taken too much of the person's soul. It's literally sucking the life right out of them and they will eventually pass away, but first, they hate me and try to kill me.

The church and I learnt that the hard way. I can hold onto the doll for three to four days if I don't get seriously hurt, and I try to wear it as much as possible but I don't want to die either so I end up sucking people's souls. Maybe one day I'll end my life for the sake of everyone else, but I'm too selfish now.

Someone bumps into my desk and lets out a snarl, which echoes over everyone's chatter. I look up to see Jayden staring at me, looking shocked. Then the class breaks into a snicker. Jayden looks like he is trying to hide a snicker too.

He looks down at the doll, "I didn't know it was show and tell today or I would've brought something."

The class goes up in a roar. Mr. Daniel barks at them to settle down but there is still some giggles going on. I can feel Mr. Daniel's eyes on me but I'm not going to look up, I don't want his pity. I just put the doll around my neck and tuck it under my shirt.

The chair next to me moves across the ground; I look over to see Jayden sitting down. There are three other empty seats in the room, but of course, he has to take that one.

Just as I begin to say something, this high-pitched voice speaks out.

"Jayden, you should come and sit over here. Alex is a nobody and she is more beast than angel." She leans over, more so she doesn't have to raise her voice and also to make her small boobs a little bigger. "You will have more fun over here anyway." She gives him a wink.

The girl looks like a little mouse that I can just step on, with mouse-like hair too, she has on way too much makeup and the buttons on her shirt are undone one too many.

He looks like he's about to turn them down but I need to put in my two cents… I can't help it.

"You know she's right, Jayden, you will have more fun over there," I say loud enough for the class to hear me. "I might be too much of a nobody for you, but umm…" I turn my icy glare on her. "I'm sorry, you know my name but I don't know yours. Who are you again?"

Her jaw just drops and her mouse look-a-like's trying to coo her. Jayden looks amused and there is a bit of approval. I curl my lip at him and turn my attention back to Mr. Daniel.

For the first time ever, Mr. Daniel can't hold my interest. I find myself eavesdropping on Jayden's and the mouse girl's conversation. It's mostly nonsense, but the only thing I care about is what his next classes are. I hold in a groan when he says he has math, then chemistry, lunch, training/gym, and his last class is just a spare.

He has the next two classes with me and thank the Lord that Eric is in those classes too. He is the only reason I am passing either of them. I am horrible at math, even though I have Eric, I am still getting a 'C-'. I am getting an A in chemistry but that's because Eric is my partner and he does most of my work. I do the entire cutting and measuring though, so it kind of works out.

I finish my work in English way before anyone else, so I try to sleep, but as soon as I close my eyes, the bell rings. Even though I don't want to go to math, I rush out of the room so Mr. Daniel doesn't have a chance to talk to me. I'm going to see him after lunch anyway to train. Where most students have two classes after lunch, I just have my training, which I am more than happy with.

Most students follow the current of the hallway like good little fishes. I walk down the middle and they go around me like the rock I am, if not, I knock them out of my way.

Sometimes the God's Guard (G.G) try and challenge me; they are usually big, arrogant, thick-headed, with a caveman way of thinking, certain they can take on anyone. They can turn into giants twice their size and their attitude grows with them. They act like the Incredible Hulk to sum it up. The stronger they are, the longer they can stay in this form... the only thing they are really good at is being a wall when you need one or a guard dog since they can be very protective.

I make it to math with seconds to spare. Our math teacher is Sister Willems; she is a very horrible woman who hates me. She is about a foot taller than anyone I know, with long bony fingers that linger over everything. Her eyes are sunken in, there are dark purple circles all around them, and when she talks, you can see her crooked, stained and missing teeth. She has so many wrinkles and loose skin around her mouth, it looks like she is forever frowning. The way she looks and acts, everyone calls her the bone keeper. If you shut one eye and squint really hard with the other, you could almost see that she was beautiful once.

To prove she really hates me, as soon as the bell rings for class to start, she asks me to solve the question on the board and I'm not allowed to say it out loud for Eric to answer. I just stare at the board and, in two seconds, all of the God's Knowledge have their hands up, and about a minute later, the rest of the class have their hands up.

"Miss. Alexandra, are you really this stupid or are you just choosing not to answer?" she doesn't give me a chance to answer. "You may go into the hallway and finish this grade one math booklet. If you do not finish, you'll be spending the rest of the year in their class," she spat the words at me.

If the class wasn't so scared of her, they would be laughing, but they remain quiet with smirks on their faces.

As I grab the booklet, I say, "Sister Willems, would you like a tic-tac or do you like having your breath smell like mouldy shit?"

She bares her teeth at me, "Get the hell out of my classroom!"

I give her my sweetest smile, "Gladly," and slam the door behind me.

I have no clue why she hates me so much; I am a delight to have in the classroom, I think to myself.

I finish the booklet in about twenty minutes, so I sleep for the rest of the class. It was the best nap I've ever had during math, and since I made her so mad, she is taking it out on everyone in there. I can hear her yelling at everyone, giving them hard questions. I would feel bad for Eric if I knew he didn't love every minute of it and she doesn't bother coming out to check up on me. She is also the teacher that doesn't believe that students should go to the washroom during their class hour, so no one bothers me, which is quite nice.

The bell startles me awake and I'm too slow to get to the door before the wave of students pours out, so I just lean against the wall to wait for them to clear the way.

Jayden is at my side within seconds of leaving the room.

"If you need a tutor, I am really great a math," he says softly.

It catches me off guard; I'm having some trouble finding my words.

"I already have a tutor, thank you," I say as politely as I can, but there's still some chill to it.

He lets out a frustrating sigh, "Look, Alex, I am sorry for this morning. You remind me of someone very special back home… really special."

I can't help it that my eyebrows shoot up. G.R.Hs aren't allowed to have feelings for any other person besides the G.D (God's Daughter).

"And you had the scratch on your cheek and I was moving your hair out of the way so I could get a better look at it." He almost looks sad and concerned.

For a second there, I almost believe him… or maybe I want to believe him. I don't answer him; instead, I just make a mad dash to Sister Willems. I'd rather deal with her than him.

As I hand it to her, she rips it out of my hands so fast, I still have the corner of the booklet.

No more soul-sucking doll for you.

I don't wait around for her to give me any more punishments and head to chemistry. By the time I get to the classroom, Eric is already at our desk reading one of his special books. I make myself comfortable in my seat; I realize that all the other tables have partners and that Jayden will have to sit with one of us. I know what table he'll choose because my luck isn't that good.

I let out a groan.

"What's wrong now? Is Sister Wilts looking for her glasses again? Or is there a big spider somewhere close?" Eric asks without stopping his fingers.

"No, Jayden is going to have to sit with one of the tables and I have a feeling he is going to sit with us."

Eric chuckles, "Maybe it will be like that vampire book where they meet and fall in love in chemistry."

Almost gagging at the thought, "He is too much of a good boy for me."

He laughs and goes back to his book and I go back to pretending I understand the notes Eric gave me. It looks like a code of numbers and letters that don't make sense and it makes my head hurt.

"So, beautiful… it looks like we are partners." His voice makes a shiver go down my back and not in a good way.

I look up at him to see his smug little face.

"Sister Wilts said I could choose which table I sit at."

"Hi, Jayden, I am Eric," he says, trying to be nice.

"Hey, Eric, nice to meet you," Jayden says, sticking out his hand.

Eric's lip twitches, "If you are sticking out your hand for me to shake, I can't see it."

Jayden's smile drops.

Eric waves him off, "God gave me the gift of Knowledge, so I see plenty without my eyes."

"Oh, awesome about being G.K, now I see why Alex made friends with you."

This pisses off both of us.

"Well, I made friends with her because she saved my butt from a couple of dicks like you pushing me around. So, from that day on, I follow her around, making sure I can repay her and so no one else bugs me because if they do, they are going to have to deal with her."

Jayden looks a little ashamed, "Oh… well, I'm sorry for the comment, I was just trying to make a joke."

"Well, it wasn't funny," I say coldly.

I hadn't noticed Sister Wilts walking up to us, "Is everything fine, dears?"

Sister Wilts looks like a plump grape; she's short, fat, but very sweet. Her eyes are magnified by her bottle glasses; her skin looks like she is always blushing. She is also one of the only teachers here that doesn't hate me, but I don't think she can ever hate anyone as she always has a smile for everyone.

"Oh, sorry, Sister Wilts, we are just bringing Jayden up to speed," Eric says, thinking fast on his feet.

Sister Wilts' face lights up and she claps her hands, "Oh, that is just splendid! Well, I will leave you to it." She turns to Jayden, "Thank you for being here and good luck with the Ultram."

He gives her a smile and she's off to the next table.

The rest of the class is uneventful and rather boring. Eric did most of the talking and explaining to Jayden. For the first time, I didn't fall asleep during the class—even Sister Wilts commented on it several times.

The lunch bell rings and the river of students starts again.

"Do you want to come up to my room for lunch or would you prefer to be alone? I'm going to go and have a nap so it doesn't matter to me," I ask Eric.

"Your room has better food than the cafeteria."

So, we make our way up to my room and all I can think of is my bed. My bed is the most expensive thing in my apartment—it feels like I am sleeping in a warm cloud. As we get to the room, I don't even bother to eat anything. I just fling myself onto the bed. It really hurts my back but I don't care.

I might have five hundred black hearts, but I have one white heart. It's my mother's. Most angels' hearts are under the churches, but as a gift, Father Jack gave me my mother's. I have it on my nightstand with a light under it and it makes light rainbows everywhere. I always turn the light on when I feel lonely and it feels like she's here. I know she's not really, but it's a nicer thought than being alone.

As soon as my eyes are closed, the dream I always have finds me in an instant.

I am flying through the night sky, and nothing can stop me as I am flying up and up. I want to touch the stars but then something grabs my ankle, I look down to see black hands grabbing at my ankle; it feels like they are branding me with their handprints and start to pull me down. The closer I get to the ground, the more hands reach out for me. I fight back and try to fly up but I can't get them off me. The pain is just as bad as someone messing with the doll.

"He's sending him, he's coming!" they all laugh and repeat it over and over again.

As we hit the ground, there is clapping all around and then the pain rings through me.

CHAPTER 5

I sit straight up, gasping for air—I've had that dream for as long as I can remember. The clapping is still going on. I look up to see Eric staring at the black hearts and they are moving a lot more than ever before. I can see his eyes through the shelf and they are moving rapidly as if there is more than just the crystal hearts in front of him... he's seeing something.

I move slowly toward him. I've never been near him before when he is having a vision; I have no clue what to do. I put a hand on his shoulder and his head just snaps and stares at me, then his mouth starts to move but nothing comes out.

"Eric?" I ask, really worried.

This doesn't feel right, I think to myself.

I keep talking, "If you can just nod to say that this is normal, that would be great."

I didn't want to say the last part—I want to say, he's scaring me. I've never been scared for someone else's life before.

His body starts to shake and twitch; blood is coming out of his nose and ears and his eyes are fluttering. He clasps and I catch him before he can hit the ground. I pick him up and pain goes up and down my back. I push my wings out, my teeth grinding together. Opening my window, it's big enough to fit both of us through. I land somewhat gracefully with my broken wings.

The first aid room isn't too far from my room, but I need to go back into the school and through a busy hallway. So, I take a deep breath and burst through the doors. I have to start flying over them, there are a couple of screams and gasps in the air. I would be freaking out too if I saw a black-winged beast covered in blood, with a dead-looking boy in its arms and blood dripping out of him. I don't stop flying even when I push past the first aid door. I don't stop flying until Eric's lying on a bed.

"Help him!" I order so loud that it shakes the windows.

The nurses jump but don't stop busting around, trying to figure out what's wrong.

"Do you know what happened to him?" one of them bravely asks.

I run a hand through my hair, "He was having a vision I think. I woke up from a nap and his eyes were moving so fast, I've never seen him have one before." I can hear my voice and I'm yelling at them, I can't calm down.

I look at her, "You need to help him, do whatever you need to do."

I've never had this fear for someone before—I can't catch my breath.

Pity fills her eyes, "Alex, I need you to take deep breaths for me... he's going to be fine. If a G.K sees too much of the future at one time, this will happen. He just needs some rest but he will be fine."

She can see the doubt in my eyes.

She gives me a small smile, "I promise, Alex. He will wake up in a few hours."

You better hope he wakes up, I want to say but I know it's not worth it.

That's when I can feel eyes on me. I look over at the doors to see it full of students and teachers just staring at me.

I need to get out of here.

43

I look down at Eric, his breath is a lot calmer and now he just looks like he's sleeping.

"I'll be back tonight," I say to him. "Remember what I said, Eric, I need you here so I don't go crazy and take it out all on the school." I lean in and whisper, "Please wake up." I turn to leave.

"Alex, you're bleeding, we should take a look at it," one of the nurses says.

I look over my shoulder and glance in the mirror at the end of the room. My back has opened up again and my white shirt is now dark red. My poor wings have missing feathers and blood dripping from them, they look like they have been in a blender. There's already a pool of blood gathering at my feet.

I make my way to the door, "I'll be fine."

The people in the doorway start to backpedal out of my way, not wanting to touch me. I leave my wings out to scare them even more. The only people that don't move are Jayden and Jennifer. I don't make any eye contact with anyone, I just make my way to Father Jack's office. I put my wings away once I get out of view of everyone, which makes my whole body shake; buckling under my own weight and I need the wall to support me.

Halfway to his office, I can see him running toward me. He eyes the trail of blood behind me.

"Are you okay? What happened?" he asks.

I've never seen him look this worried; I can't help but tell him what happened. With each word that's coming out of my mouth, it is making my throat tighten a little more.

He looks at me, "You need to go back there so they can take care of you, Alex."

I shake my head. "I don't feel like being put on display any more than I have. And it doesn't hurt that much. I was coming to see you so I can get a job, I don't want to be here."

He leads us back to his office, "Alexandra, I don't think that is wise, you need to have a night off… you can barely stand."

"I don't need one, and I promise I won't go in unless I think I can handle it," I say, being persistent.

He lets out a sigh and looks very tired, "Well, if you don't have a day off for you, take a day off for Eric. You two have a special bond, and if I was a betting man, I would say whatever he saw has something to do with you."

I sit in one of his chairs, not saying anything, just staring at the angel and the demon. *Maybe I'm the demon. When I was younger, I thought I was the angel just because we had the same hair.*

"If you haven't noticed, all of his visions are about you. He is here to protect you before you know you are in danger, and if he just had a huge vision like this, something is going to happen to you and I don't feel comfortable sending you out until you know what is outside these walls."

I didn't know all of Eric's visions were about me, I knew a lot of them were but not all. I feel a little guilty and shameful that I didn't listen to him more.

I know I should stay in tonight, the little voice of common sense is telling me, but it doesn't want to stay in the school walls.

"Can I please have my next target? I won't attack him unless he is alone."

He lets out a soft chuckle and goes to his desk to grab the thinnest folder I've ever seen. "There is no stopping you, is there?"

"Anna didn't find much on this guy, they only saw him once with five women, and then he vanished with them. He had two she-demons with him," he looks a little worried. "Anna said that she was following him and they just lost the scent of him and the she-demons. So, be careful with this one. We haven't seen a demon this strong in a long time."

"Don't worry about me. I can take care of myself." Before I leave his room, I say, "Thank you."

He nods. "I know you are going to go out tonight but can you just do a scouting job? And if you are just going on a scouting job, you don't need to bring Anna with you. You two need a break from each other." After saying that, he goes back to his paperwork.

All the students are in class now so I don't have too many eyes staring at me. As I move my shoulders as I walk, I can feel the blood drying the shirt on my back and pulling my skin.

When I get back to the first aid room, they don't say a word to me and they are trying really hard not to stare at me, I don't blame them.

I push another bed closer to Eric's and sit and watch him for a while. I zone out on him so hard, I don't hear her coming up.

"I am sorry about Eric." Her voice is so soft and nice to hear.

I blink a few times and look up at her but turn my attention back to Eric. Her face has too much pity and sadness in it… I can't take it, especially since Eric is in here because of me.

"What do you want, Jennifer?" I sound so exhausted.

"I came over to see if you needed anything? You know I am a healer and I can have you back together again in no time."

I want to laugh. When we were younger, we would play games all the time but most of the time we would dare each other. One time, she dared me to climb a huge tree out in the courtyard. Well, I slipped and broke my leg in several places and split my head right open. She rushed over and tried to heal me but it didn't work. She started to freak out because there was so much blood. Even though Jennifer was young, she was one of the top healers and she couldn't even help me but it didn't take long for me to heal because of my doll, and the person who was wearing it passed away that day. I didn't have control over the doll and how much I could drain from someone. That's also the day Jennifer and I stopped hanging out really.

Coming back from that memory, I can see it in Jennifer's eyes that she remembers it now and is fighting the urge to take a step back.

"It's all right, Jennifer, you don't have to be nice to me because you feel sorry for me, and I am sure there is someone else who needs your attention more than I do." I give her a fake smile, "If it makes you feel better, I can feel it already closing up so I'll be fine."

She doesn't know what to do and she gets saved by someone else coming in from training. She tries a few times to take care of my wounds, but I turn her down as nicely as I can.

As the day goes by, there's less and less people in the first aid room. By nightfall, there's only three of us in here—Eric, the night male nurse, and me. The male nurse is asleep at his desk.

Eric's breath flutters a little and I can't help but to slide in the bed next to him and hold his hand. His face is still pale and he's a lot smaller than I thought.

"Is it really my fault that you're like this?" I softly whisper. "I'm sorry that I cause you so much pain."

I hate myself for what I've done to you, why is God making you see these things and causing you so much pain? I feel so angry.

Eric shifts with a groan, then says, "You don't have to squeeze my hand so tight."

I didn't realize how hard I was squeezing his hand... I look down to see that my knuckles are white. I let go, apologizing.

He offers me a small smile. "No need to apologize to me." He sits up a little. "Now that was a rough vision, I've never had one that harsh before."

My hands start to shake and I don't know if I'm mad at him or at me.

"I don't want to know what you saw! Why haven't you told me about your visions?" I say through my clenched jaw. "Why didn't you tell me that they are all about me?"

His smile drops, "I take it Father told you that you're the only one I see?"

"Why haven't you told me?" I ask harshly.

He shrugs a little, "I don't know... I thought you would have figured it out. I had visions of you before I even really met you. That's why I had to become your friend. The first time I had a vision of you was when you were standing over an empty circle, you just ended your first demon. The only injury you got was a small scratch on your arm. And unlike the other Saviours, who were cheering about their successful hunt, you were livid. You were so mad. Why were you so mad?"

This question catches me by surprise. Stumbling over a lie so I don't have to remember what happened. But not one single lie comes to my mind, so I tell the truth.

"I… umm, was disappointed that I couldn't save it."

The memory of the fight flooded my mind.

"That's why I got the scratch, you know. I was buying the demon time to change its mind." *I was such a fool back then*, I think to myself. "The other Saviours made fun of me for holding out for so long. Even a whole demi-angel didn't have as much hope as me."

Eric holds out his hand for me to grab. I hesitate for a second before taking it.

He shakes his head to the side, "Why did you give up hope?"

A harsh laugh escapes my throat, "Do you have any idea how hard I tried saving my first fifty demons? More than half of the scars I have are because of them, and it wasn't because I was not skilled enough… no, it was because I waited for a long time before I finished them off. It became a waste of time to try to save them." I take a deep breath, trying to calm down. "I stopped caring about them, and they obviously wanted to stay in Hell, so I granted them passage back to it."

He doesn't say anything, just sits there thinking and I have a feeling I'm not going to like whatever he has to say.

"Why did you have so much hope for a demon?" he asks slowly.

Nope, definitely don't want to answer that question.

I let out a frustrated sigh. "Honestly, I don't remember anymore. God put them down there for a reason, so I don't think I should be the one to decide if they get to stay."

He shakes his head, knowing very well that I'm lying to him, but before he can say anything, I get up very slowly. Every bone in my body begins to scream, but I've had enough of this conversation.

"I'm happy you are awake and everything, but I got another job from the church to do." I wave the folder at him, ignoring the fact he can't see it. "I better be going."

He frowns, "Well, be safe. I'll call and let you know if I see anything."

I hope you never see me in a vision again.

I leave without saying another word to him. I can't look at him without feeling so much guilt. The school's hallways are so quiet and dark at this time of night. The only light comes from the full moon without any signs of a cloud. I stop to look at the sky—it's such a beautiful night to go for a fly. Before I continue down the hall, I see a few students flying around the grounds.

Jealousy and envy wash over me, just the thought of not being able to fly makes my heartbreak. My eyes begin to feel heavy and my head starts to spin. The chain on my neck is starting to feel heavy, almost weighing me down.

I always forget how much this stupid doll affects me when I wear it!

"Fine, I'll stay in tonight and go out tomorrow!" I grumble, turning around to go to my room.

I look out the window one more time and I can see Jayden walking around and watching the couple flying around.

Good thing I decided to stay in… he would have seen me and tried to talk to me. I might have killed him.

It took me forever to get to my room, but now I'm here, I don't know if I am sleep deprived or I'm just going crazy, but it looks like my bed is calling me to it with open arms. I take off my pants and tie but leave my school shirt on—too lazy to go find another baggy shirt to sleep in. I get comfy under the covers, and before closing my eyes, I lay my head on the back so I can look out my window, up at the stars. Loneliness surrounds me.

This is why I don't like being here at night. If I am out on a job, my mind is on that, not how alone and pathetic I am.

"Hey, Mom, sorry that I haven't talked to you in a while, I have been busy with work and school. I was able to get a few more hearts last night… don't worry, I'm not hurt too bad. Erik did a good job at fixing me up. And school is going okay, still hate math though, but Erik is still helping me with that. I owe so much to that kid!

"Why is God punishing him so much? I am really worried about him. I wish you were here, maybe I wouldn't need to rely on Eric so much. I hate that I have to do that too, but I don't have anyone else to help me. The Saviours don't want me and the kids and teachers are terrified of me… Eric is the only one I really have. Anne is always busy and we don't really have anything in common. I'm sure if she wasn't my G.C, she wouldn't talk to me either."

I sigh, "Sorry for the pity party, Mom. Hopefully, I'll have better news for you next time. Oh! Speaking of news… the other G.R.Hs are starting to show up. There is only one here right now and he is way too friendly, I feel like he wants something from me. I figured most of them would hate me and try to beat me down, but if they are all like him, I'm going to be creeped out a lot."

My eyelids are starting to have trouble staying open. Before I can say goodnight, my world is black and I'm in my dream.

I'm flying through the night sky. There are less stars out and there is no moon tonight but the air is still fresh and calming. A smile spreads on my face as I am flying up and up. I want to touch the stars but then black hands grab my ankle… it feels like they are branding me with their handprints and starting to pull me down. The closer I get to the ground, the more hands that reach out for me. I fight back and try to fly up but I can't get them off me. The pain is just as bad as someone messing with the doll.

"He's sending him, he's coming!" they all laugh and repeat over and over again.

I sit straight up, my neck and back all protesting about how fast I moved. I let out a groan.

"Had the dream again?" Anna's voice breaks the silence in the room.

"What the hell! What are you doing in here?"

She snickers, "I haven't been able to scare you in a while."

She looks tired and worn out, even with all the makeup on and her hair done perfectly. She's also wearing the same clothes she was wearing yesterday.

I curl my lip at her, "What do you want? What time is it?" I reach for my phone, and it reads seven am. *Not bad.*

Anna shrugs, "I wanted to check up on you, I heard what happened to Erik and I knew you were hurting from your last hunt."

I glare at her, "How long have you been sitting there?"

"Umm, a few hours. I slept at the foot of your bed for a few hours but then you kicked me off," she glares at me. "Rather hard, I might add, but I noticed you were having your dream again."

"It's kind of creepy that you were watching me sleep, and how do you know I was having the same dream?"

She rolls her eyes at me. "Well, I've slept in this room with you for so long that I know you talk in your sleep and it sounds like you're struggling against something. You say the same thing every time."

It's kind of annoying that she knows so much about me.

She sighs, "Do you want to talk about it?"

I narrow my eyes are her.

She raises her hands, "I knew you were going to give me that look… I was just trying to help." Her face softens, "You know you can tell me, I won't tell anyone."

I get out of bed, "I know you mean well, Anna, but I'm fine. I've been having this same dream since God's Right Hand training."

Wow, it's been so long but yet it still affects me so much. Pathetic.

She opens her mouth to say something.

"Look, Anna, I need to get ready for school. I'm fine, okay? Stop worrying about me or I'm going to give you wrinkles."

She gasps, "I am too young to be getting those!"

I raise an eyebrow. "Are you sure?" I lean in. "I think I can see some forming on your forehead."

She shoots up, glaring at me, "Go to Hell, Alex!" She then shifts into a cat and runs off.

"See you there, Anna!"

I have less than an hour for school. I sniff my armpits—I'm good, don't need a shower. Change of uniform and brush my hair and I'm calling it good.

CHAPTER 6

My back is still killing me but the wound is all healed, so I won't be bleeding today. I need to see Eric before classes start. I'm not looking forward to going through the school hallways, but there's nothing I can do about that. I open my last door to the hallway to see Jayden standing right in front of me. He's wearing the school uniform and his hair is a blonde mop at the top of his head. *Doesn't look like he slept much either.*

I raise an eyebrow, "What are you doing here?"

Everyone else is avoiding my door like the plague.

He shrugs, "I was worried about you, you were in really bad shape yesterday and I just wanted to make sure you were okay. I know we just met but I can already tell you love Eric, and I also can tell that no one would ask you if you were okay."

I start walking to the first aid room, "You have only been here for one day and you already picked up on that? Thought guys couldn't see as far as their penis."

Jayden snorts a laugh, "I'm not like most guys, I guess. I'm one of the lucky ones."

I shake my head, "You better be careful what you say about that subject. They will remove your wings."

We both shiver at the thought.

"They can't do anything… I'm going into the Ultram without a fight and also pure so they can shovel it."

Listening to him in his English accent, I can't help but snicker as we walk in to the first aid room.

"Well, it's good to see you laughing, Alex," Eric says from his bed.

I rush over to him, he's looking a lot better; his skin actually has some colour to it.

"How are you feeling? When did they say you could leave?" I fire the questions at him.

"I'm feeling better and they say I have to stay one more night just to make sure." He looks towards Jayden, who hasn't made a noise.

"Hello, Jayden, I didn't think you would come and see me," Eric says.

"Umm, well, I wanted to make sure Alex was okay and she was headed here so I thought I would check up on you too." He comes over to the bed. "How are you doing?"

Eric shrugs, "I'm still tired but I am doing better, thanks. You guys should get to class… the bell is going to ring."

Before we can say goodbye, the first bell rings and the nurses rush us out. We don't say anything to each other as we walk to English class. The other students still move out of my way as they rush to class, but I don't see fear in their eyes today… I see disgust and hatred.

"You really shouldn't be walking with me, Jayden. They might hate you just as much," I snarl at him.

"I think it's my choice who I hang out with," he sneers his answer to me.

I don't fight with him. If he wants to ruin his life by being close to me, that's fine.

A group of five God's Guards stand in the middle of the hallway. I curl my lip at them and shoot them my death glare. The two at the back are the only ones who look a little scared. I know the first guy… his name is Kyle. We've butted heads a lot over the years, he hates that

I'm stronger than he is. He's either hitting the gym or on the girls in the school. He has a gross amount of muscles, where if you stick something in the middle of his back, he's unable to reach it.

The rest of his features are boring—dull, short brown hair and dark brown eyes. He's tan from being outside all summer. And the four idiots that are behind are a bit smaller than him but there's nothing really special about them either—all jerks.

"Get out of my way, Kyle!" I bark at him.

He narrows his eyes, "No, you will no longer put fear into the students here, and we are standing up to you. You don't own this school."

My temperature spikes, my nails dig into my palm, and my canines start poking at my lip.

"I have no patience today, get the hell out of my way before I make you," I sneer at him.

Jayden steps in, "Oh, come on, guys… calm down, we don't want to get kicked out for fighting now, do we?"

"Get out of our way, pretty boy," the one on the left shoves Jayden.

Without thinking, I flash in front of him and punch him square in the jaw. I can feel his bones breaking and I send him flying into the lockers. Some girls scream as they run out of the way but even with them screaming, I can hear the rest of the God's Guard's clothes starting to rip as they grow in size and their skin is turning a gold colour. They are snarling like beasts too. When they all Hulk out, I never understand why people don't think of them as beasts too because that's what they remind me of.

I crouch down, snarling, "You guys need to back off. I don't want to fight you."

Kyle barks a laugh, "Whatever, Alex… you've had this coming for a long time and you know it," his voice is deeper, almost sounding like he just woke up and hasn't cleared his throat.

"Come on, guys, the Sisters and Father Jack are going to be here soon. We shouldn't be doing this. Someone can get really hurt," Jayden says calmly.

One at the back, "You think we are that weak, we'll get hurt by her?"

He doesn't give us time to answer before all three of them charge toward us. G.G are very top-heavy, so it's always easier to go low. Kyle and another one comes at me while one goes for Jayden. Kyle swings at me, making me move back. There are students scrambling to get in my way and I trip over one of them. Making me fall back, both Kyle and his buddy start stomping their feet, trying to crush me. They are leaving crack marks in the ground. If I let them hit me, there will definitely be broken bones.

Kyle's buddy is getting worn out already—the lesser G.G can only be in their full form for a few seconds. The stronger you are, the longer you can stay in it. Kyle is one of the strongest in the school. I heard some of the girls gushing over him, saying he can last five minutes and that's pretty impressive.

As his buddy slows down, I sweep my leg under him, knocking him into Kyle, giving me time to stand up. I rush to Kyle. His buddy recovers a lot quicker than I thought he would, he grabs my ankle, bringing me back to the ground. Kyle grabs the back of my neck and picks me up—I'm a good three feet off the ground. I claw at his hand and try to kick him but my legs are too short to reach him.

"See, she's no better than the rest of us," Kyle showboats me around to the group of students squeezing my throat tightly, making it impossible to breathe.

My vision is already starting to blur. I can see some students looking my way to amuse about my suffering.

"Alex!" Jayden roars.

He sounds hurt.

Kyle laughs, "How pathetic! What kind of God's Right Hands are you? You can't even take care of three God's Guards?"

He's starting to really piss me off!

Even with his hand around my throat, a deadly growl rumbles through my body. My wings erupt from my back, scaring Kyle to let go of me.

I draw a raggedy breath. "You want to see a true G.R.Hs gift, Kyle? I was trying to go easy on you because I didn't want to hurt you, but to hell with it."

I take off right in front of him and give him an uppercut, sending him flying straight up. Before he can start coming down, I catch up and punch him in the gut, sending him down harder and causing him to crack the floor. I follow him down and slam my knee into his chest, grabbing his throat and digging my nails into his neck, drawing back my other hand in a dagger position. My nails are too long to make a proper fist.

"Alex, that's enough!" someone shouts in my ear and grabs my shoulder.

Without looking, I grab their hand and flip them over my shoulder without taking any pressure off of Kyle. I go to hit Kyle again but, all of a sudden, I am flung through the air and hit the ground. It feels like a huge weight is pinning me down. I can't move, I can't even turn my head. Only one person can do this to me…

"What is going on here?" Jennifer shouts.

"Alex went crazy and started attacking them!" a girl says.

I snarl, trying to move.

"Hey! That's not true!" Jayden shouts. "Jennifer, that is not true! They attacked us!"

The weight lifts off of me. I jump up and anger is still coursing through me. I want to rip Kyle's head off. I look around to see Jayden has blood running down his face from his brow and a nice bruise forming on his cheek. The G.G that he was up against is unconscious on his back. It looks like Jayden only laid one punch. I'm a little impressed. Jennifer is standing between Kyle and me. Kyle isn't moving and there is blood dripping from his mouth and neck where I was digging my nails.

I glare at Jennifer, "Move out of my way, I need to teach that asshole a lesson."

She puts a hand up, "Alex, calm down. He's not coming after you anymore."

I snarl at her, "What makes you believe Jayden that I didn't start this fight?" My blood is still boiling… I want to keep fighting. I want to sink my teeth into their necks.

Her face remains calm but I can see in her eyes that she is terrified, "I have never known you to start a fight but I've seen you end plenty, and this fight is done. We need to get him and his friend to the first aid room."

"Why aren't you all in class?" Father Jack's voice booms across the hallway.

Students move out of his way as if he is Moses parting the red sea.

He looks at Jennifer, "What is going on here?"

"Some of the God's Guards came after Alex and Jayden. I just got here in time before it got too out of hand," Jennifer answers him.

Father Jack's icy glare looks at the three G.G. Two are still not moving and one is slowly moving into the crowd, but Father Jack calls his name out.

"Jennifer, take these two to the first aid room and, Jayden, I'm assuming you are well enough to help her?"

Jayden just nods.

"Alright, everyone else to class… now!"

Everyone scrambles to get to their classes.

Father places a hand on my shoulder, "Good job at controlling yourself, but you go to class too and we'll talk after school." He looks over to Jayden, "You need to go to the first aid room as well."

He looks like a sad little puppy, "But it's just a scratch… I'm fine. I can already feel the blood stopping."

Father Jack just points back down the way we came. Jayden lets out a sigh in defeat—it almost sounds like a little puppy whine. I can't help but crack a smile at him. Father Jack falls in step with him.

I'm left standing in the middle of the hallway by myself. I am no longer in the mood to go to class, but I have nothing better to do, so I slowly make my way to English.

I walk into class and I can feel everyone's eyes glued to me as I move to my desk. Mr. Daniel doesn't stop his lesson or even give me a head nod.

"We are going to start a new novel today, I want you to pick a book where the villain is the main focus."

A girl puts up her hand.

"Yes, Sarah?"

"Why a villain? I feel like that wouldn't be good for us."

Why do I find every female's voice so annoying!

Mr. Daniel sighs, "Why not? I want your point of view at the end of the day about why you think they're a villain? What makes them a villain? Is it how other people made them look? Does someone influence us so much that we are willing to villainize someone? These are the questions I want you to ask yourselves as you read your books and while you write your essays. I also want you to try and convince me that they are actually a good guy."

I raise my hand, "What do you consider a villain?" I ask.

His lip twitches, trying not to smile, "That is for you to decide."

"So, who is going to make Alex a villain?" one of the boys chimes in.

Everyone snickers.

Mr. Daniel's face shoots daggers at him, "You can use her, but do understand I want you to try and convince me that your villain is a good guy, and if you can't do that, I will fail you."

The room falls silent.

"We are going to the library so you can pick out your books, I want this done by Monday."

Everyone stands up and follows Mr. Daniel out of class; I'm waiting for the last person to be out completely and then I slowly follow them. I already know what book I'm going to use, just because I like stirring the pot. I'm going to make Lucifer a good angel.

My lip curls into a smile.

"You are scaring me with that look," Jayden says, coming up beside me.

"I'm smiling at how much trouble I'm going to get in." I look at him, "Are you okay?"

He grunts, "Yeah, I didn't need to go. You were the one who caused more damage than the G.G."

"Huh? What do you mean?"

He looks a little confused, "I was the one who you flung over your shoulder, I was trying to stop you but it didn't really work out as planned."

I look down to my feet, "Oh, I'm sorry, I didn't know."

He shrugs, "Meh, you didn't know who I was, so it's okay. Umm... so what are we doing anyway?"

I explain to him what we are doing.

"Ugh, I really don't like English. Like, how am I supposed to do that?" he whines.

I roll my eyes at him, "I already have my booked picked, it's not going to be that hard."

"What book? Maybe I can do the same book and we can work together?"

I shake my head, "No, you won't like what I'm doing."

"Oh, didn't take you for a romance novelist but that's cool, to each their own, I guess."

I shove him, "Ha ha, so funny."

We enter the library, most of the class are in the rows of books but I just beeline it to the corner of the library where there are beanbags and pillows to sit on. This is where they keep Eric's books for him, so we are the only ones that really come to this area. I sit down and start to write. For the title, I put N/A, deciding not to put Lucifer's name down. I don't want Mr. Daniel guessing who I'm writing about right away.

Jayden flops down onto the bag beside me, "I really don't like reading. Why don't you have a book?"

I smirk, "Because I'm cheating and using a book I've already read."

"That's smart. I wish I could do that but the books I've read aren't interesting enough for me to remember or they don't have a villain that I need to turn into a good guy. What book are you using?"

I sigh, "I told you that I'm not telling, I'm going to get into trouble using it so it's better that you don't follow my lead."

He laughs, "You really like getting into trouble, don't you?"

I just smile at him and we get back to work on our projects. I finish my paper before the bell rings and it looks like Jayden hasn't even finished the first chapter before falling asleep. The bell startles him awake.

Jayden stretches, "Mmm, that was a good nap, got to love English for that."

"Yes, it is, now it's time for math. The old hag better be in a good mood," I mumble.

"No, Alex, that is in no way to talk about a Sister," Mr. Daniel says, coming up behind me.

I turn my head to look over my shoulder, "I'm sure God would agree with me on this one. She may be a Sister but if she makes it to Heaven, God is a lot easier on the whole sinning thing."

Mr. Daniel hits the top of my head with the book in his hands.

No big surprise I get kicked out of math again and am sent to sit in the hallway. I finish the booklet she gave me a lot faster this time and close my eyes to have a nap while I wait for the bell. I can hear some girls walking up the hallway whispering. I don't open my eyes, but I can feel their eyes on me.

As they get further away, one of them whispers, "I almost feel sorry for her. She seems like she's always alone."

"You really shouldn't, it's probably just as bad as feeling sorry for Lucifer," the other one says.

I let out a frustrated sigh. *I brought this onto myself. I shouldn't expect anything different.*

The rest of the day goes by rather boring. I try to pay attention in chemistry and take notes, mostly for Erik. I walk to the gym slowly, not really in the mood to work out because I know I'm going out for a hunt tonight. Mr. Daniel texts me to tell me he can't make it to practice, but he still expects me to do my drills. I just decide to do laps. On my fifth lap, Jayden walks in.

"What do you want?" I ask a little too harshly.

"I have this period free too and I'm allowed to come here and work out and train with you."

I narrow my eyes, "I don't really feel like training today, but you are more than welcome to use my gym."

He nods and goes to get changed. When he comes out, we don't say a word to each other. He does a few laps with me, then goes to the weights. When the last bell rings for the day, I do about thirty laps and walk over to get some water and cool off before getting changed.

"You run a lot," Jayden says, coming up beside me, smelling like sweat and whatever cologne he has on, which is a nice combo.

"I didn't feel like lifting weights today, I haven't been working on my cardio lately. I can feel me getting slow out there."

"Mmm, can I come with you on your next hunt?" he asks.

I scratch the back of my neck, "I don't know, I don't really like having people come with me. Anna doesn't even stick around. Maybe next time," I say as I walk into the changing room.

When I come out, Jayden is no longer in the gym. I walk back to my room and skip out on having dinner in the mess hall. I'm feeling like having some greasy pizza in town when I go. I have another shower and get dressed for my hunt. I wear dark jeans, a baggy long-sleeve shirt, my leather jacket, and my 'kicking ass' boots. I tie my hair out of my face and call it good. I grab my keys and cell phone and head down to visit Erik until nightfall.

As I enter the first aid room, Erik is the only one in there, which is good. I don't want to see the G.G. glaring at me the whole time.

"It's supposed to be a full moon tonight… perfect for flying," Erik says as I sit on his bed.

"Unfortunately, that means everyone will be out flying tonight. But I plan on taking my car. If something happens to my wings again, I don't want to walk back or have anyone coming to get me."

He nods, "I think I'm finally rubbing off on you, you are actually thinking with that brain of yours."

"Ha, ha. I do that once in a while. I did take notice in chem today, for you. Although most of it was gibberish to me, it might make sense to you."

He gives me a pouty face, "Soon, you'll no longer need me."

"Oh, shut it."

"So, you put some G.G in here this morning. Want to tell me your side? They were rather annoying, by the way. Coming in here crying like babies. I think you should have more consideration for me."

I laugh, "Sorry, next time I'll ask them to wait to fight me until you are out of here."

"Thank you, it's all I ask."

I tell him what happened and how Jayden helped me and had my back, even Jennifer did too. After a while, he drifts off to sleep. I sit with him until the moon is high in the sky. Making sure he is all tucked in and has water by his bed. I whisper, "Goodnight," and leave for my hunt. As I walk out of the school, I can see kids flying about. Some of them look so peaceful and beautiful while they fly, almost like they are dancing.

CHAPTER 7

The garage looks like an underground parking lot, normally just teachers and the older Angel Saviours can park their cars in here, but I bet one of the Saviours that I could kill ten demons in one night. Not all at once, of course. I got all ten before the sun rose in the morning and now I can park my baby in here.

I can smell her before I see her. Anna is leaning against the side door of the garage with her arms crossed under her boobs. She says it's to take the weight off her back but I think it is just because it makes her boobs look even bigger.

"Where do you think you're going?" she asks.

"Father Jack said I was allowed to go out alone. If you don't like it, take it up with him."

Even in this dim light, I can see her green eyes shooting daggers at me.

"Just be careful, if I hear you get hurt again, I'll tell Father Jack you've been sneaking out almost every night to go and hang out and hunt on your own."

I snarl, "If you get me grounded, I will make your life a living hell until I get out."

"Just try me, Alex. Unlike you, I am allowed to leave the school grounds whenever I please." She starts to walk away, "Just be careful, okay? Especially with you driving that car. I worry about you sometimes."

I smirk, "You always worry too much."

I can see a small smirk before she walks back to the dorm.

I unlock the garage and flick on the lights, my car is standing out from the lot of mom vans. Just looking at her makes my heart race. She's all nicely polished. In fact, she's so polished that I can see my reflection in the black paint. I open the door and slide in, the leather seats fit me perfectly, even with my back killing me.

"Hey, girl, sorry that I haven't taken you out in a while," I whisper to her.

I turn the key and she rumbles to life; when you hear it, you can't help but rev the engine. I open the garage door, and as it goes up, I can see a pair of legs. My smile turns into a sneer. I can smell who it is before I can see Jayden's face. It takes every bit of energy I have not to floor it. Once the door passes over his head, we make eye contact and I notice that his jaw is hanging open. His mouth starts to form words but nothing is coming out, he looks like a fish out of water. His loss for words amuses me.

He rushes over to the passenger side before he can lay a greasy finger on the car. I honk the horn, making him jump back.

"You have to take me for a ride!" he begs, opening the door and just taking a seat in my car.

That's when my canines start to poke out, "Why would I take you anywhere, Jayden? Get out of my car."

He waves his hand at me... I so want to break it.

"You should take me for a ride because you have a Boss 429 Mustang!" he looks at me with pleading eyes.

"I'll sit somewhere else for chem and I will never talk to you again until the Ultram."

I think about it before saying, "Deal... if you become Eric's friend."

Jayden looks a little confused, "You want me to become the G.K's friend and not talk to you and you'll let me have a few rides and help kill some demons?"

"No demons, but I'll take you for a few more rides... but no talking, just music and the car." I stick out my hand.

He grabs it, "And I can drive it?"

I laugh harshly, "In your dreams, pretty boy."

He shrugs his large shoulders. "Can't blame a guy for trying."

With that, I take off, leaving some of my tires behind. Jayden gasps and rushes to get his seatbelt on. I laugh at him.

The gates of the school open just enough for me to squeeze through and the school disappears within seconds.

I love this car!

Jayden's silence doesn't last long again.

"So, how does an orphan high school student afford a beast like this? And your G.C is really hot but I didn't see her in school. Is she older?"

My jaw twitches at the word orphan. *I hate that word.*

Because you are one. The dark voice laughs.

"I get paid to kill demons," I shrug. "And I saved up for it. Although it didn't take me long to save enough money. And let's not talk about Anna, okay?"

I feel the mood change in the car.

"What makes you so much better than the rest of us? We aren't allowed to fight demons until graduation. Are you really that good that you started four years early?"

I give him a sideways glance, "I can't be killed."

"Come on, Alex, tell the truth. Why are you so different? You have the same teeth as they do. You heal faster than anyone I know. I literally saw the gash on your back sow itself together."

"That's odd... normally, it takes forever for me to heal when I am wearing it," I mumble to myself. *Shit, I shouldn't have said that out loud. Shit, I should have left him and the doll at the church.*

I am not allowed to take the doll off the school grounds, but I forget sometimes. Even though the doll is slowly draining me right now, it feels good to have the doll on me for the first day. It feels like I am whole and I can relax a little bit too because I don't need to worry about draining someone completely. So, I forget a lot of the time.

"Wear what? Is that how you are so good? You have something that increases your abilities."

I've never had someone ask me so many questions about myself before; I don't like it.

"Look, Jayden—"

"And why are your wings black?"

I slam on the breaks. "Will you shut up! Do you think I really know why I am so different from everyone else? I don't... and if I could look and act different for people to like me, I would never change who I am! I love that my wings are black and I love that I can make a lot of money on my own because I know how to fight better than more than half of the Saviours combined."

Taking a deep breath, I start to drive again, "The only thing I would love to change is how people look at me with so much fear— they are more scared of me than the demons. When people look at me like that, that's what makes me hate myself. No matter how hard I tried to be part of everyone's lives, it just scared them more, so I just stopped trying. It became easier for me to stay away from people."

Jayden moves his hand over to put it on mine, but I draw mine away.

"I'm sorry, Alex, I shouldn't have asked so many questions. I didn't know you were going to react that way."

My eyebrows rise, "Really? Why do you think I have one friend in school? Once I became part of the Angel Saviours, no one talked to me. Teachers didn't take long to start fearing me too."

I look over at him and there is so much pity in his eyes.

I snarl, "Stop feeling sorry for me. People keep feeling sorry for me. I see pity in people's eyes when they look at me. I might not like it all the time, but I'm used to it and I'm not allowed to let anyone know what I do, so it makes it easier to keep a secret."

He shakes his head, "That's not right. People should be kissing the ground you walk on."

I laugh, "Yeah, too bad, while they are kissing the ground I walk on, can they bring me food too?"

"Why not? They should carry your bags too. I have one more question… why aren't you allowed to tell anyone about what you do?"

I shrug, "I asked Father a few times but he just told me it's so the other kids won't ask questions, but I always thought there was more to it than that."

I take a sharp corner—way too fast—and the job folder slides across the dash onto Jayden's lap. He flips it open. I look down and my eyes glue to the demon's face. My heart starts to pound so hard, I'm sure that Jayden can hear it. My palms are pumping out sweat like crazy.

His hair is white as snow and short, just long enough to flip up the front. By the look of his jaw and cheekbones, he is very well fit. And his skin colour is on the lighter side of olive, but on his cheeks and nose, he has freckles. I find it amusing because I've always called them angel kisses. I look at his eyes, they are like emeralds—something about them scares and excites me, I can't look away. I don't want to look away.

Jayden jerks the steering wheel, breaking me out of my trance.

"What the hell, Alex?"

I didn't realize I drifted into the other lane. I mumble, "Sorry," and grip the wheel so hard that my knuckles are turning white, and with my other hand, I wipe the drool from my mouth. I almost cut myself on my canines.

God damn it, I am more beast than angel.

Let's have another look at him, my inner voice whispers.

"What was that about? Are you okay? I could hear your heartbeat. Do you know him or something?"

I want to know him. "No, I've never seen that demon before."

I can feel his eyes on me... I can also sense he wants to ask me more questions but I just ignore him. He is, unfortunately, only quiet for a few seconds.

"So, where do you go first to find this guy?" he flips open the folder again and tilts it so I can't see it.

I glare at the folder, wanting another peek. "Where does it say that Anna saw him last?"

"Umm, it says she saw him enter a club named NOW. Do we get to go to a club?" he asks, sounding way too excited.

"Not really, we sit outside it. Angels aren't welcome there anymore. Ever since the huge fight that killed two angels, three demons, and about seven humans."

"I don't understand... we are the good guys. Why would they kick us out and not the demons?"

I roll my eyes, "The only reason a Saviour would go in there is to start fights with the demon on their list. Demons go in there to have a good time and, of course, to find their next meal. Angels don't drink and party like that." I snicker at the thought of never drinking again. *I wonder if the church knows how much I drink when I'm out hunting.*

"And, of course, since angels don't go there, guess where all the demons like to hang out? Last night, there were over thirty of them in there. I don't even understand why people love going there. The music is horrible and the line is always long, and don't get me started on how the women dress."

Jayden chuckles, "I take it you're not big on clubbing attire?"

"Why would I be? There is no place to put my blades."

He laughs this time. "Of course that's all you care about. Do you ever leave without them?"

"No," is all I say.

A memory flashes through my mind. I had forgotten them once a few years back. I was just going scouting like today when I came across a human being attacked by two demons. I didn't think, I just flew over and fought them, but without my blades, I couldn't open up the door for them to pass through me. They just looked like two mangled bodies by the time I was done with them. They healed and tracked the human down; I didn't know they were tracing us. I healed the human and got him home, in his own bed.

I wasn't even a block away when the screams echoed off the empty street. I rushed back but the demons already took him. I followed the trail of blood to an alleyway, but by the time I found him, his body had chunks of flesh missing. But his face was ghostly white, his eyes were hollowed, and his mouth was ripped open and just hanging open. I didn't know what to do... I panicked and ran. He was the first human I lost because I forgot my blades.

Anna tracked me down a few hours later. She found me by the river, I was so furious with myself. I was breaking rocks over my hands (it makes them stronger) when she found me.

She didn't say anything but just wrapped her arm around me and held me tight. I'm not sure how long we sat there for, but our bodies were stiff and the sun was coming up. She whispered to me that I would do better next time. Those words stuck with me, and I will always be better. And she was right—I have never forgotten my blades again.

Jayden feels my mood go dark and lays his hand on mine, which brings me back from the dark memory. I jerk my hand from his and glare out the window.

"I will never leave the church grounds without them ever again," I whisper more to myself.

Jayden leans forward and pulls out twin desert eagle pistols with what looks like rosary engraved on the grip and names are engraved in them too. He notices me looking at them.

"The names are for the people I care about and to remind me why I fire them. I'm not that great with swords or any other weapon like I should be. My trainer is rather hard about it, more like pissed and disgraced that I'm not like you, but with these, I haven't missed a target yet. Not like that would make him think any better of me. I've only been on a few hunts with a party, but to be honest, I've never liked killing. I really hate it when the demons pass through us. I actually hate it and I hope I don't win the Ultram." He runs his thumb over a girl's name—Sharon.

Us G.R.Hs aren't allowed to fall for any other person than the God's Daughter, we are supposed to stay pure for her and she will stay pure for us. I'm not entirely sure where I come into this, but I didn't argue when I got told this rule, I thought it would be easy to stay pure for her.

I'm sure everyone is wondering what's going to happen if I win and so does Jennifer—she even told me once when we were really young and didn't understand how life worked yet that she would like to have our baby and be my wife. Father Jack heard her say that one day when we were playing in the garden. He has never been mad at her but he was furious that day at her. He started to yell at her, telling her she should never think those thoughts again. I didn't do anything until I could smell that she was scared.

I stepped in between them and shoved Father away from her. I shoved him so hard that he went ass over teakettle. That's the first day that my fingers grew like the demons. All three of us were surprised that I was that strong at such a young age and Father just stared. I could smell some fear on him too that day, and I think I had some fear of my own. I didn't wait around for Father to say anything, I just grabbed Jennifer's hand and we ran. To this day, I'm still surprised that I didn't get in trouble for that or that Jennifer isn't scared of me yet.

CHAPTER 8

Jayden and I haven't said anything for the rest of the trip into town. Most streets are quiet, but as we get closer to the club, there are more cars and people walking on the broken sidewalks. The club is built on the wrong side of town—they are hoping the club will bring more business down here. We can hear the music before we turn the corner.

I inhale deeply. There are three demons close to us, but I know there are going to be a lot more the closer we get to the club.

"Why are your nesters flaring? Did you fart or something?"

My lip twitches, "They are dancing to the music," I say. The sarcasm rolls off my tongue.

He snorts, "You have a bit of a funny bone, don't cha? But no, really… why are you doing that?"

I roll my eyes, "I'm sniffing for the demons."

I can see his eyes popping out of his head.

"You can smell them in a moving vehicle? I don't even think God's Creatures can do that!"

I shrug, I can't share with him anymore.

"You know what… you are like a super angel! What else can you do better than the rest of us?"

I can't tell if he is joking or not.

I change the subject, "Is there a piece of clothing in the folder? I need to smell it."

"You're like a bloodhound."

"I've never been called that before, I think I like soulless bitch more," I mumble.

"Why do you need to sniff him out? Why can't you just look for him the normal way?"

I hit my steering wheel, "Are you writing a fucking book about me or something?"

"No, you are just interesting is all… and different. I just want to know more."

Yeah, I'm sure you are just here to find an opening to stab me in the back like the rest of them do. And to find out what my weakness is.

You're wearing it, the dark voice laughs.

My hand goes up to my chest, where it's tucked nicely in between my breasts. "Shit!"

Jayden's hand flies up, "I didn't do anything."

"It has nothing to do with you! I just forgot something back at the school." Before he can say anything else, I add, "Did you find the fabric?"

"Umm, no, I can't find it."

"Great, how am I going to find him now?"

"What do you mean?"

I am really regretting bringing him with me.

"It's none of your business, Jayden. I have a feeling we should just go back before I get you into trouble."

"What? Come on, we should at least go in and look around."

I glance at him like he's crazy, "We were never going in there, and even on my best day, I would never go in there."

"You're not going in there because there are too many demons? That's a terrible excuse."

I finally park the car in an alleyway, hiding behind a garbage bin. I've never wanted to get out of my car so badly before. I grab my blades that are in my back sheaths and get out, and unfortunately, he's following me.

"Are you a special kind of stupid? It would take one swift movement to make every human in there reek of fear. So, you are planning on going in there to take down all the demons but you'll just cause death and make them stronger," I snarl at him while putting on my blades.

I narrow my eyes at him, "As we passed the club, I smelt about fifteen demons in there. I know I can take about five demons if they haven't eaten yet and if there isn't any fear to feed off of. How many can you take? And I also know I can't put that many humans out. How many can you do?"

He holds my gaze for only a few moments before looking at the brick wall in front of us.

"That's what I thought."

I look up and do not want to climb all those ladders.

"Maybe I can use you after all. Do you think you can fly us up there?" I point to the same roof I was sitting on last night.

His eyebrows shoot up, "You trust me enough to fly you up there?"

"If you drop me, I'll bring you down with me."

The corner of his lip twitches.

"What are you smirk—"

He scoops me up and takes off so fast that it takes my breath away. His wings are so white that they glow in the dark. As he is carrying me, I can tell his wings are strong and that they are very large. You know what they say about a guy's wing size...

I didn't realize that we have landed. I move a little and the doll touches him.

His soul flowing into mine gives me such a rush, I become lightheaded. He is staggering, almost falling over. He tries to hold onto me but I jump away from him. I have to hold onto the railing of the building until the world decides to stop spinning so much.

I start to laugh. "Holy shit, this feels awesome," I whisper under my breath.

"What is going on?"

I glance over to Jayden, he has his head between his knees and I can smell his vomit from here.

I don't think the doll has ever affected someone so badly before. I can feel it pulsing under my shirt. Although the doll has never been near another G.R.H.

I want more!

No, it's definitely more of a reason to stay away from him, I think to myself, taking a few steps back. "I'm not allowed to tell you. But trust me when I tell you that you should stay away from me."

He slowly gets to his feet, "What is it, Alex? There has to be something you can tell me."

I shake my head, "I literally can't, and I made a blood oath to God. God has chosen only Eric to know. And trust me, I wish he didn't know."

His eyes narrow at me, "What are you holding on to?"

I look down at my hand—the doll is staring up at me. *How the hell did it get in my hand?*

"It's just a stupid doll," I put it back around my neck.

He scoffs, "I'm not great at a lot of things, but I am great at reading people and that thing is important, whatever it is. The way you were just looking at it, you almost looked scared."

Frustration starts to nip at my mood. "I've told you I can't say anything." The itch to hit something washes over me.

He glares at me, "There has to be a way. I've never seen someone hold on to a blood oath before."

My canines start to poke through my lip, and my growl rumbles in my throat, "Please stop asking me questions."

"You took the old blood oath? We aren't allowed to do that anymore. If the high church finds out, what will they do to you?" he asks, just realizing what I said.

I scoff, "Guess who gave the order to do it?" I smile. "I don't follow the normal rules like the rest of you. For me to do what I am doing, I had to give the blood oath, and yes, sacrifice a lamb and my own blood."

He runs his hand through his hair, "What the hell is going on? All of this doesn't make sense!"

I shrug. "It's just easier to forget about it, there is no way I can tell you anything more than I have. You should be grateful that I have told you this much."

I turn my back to him and walk over to look at the club—I become lost in the light show and the noise of the people. He walks over and turns me to look at him.

"What did they turn you into?" his words are so gentle.

My head moves to the side, "You will never know." My own voice is so soft, it surprises me.

Without realizing it, he grabs the doll. I gasp more from the rush that he's giving me and not because he is squeezing it a little too tightly. He begins to sway again and tries to shake it off.

"What... the hell... is this thing?" he slurs his words.

"What you are holding is my soul... so, if you don't mind, can you please loosen your grip?" My eyes widen. *I told him... I told him the truth.*

"What are you talking about? Why does it make me feel like this?" he falls to his butt.

Feeling his soul draining into mine like dry dirt soaking up water, my back already feels completely healed. And I feel high off of it—I definitely could get used to this rush. My wings shoot out of my back and they are healed... it doesn't even feel like they were ever hurting. I've never healed this fast, my heart rate keeps rising. I feel like I can hear more clearly too, and my eyes are seeing different colours, they can even see particles moving.

Can music have life too? Because I think I can see it right now.

I don't want to tell him to let go; I want to always feel like this. I also want to tell him to let go. I want to tell him the deepest, darkest part of my life; I'm so used to keeping everything in and not letting anyone know, but I spill my guts to him.

"My soul is in that doll, and as of right now, it's draining yours so fast. If you don't give it back to me soon, you will die, but before that, you will want to try to kill me. And the high church has given me permission to dispose of anyone who tries to kill me." I cock my head. "I'd rather not kill you because of my soul, so give it back now," I request, holding out my hand.

He flings the doll out of his hand like it just stung him. As the doll hits the ground, it feels like I hit the ground with it too, it's difficult to not show him how much that hurts me. I pick it off the ground so slowly, as if it's going to break. I tell him the rest of it, the blood oath for him is no longer holding me back. Him holding the doll must have broken it. I haven't decided if I like it yet or not. But I am glad that I can finally tell someone everything, even if it has to be him.

His eyes are closed like he's soaking everything in. I tell him everything. From my father selling my soul to the church partially controlling me, and whoever has the doll can make me do whatever they want me to if their soul can last that long.

Even a blood oath can't save me from the doll.

"Why is it affecting me more than other people?" he whispers.

A real laugh escapes my lips, "That's the first question you're going to ask me? I think it's because you are a G.R.H too. My soul has never been near another one before."

"How does it feel?"

"How does it feel to drain someone or to have people have control of me so easily?" I sit beside him, expecting him to move away from me but he doesn't. "In the beginning, it's a rush and I want more, I want all of it. There is a dark side of me that doesn't want to stop; it was a lot harder to slow it down from taking all of yours. And for letting people control me, how do you think it feels? I don't even know if an action is mine sometimes. The church says that they don't make me do anything I don't want to, but how do I know that?"

He shifts a little bit. "You can control it?"

"I've never been able to stop the flow, but I can slow it down or speed it up. It's like a dam that I can control most of the time. I normally have it at just a trickle but if I get hurt, it's harder for me to control and there is more demand for me to open the floodgates."

"So, you can die? But just through your soul."

I glance over at him with a smile on my face, "Do you want to be the one to do it? I'm sure there is a huge queue for it. Did I drain you too much? I hope you know I didn't mean to, I couldn't stop."

He leans his head back, chuckling. "I don't think I want to kill you just yet."

I look up to the sky hoping to see stars, but the sky is just black as if there is no hope for anything in this world. The energy of his soul is still making me feel like I have a buzz, and without realizing it, my foot begins tapping along with the music. It's not like it's that great—I think I heard the same song yesterday. All club music sounds the same to me. I watch my foot for a while, not paying attention to anything.

"I'm in love with someone back home, that's why I don't want to win the Ultram. I don't think I can win, especially if my heart belongs to someone else." He takes a deep breath, "It's not like I can refuse to or they cut my wings off."

We both shiver at that thought—at least they put us to sleep now. In the old days, they would do it as a punishment and have us awake with no pain meds and cut them off slowly, in front of everyone to watch. Most angels didn't live long after that and I don't blame them.

"My girl back home understands what I must do but she's not happy about it. I'm not happy about it either. I hate training, I hate killing. My trainer pushed me harder and harder every day. Nothing

I did was good enough and if it wasn't for her, I would have given up a long time ago." He looks over to me, "She's the one who came up with the idea that I train—not for me, not for Jennifer, but for you. Help you win, be the first girl to be G.R.H. and that's what I did. I heard stories about you since I was in junior high and how amazing and terrifying you are to everyone. She felt sorry for you and would always say that you must be so lonely, and once I get here, that I have to help you."

I let out a snicker, "She sounds too good for you."

He gives me a true smile, "Oh, she is and I want to give her everything. She is my world and I want to keep her as happy as possible or she'll realize that she can do so much better.

"The reason I was acting the way I was this morning is because I wanted to see how you would act. I wanted to see how people treated you and to see if you deserved my help. Even though I don't want to be God's Right Hand, I still want well for the world. And Jennifer deserves the best to protect her."

Stretching my legs, I say, "So, do you think I'm the best because the other G.R.Hs might be a better pick?"

He shakes his head, "No, it's you or no one. God made you for a reason and I think it's for this."

I look forward, "Yeah, maybe."

CHAPTER 9

Taking a deep breath, the smell hits me, and before I know it, I'm standing on the edge of the apartment building, looking down. Rubble falls to the ground I don't even watch it, not caring if it hits someone. I feel his eyes on me—those eyes that can hypnotize anyone... anything. We both look at each other, unblinking. If my heart reacts to his picture, my heart is stopping and my breath is getting caught in my throat.

His face looks surprised, maybe a little shocked too. Everyone around us vanishes, I can't even hear the music anymore or the traffic. I can hear his heart though.

My eyes are so amazed, "I see you," I whisper.

A heart-dropping smile appears on his flawless face—he has perfect teeth and two matching dimples on either side of his freckled cheeks.

I tilt my head. "I can see you," I say a lot louder.

He raises a hand slowly and begins beckoning me, just as I take a step towards him, arms wrap around me and the green eyes disappear behind a wall.

Jayden starts to shake me and cracks a side of my cheek, "Snap out of it, Alex."

I shove him off of me. "Why did you do that?" I rush to the edge and there's nothing there besides humans.

I can't even smell one demon down there. *What the hell is going on?*

"We need to get out of here," I say as the hairs on the back of my neck rise.

I grab Jayden by the shoulders and take to the sky. With Jayden's soul healing me, I don't feel any pain; even flapping my wings like this isn't hurting. As we reach about twenty feet in the air, three demons crawl over the edge of the roof.

"A demon hunting party," Jayden whispers.

"If I let go, will you go after them?" I snarl the question at him.

"I just told you that I hate hunting, so what do you—"

I detach myself from him before he can finish his sentence. He drops about five feet before his wings catch him.

Well, now that I am all healed, I can take on these demons with no problem.

Jayden flies up to me, "What are you thinking?"

I sniff the air. "Well, I can't smell any other demons besides those three and it would be a shame to go back to the school empty-handed. Even if we went to my car now, they would see us."

He looks back down at the demons, "Umm, I don't think that's a good idea."

I put my hand on his shoulder, "Look, you can be my backup if I have trouble, which I doubt I will, and I'll be the door too so you don't have to worry about that."

He groans, "You're going to do it even if I say no."

I smile, "You know me so well already."

I reach up and pull out my God's Blades and my smile grows.

"Can you stop smiling? You are creeping me out," Jayden mumbles.

I flip him the bird and fall silently towards the demons on the roof. They don't even look up once; they don't know I'm here until I slice one of their heads off. The other two are on me immediately, slashing at me with their claws. I play with them for a while. One of them is able to scratch my arm and rip my shirt.

I snarl, "I am getting tired of you guys ripping my clothes!"

I am done playing now. I advance on them and they split up, and one of them tries to attack me from behind. I'm able to block both of their attacks by dropping to my knees and cutting through their legs. As they fall, I stand up and raise my blades over my head and pierce both of them. My blades go through them before they can hit the ground.

Jayden lands right beside me. "Wow! That was amazing, did these demons suck or are you that good?"

I don't answer him, "Can you drag that other one over here?" I ask as I draw the circle around the two demons.

He does as I ask.

"I have a feeling we need to get out of here as quickly as possible. These three demons were after us, and I don't want to push my luck with any more," I say.

I do the prayer and the demons pass through me with no problem, and all that's left are three black hearts in the circle. I pick them up and hand one to Jayden.

He raises an eyebrow, "Why are you giving me one?"

I shrug, "Well, it's not like I get paid for every heart I collect, and you're oddly the first person I trusted to have my back."

He looks in awe.

I frown, "Don't make me regret giving it to you."

Before he can say anything, the alarm on my phone goes off, telling me it's three am.

"Damn, it's that late already? We should get out of here before more trouble finds us."

Jayden laughs, taking off towards the car, "Please, I think you're just a magnet for it."

I smile in agreement.

As I follow Jayden, I can feel someone watching us. I look around to see if I can see anyone but I can't.

"It's probably the lack of sleep," I mumble to myself.

Nothing happens during the car ride back to the school, but I do find out that Jayden is a loud snorer. He passed out not even five minutes into the drive. I'm not sure if it's because of all the soul-sucking I did or the fact it's so late.

As we're pulling into the school, Jayden's buzz that he gave me has worn off and exhaustion is washing over me. My eyes close with the garage door. The dream is the same as always but there are flashes of emerald and white, not just black hands grabbing my ankle.

I jolt awake once I hit the ground. A groan rumbles in my throat. I try to rub the kink out of my neck—a soft snore makes me freeze. I look behind me, and in the back seat, Jayden has crammed himself into it. His legs are stuffed under the passenger seat and his head is at a ninety-degree angle, his large arm is under his head as a pillow.

I go to shake him awake, and just as my hand rests on his shoulder, his eyes fly open and his blue eyes lock onto mine. He sits up, just as I draw my hand back.

"What time is it?" his voice is a low, husky rumble in the morning, almost sexy—almost.

I look at my phone, "Holy shit, it's nine am!"

I jump out of the car and my legs give out a little from being cramped up in the car for so long.

Jayden is smarter and gets out a lot slower, "Why does it matter if we are late for class?" he says in between a stretch.

"Because I'll be grounded if I leave the school grounds and late. I can't be late or no more going out for me," I say, annoyed because I know I am going to get in a lot of trouble for this.

I don't even get to the garage side door before it opens with a pissed-off Father Jack looking at me, and Anna looking at me with worry and sadness.

I look down and mumble, "Here we go."

I feel his rage before he even starts talking. "Where have you two been?" he looks at both of us. "You've been together all night! Alex, this is not what I meant by showing him around!"

Jayden steps forward, I try to stop him but he just shakes my hand off. "Father Jack, it's not her fault, I practically tied myself to her car."

Father Jack turns his icy glare to him, "Oh, don't worry, Jayden, you are in trouble too. I called your trainer and he's on his way."

Jayden flinches and takes a step back. I almost want to say that he looks scared.

"Both of you know better than to go out with each other!" Father yells so loud that I'm sure the whole school can hear this.

I glare at him, "So, you're telling me I have the same rules as the other God's Right Hand! Would you be so furious if I was a male?" My canines are showing. "I've been obeying the same rules as them, I have not shown any interest in the opposite sex, I have been loyal to the church, I have not swayed in my faith of God, I've dedicated my life to God's Daughter! I have not once broken my blood oath! So, don't you dare make me feel ashamed that I was doing my duties and for being a female!"

I take the doll off, my blood is boiling, I can feel my saliva foaming at my mouth and my vision turning red. I storm past Father Jack and give him the stupid doll and leave Jayden before I do something I regret.

Anna reaches out her hand but draws it back to let me go. I can also hear Jayden asking why they are so hard on me and where I was going. Shooting off all of his annoying questions, Father Jack doesn't say anything but I can feel him trying to burn holes in the back of my head.

I march straight for my gym. I have my own gym so people don't question why my training is more advanced than everyone else's. I begged Father Jack for it once I started the Angel Saviours and he agreed, but my first couple of payments went to the renovations of it and I was able to build it how I wanted it.

My gym has a running track, which I have to run four times to make a mile. The running track I made into more of an obstacle course. I keep the temperature high in here too, almost like a heat wave every time I open the door to the gym. In the middle of the room, it's split in half. On one side, I have my weights, climbing rope, a rotating rock climbing wall. I used to have a punching bag but I would go through them so fast that I was sending whole paycheques on them, so I just stopped using them.

On the other half, I have my sandpit where I work with my blades, other weapons, and hand-to-hand combat. I'm sure there is more of my blood in the pit than there is sand. Daniel keeps telling me to change out the sand because it's rather disgusting, but I leave it as a reminder that if I don't move fast enough, I'll bleed—even if I don't have a soul. On the edge of the sandpit are three 12X12 posts that are wrapped in thick cotton rope. And on the opposite side is a large board for target practicing.

There is a table close to the sandpit with some of my favourite weapons—my blades, daggers, throwing knives and axes, a couple of staffs, and mostly just for fun, a bullwhip too. There are also some sharpening stones and a case of water.

Anna used to train with me all the time when I was younger, but now that I'm too good for her, she usually just runs with me but will not get in the sandpit with me. Mr. Daniel is the only one who does, and even now, he isn't that much of a match for me anymore.

I run on the track until the sweat soaks through my shirt and my feet become sore (I run barefoot—it keeps them tough). My anger levels are still really high, so I work on my back muscles, especially my lower back as I use those muscles the most while I'm flying. You would think it would be my shoulders but I need to keep myself up and tight in that area or I will be all over the place.

Next, I work on my arms, lifting weights until my arms became numb. Once they are like this, I pick up my God's Blades and start going through the steps and swings. My favourite dance—no, this is far more beautiful than any dance. There are turns, flips, and throws, and my partners are my blades. I get faster and can do it longer, but there is always room for improvement. When I first started, I would get deep cuts on my arms, legs, and my back. I was never allowed to stop until I at least did it right once, no matter how long it took me.

I do my dance until I can't hold them up anymore—even though my arms are relaxed at my side, they shake, barely holding on to the God's Blades, and my breath is ragged. The sweat is dripping off of me, and it burns my eyes. Whoever Father Jack gave my doll to is going to feel like shit for a while.

I go over to a small table just on the edge of the sandpit, where I keep towels and water. Wiping my face with a towel doesn't help, it just makes a white towel brown. I crack open a water bottle, my muscles scream and make my hands shake, causing me to spill water down my chin. I can feel it seeping into my shirt.

"If you keep doing that, I will be able to see through it."

The water spires out of my mouth. I turn around but the coughing fit I am having is causing my eyes to blur up, so I can just barely see him. Even though I just see the outline, I can tell who it is.

"Surprised to see me?"

I can't speak, he's stealing all my words from my mouth, and there are thousands of questions going through my mind. I'm trying to keep my face neutral, but I'm sure he can see that I'm surprised, mad, and a little scared that I didn't hear him until he wanted me to.

How long was he here? How did he get here? What the hell is going on?

The white-haired demon holds up a hand. "Now, I know you must have some questions about how I got here. And that boring stuff, but before that, I just want to say you are amazing," he says, taking a few steps towards me. "I have watched you for about an hour and was not even the slightest bit bored. Do you know how hard it is to entertain me?"

I snarl, "I am not here for your entertainment." I'm a little surprised that my voice didn't crack.

His lips start to turn up in a smile, "Even if you're not, you do a good job at it." He cocks his head to the side and looks me up and down. "I wonder why my father wants you so badly though. I'm sure he can make another one of you if he really wanted to."

"Well, it's good to want things. Now, what the hell do you want?" I spit.

"Well, we want you."

I narrow my eyes, "We?"

As the words leave my lips, two twin female demons appear behind him. I can see them too, they aren't just black shadows. Their hair is dark as a raven's feather; one has it up in a high ponytail and it falls well past the middle of her back; the other one has two French braids that are brushing her hips. Their eyes are just black with no other colour to them, the skin around their eyes are all red, like they have been crying, but I know better—they are very hungry. The other angels say that the hungrier they are, the redder their eyes get. I've never seen it before.

One twin does have darker skin than the other, but they both have the same burn mark on the opposite cheek. They stand a head taller than him, so about a foot taller than me. They are just mostly legs and remind me of a python... if they get a chance to wrap their limbs around you, you are never going to get free.

My mouth is dry and I can feel my heart racing—not because of lust, but because of fear. I don't think I have ever been this terrified before. They can smell it, and all three of them have smiles growing. It just pisses me off.

"Did you know that an angel's fear is probably the best-smelling thing in the world? It's almost sweet and pure; we demons really can't get enough of it."

The lighter twin demon scoffs, "She doesn't smell like any angel I've smelt before."

The darker one crosses her arms and nods in agreement.

Confusion washes over his face, "This is true. Why do you smell better?"

The twins both huff. "She smells rotten," they echo each other.

Okay, now I'm the one who is confused.

He turns his back to me and faces them, "Really? She smells horrible to you two? She smells better than a full angel."

I don't wait for the twins to answer; I pick up two of my throwing knives and whip them at him. The twins shove him out of the way. Where the twins now stand, the knives should make contact but they catch it. They smile at me, showing their canines, which are starting to grow. They are twice as long as mine and almost remind me of a saber tooth tiger—they can't close their mouths. Their black eyes shift to a dark red and the red around their eyes takes up more of their face as if they are crying and the red is running.

I can't hide my shock, "What the hell is going on?" I snarl. "I've heard people say they get so angry that their eyes go red, but damn, you should get that looked at."

The white-haired demon flashes in front of my face so fast that I don't even have time to blink. I have to tilt my head up as he towers over me to see his emerald eyes staring into mine. His eyes aren't completely green, there is a black ring around the iris that makes them pop more. There are also some yellow and dark brown specks throughout them. His eyes lock me into place and I can't move. I always thought demons smelt like death, pretty much like a zombie would be, but he smells like brown sugar and fresh rain.

He runs the back of his hand down my cheek; I can feel his cold, clammy hand. I want to move away, slap it off of me… I want to do something but I'm frozen.

"If you do something like that again, I'm going to make your life a living hell." His smile curls up and it makes me think of a porcelain doll's face breaking, "No, I have a better idea… I am going to take your beloved friends to Hell, especially if you tell anyone that we can walk on Holy land like this. It's kind of a top-secret thing."

Something snaps in me and I realize I'm only a few inches away from my target; I reach for one of the God's Blades and drive it into his stomach before anyone can move.

"Dumb girl, don't you learn? You can't hurt us in this form," the lighter twin snickers.

As I slowly pull the blade back, I can feel it doing something to him. As I let go of his shoulder, he drops to the ground holding his hand over his stomach, keeping his insides in.

"What the hell?" the twins rush over to him.

As soon as their hands touch him, they disappear.

I twist around to make sure that they actually left—to make sure I am alone. I can feel that I am… I can feel my breath returning and my heart rate slowing down. I run my hands through my hair.

"Okay, don't panic, keep calm. You just got your heart rate down. Keep calm."

Should I go and tell Father? "What's the point? The whole school will be on alert and he doesn't need to worry about this too. I should tell him, but Eric…"

I put my blade on the table to see some black tar eating away at my blade. I have never seen this before. I rush to the bathroom and put the blade under cold water.

"Where the hell did this come from?"

The blade is in bad shape, there are holes right through it! It's totally ruined, I can't use it anymore. I do have a few extra blades but I hate losing or wrecking them.

After giving up on my blade, I walk back to my room thinking about whether or not I should tell Father Jack. I decide that I will tell him if I don't kill the white-haired demon in a week. I give myself some time because of the fact that they can disappear and reappear, which will make it hard to track them down.

CHAPTER 10

Walking up the stairs is becoming really difficult, my muscles scream in pain, but I love this feeling. I take a long shower and crawl into my wonderful comfy bed. And what feels like two seconds later, a knock on my door startles me awake. I am surprised that I didn't hear them walking up the stairs. I let out a groan as I sit up.

"What do you want?" I yell.

"I'm just making sure you are alive," Mr. Daniel's voice muffles through the door.

I look down at what I am wearing—a baggy old shirt with some holes in it and short shorts, and I am sure that my hair is a mess and crazy too, with some of it still sticking to the side of my face because it is damp. I run my fingers through it, probably making it worse and puffy. I can also feel the bags under my eyes; I am well on my way to becoming a zombie.

I shuffle to the door and unlock it. "You're not allowed up here." It's the first thing I say to him.

He doesn't look that tired today—he is wearing a black button-up shirt with dark blue jeans and black runners. Something is different about him but I don't really know what.

"What kind of greeting is that? You didn't show up to class and now you are missing our training section... again, I might add." He smirks.

"Well, I've been busy and I need at least two hours of sleep every twelve hours. So, I think I can miss some training and English. And I did about five hours in the gym today."

He looks at me with concern. "You look a lot better than you did yesterday, so I don't understand why you need to miss today. Get some clothes on, we have to be outside the dome soon and meet up with Jayden and his trainer." He turns to leave; I almost have the door shut. "And wear something that you can kick Jayden's ass in, please. His trainer is the G.R.H of the God's Daughter and he is so certain that Jayden will win because God favoured him last time."

I answer him with a snarl, shutting the door and the snarl echoes off the demon's hearts.

"Why are you guys acting so weird lately?" I whisper to them.

If they ever answer back, I'd probably piss myself.

You're not crazy for talking to them; you're just crazy if they talk back. The voice in my head laughs.

"I'm pretty sure I'm already crazy," I mumble to myself.

I look over to my beautiful bed and can't help but pout. I send out a silent promise to it that I will be back soon to give it some company.

I'm going to take my sweet ass time getting ready, I have no problem making the boys wait for me while I get my armour on. Mr. Daniel wants me to put on a show... I can put on a show.

I rarely wear my armour, it is mostly just for show for me. The other Saviours wear theirs but I feel like it slows me down. But my armour is probably my favourite piece of clothing I own though, and of course it is different than the rest of the Saviours' armour.

I wear a turquoise long-sleeve shirt and black tight jeans but I can move easily in them—they hug my legs but I can easily do the splits in them. I have a matte black belt that has two sheaths for my God's Blades, they rest at my sides and in the back, I have a hidden sheath where I keep a small dagger. It is really uncomfortable, especially when you land on it, but when you do a pat down to find all of my weapons, you can't feel it.

The chest plate has buckles on the front so I don't need anyone to help me to do it up; it's all matte black with feathers carved in it and a turquoise line that outlines the chest plate. That's the only colour on it. And the plates for my arms run from my elbows to my wrist, but the top of it ends at a sharp point on the back of my hand. There is a little loop that goes around my middle finger. There is one long turquoise feather on top of it. My high heel boots go up to my knees—the turquoise starts at my knee and fades into the matte black.

I put a French braid down the middle of my head and leave the rest of it down. I do have a helmet too, but I only wear that when a Saviour has fallen and we have to be in full uniform, usually graduation or a promotion. The helmet is all matte black with a feather on each side of my head right by my ears. They are extremely sharp—if you don't put the helmet on properly, you can really hurt yourself. I learnt this the hard way...

It once cut right through my armour; the only thing protecting my lung was my rib. I knew what my commander would have done if I left rank—the punishment would have been worse than standing there bleeding out. The other Blades that were standing beside and behind me snickered and didn't offer to help. I know... for angels, they are all dicks. I saw Father Jack holding Anna back; she wanted to come and help me to make sure I was okay but Father Jack wouldn't let her.

I was pretty much done bleeding by the end of the ceremony and extremely tired. Then I got in trouble for bleeding on the floor. My commander should have counted his lucky stars that I was drained of blood or I would have socked him.

That was also the first time I got Eric to stitch me up—there are large needle holes where he sowed it up. And it took forever for it to heal properly. Anna offered to help out but she started to gag when she saw the needle go through my skin.

I have a dagger sheath in each boot. I only use them if I absolutely have to—I am not really good at throwing them at a far distance.

I put on a thick line of black eyeliner around my eyes and paint my lips black. I always aim to look like death coming to collect you.

I push my wings out and tuck them behind me tightly so they aren't dragging on the ground, then make my way down the stairs. With each step, I let my anger and focus set in and my resting bitch face is now dark and terrifying. I know how I look and I know I look like hell among angels. I know it would be faster to go out the window but I want people to see me.

Just as I reach the last door into the school, the last bell rings. I walk out and everyone stops everything. I'm used to people whispering but I'm not used to the silence. But I keep my head held high and glare at anyone who is brave enough to look at me. I walk through the crowd, the kids scramble out of my way, tripping over themselves.

We aren't allowed to have our wings out while we are inside, it's considered rude, like wearing a hat at the table. A smile pulls at my lips as I watch the mice scurry away. I know that they are not used to me wearing my full uniform and seeing my wings, but by the looks on their faces, they forgot that I am an Angel's Saviour, too.

I walk to the top of the step of the school, stretch out my wings, and take off. I knock a few kids down that are closest to me. I can hear them cussing at me and I can't help but laugh at them.

Outside the gym is a large field, probably the size of three football fields with a normal running track. They also have the free weight gym, some of the girls add a beach volleyball court. I was surprised that Father let them put it in, I use the sandpit to train when it's a nice day and I don't feel like being inside.

93

The girls and most of the guys hate it when I get there before them because I won't let them use it. In the middle of the field is a large bulletproof glass dome that takes up most of the field. It's about the size of a baseball stadium, but with no bleachers—if you want to watch, you have to fly or stand.

The students here are allowed to use it for training and fights. Where most schools have football tryouts, we have our fights. They call the game Angelless, not very angel behaviour beating the crap out of your comrades, so some clever bastard came up with the name. It's to help us train and defend ourselves, everyone has to do it. And the best ten have to go to different schools and beat the crap out of them.

I never got to be in the Angelless—Father Jack said it was because I was already an Angel's Saviour and I already "won". I thought it was unfair at the time; I wanted to show the other boys I could kick their butts. But then I started to collect the hearts and I was more than okay with that prize than a trophy.

I can see the boys and Anna waiting for me. Anna is wearing business clothes, her grey skirt is a little short and her white blouse should be done up a few more buttons. Her long red hair is down and curled at the bottom. Her high heels keep sinking in the grass.

Mr. Daniel is nodding his head, I can tell he approves. Anna smirks at me, knowing that I am overdressed. I know she is going to make fun of me later. Jayden is looking at me with awe, and Jayden's trainer is the only one who looks unimpressed.

I've seen him a lot, but I can never remember his name. Whenever the God's Daughter comes here to see Jennifer for her training, he is right next to her. If he is here, so is the God's Daughter. There can only be one G.D at a time—well, a full one—once the Ultram is done and Jennifer has her God's Right Hand. The full G.D will gift her powers to Jennifer and the old hag can retire.

Apparently, once they retire, the G.D get to pick any place they want to live and get a fat paycheck every month and they can get their own staff to clean it and a cook. None of them are greedy about it, of course, and they donate a lot of their stuff. I would take advantage of it, so that's probably why I am not a G.D.

I don't think I have ever seen that man smile. He is always looking displeased with everything. He has that military haircut, he's standing like he has a stick up his butt, with a box-shaped head and his eyebrows love each other so much that there is no space between them. He has a shirt that is a size too small and he's even wearing military boots with khaki shorts.

God, please help this man!

While landing, I give my wings a couple of good pumps to cause some dust to kick up. Mr. Daniel and the G.R.H don't flinch but Jayden gets most of it and has to lift up his arm to cover his face. Taking the few steps between us so I can be standing beside Mr. Daniel, I mimic how the G.R.H is standing—my hands behind my back with feet shoulder-width apart and I'm looking straight ahead.

Mr. Daniel clears his throat, "Mr. Kim, this is my entry for the Ultram, Alex," he says as proudly as he can. He's even resting a hand on my shoulder.

Mr. Kim lets a sound of disgust escape his big mouth, "Daniel, I can't believe you agreed to take her under your wing. How can you not be ashamed?"

A growl vibrates in the back of my throat and my canines poke me in the lips—they are so much longer than normal, I have to keep my mouth open.

"I assure you, Casey, that my God's Right Hand is more than capable of winning and she can beat all of them in a fight."

"Will you two men stop talking as if we are not here? I did not get woken up to please any of you. I am here to see if Jayden is even worth my time." Some spit comes out of my mouth, I'm sure I'm foaming at the mouth.

Mr. Kim starts to open his trap to say something else, but I hold up my hand.

"Jayden, want to get this over? Once we are done, we can let our mentors have at each other in the dome."

Jayden's eyes are the size of watermelons, so is his mouth. I'm sure I can fit my whole fist in his mouth and there would still be room.

"Why, you little bit—" Mr. Kim says, raising his hand to hit me.

As it comes down, I catch it right before it touches me. From the corner of my eye, I can see Anna taking a step towards me but she stops when she sees that I can take care of myself.

"Now, God's Right Hands should not be acting this way," I squeeze his forearm so hard that I am able to get his jaw to twitch. "Casey, I've fought bigger and stronger demons than all three of you. And if it wasn't for the fact that we are on Holy ground, I would beat you to a pulp right now, but I promise that if you raise your hand to me or anyone on this school property again, I will introduce you to our maker."

Stepping closer to him, I finish, "Do I make myself clear?"

Nodding with a grunt is his answer.

I give him a smirk; shoving him out of my way, "Let's see how well your trainer is, Jayden."

Walking into the dome is a lot less dramatic; the entrance is just a normal size door that is glass—if you didn't know it was there, it would take you forever to find.

I can hear Jayden following me. "I can't believe you just did that," he whispers as if they can hear us now.

"What I can't believe is how he got to be G.R.H. I also can't believe that he thought it was alright to strike me." I look back at him, "Does he hit you?"

Shaking his head, he says, "No, not really… only when we are sparring but I have never seen anyone talk to him the way you just did."

"If people don't show me any respect, I don't show them any."
I hold out my hand, "Don't go easy on me, I can't die." I give him a
wink.

Smirking back, he says, "Don't go easy on, there are two G.D
here." He takes my hand and gives it a shake.

CHAPTER 11

A crowd is starting to form around the dome—the glass keeps out the noise. I can see Mr. Daniel rolling his eyes at Mr. Kim, who is obviously yelling at him. Anna is ignoring them and not taking her eyes off of me. The crowd is making it obvious that they are betting on who is going to win.

Jayden shakes his head and says, "That is so wrong, they shouldn't gamble on who is going to win."

"Don't be too upset, they are betting for you to win. There are going to be a bunch of upset people in about ten minutes," I say while stretching.

Shrugging his shoulders, "I'm used to being a disappointment."

Giving him a small nudge, I say, "Hey, there might be a chance I trip on my own footing, you never know. But let's get this done and over with."

In the dome is thick green grass that looks really nice to lie on. *I guess the blood is good for it.*

We walk to our spots. There are two large poles on either side— one is painted white and the other is painted black and, of course, I'm on the dark side.

Looking up at the crowd that will be behind me, I am surprised to see Jennifer standing there with worry all over her face, maybe some concern for me. My eyes only linger on her for a few seconds before I continue looking over the crowd, a little surprised at how many people came to this. I turn back to face Jayden.

He looks a little pale and uneasy.

I wonder if he's even fought in the dome. I don't even want to fight him, oddly.

The feeling that you get when you know you shouldn't do something, but you know you are going to have to swallow it and just do it anyway. I really hate this feeling. I can feel someone's stares more than anyone's. I look over and make eye contact with Mr. Daniel. His face has the emotion of a stone; I know he can see the doubt on my face. His lip starts to switch and he gives me a slight head nod.

I let out a sigh and my shoulders sink a little.

Father Jack's voice startles me as he begins speaking through the speakers, "Alright, everyone, we all know the rules of the Angelless—you keep fighting until one person is standing, and you need to finish it. If we think you are going to kill each other, we will stop the match and you will spend twenty days in the training dungeon with only one meal a day. You get the weapons you enter with, nothing more and nothing less. In God, we trust, in hopes you become stronger."

I've heard this speech a thousand times. Even though I am in the dome, this time I still find it stupid. But the threat of the training dungeon is not a threat you want to ignore, I have only been sent there three times. It is your own personal hell, especially with only having one meal a day. The third time I was in there was when my soul had killed one of the Sisters. I became so drained that I started to use more of her energy without realizing it. I don't even remember why I got sent there, but with the fear of killing someone again, I tried to be on my best behaviour. My worst punishment now is just getting grounded from going outside.

The beeping of the countdown starts, there are five beeps and then the large church bell rings and that's when it starts.

One deep breath in. Two exhales. Three breaths in. Four exhales. Five breaths in. The church bell rings its sweet sound.

I don't take my eyes off of Jayden as I zigzag toward him, he has his two guns with him and a few small daggers wrapped around his hip and small God's Blades on his back. When the bell rings, the vibe he gives off totally changes, following me with his eyes and guns. I'm not looking at him anymore, instead, I glue my eyes to his trigger finger; watching for him to pull it back.

I'm slowly making my way to him, trying to keep my movements a guessing game for him. But as he said, he doesn't miss a target when he shoots. Moving closer, I can see him breathing more calmly; taking a deep breath, and on his exhale, firing a shot. I hit the ground with a burning, stinging pain on my right cheek. I don't give him enough time to get another shot. I get up and take off after him in a straight line this time.

He looks mad and a little bewildered that I'm able to dodge his attack. I can't help but smile at him—this is way too easy for me. I am about five meters away from him when something white flashes in the corner of my eye. Turning my attention from Jayden, the white-haired demon is standing in the dome with us, smiling.

Starting to change direction and head toward him without thinking, Jayden realizes that I'm distracted and punches me, sending me flying a few feet. As I hit the ground, I eat some dirt. My jaw is dislocated and I know I am already getting a huge bruise on my cheek. The crowd have their fists in the air, cheering for Jayden.

"Will you start being serious?" Jayden says, yelling running toward me with his guns pointing at me.

The demon is running right beside him, smiling with his razor-sharp nails out; they look longer than another demon's I've seen before and there is something dripping from them. It looks like thick black tar. I don't know what it is and I don't want to find out.

The click of a gun brings my attention back to Jayden, lifting my arms up, protecting my face, his bullet bounces off me like wonder woman. I can feel the welt already forming. I lower my arms in time to see five razor-sharp nails coming at me. I move out of the way just in time to miss the nails but some of the tar splatters on my face.

I do a couple of back handsprings away from them; I can feel the tar eating away at my skin, the burning is making my eyes water and very hard to see again. But thank the Lord I can hear just fine because as I'm stuck in the air, I can hear Jayden fire a few more shots at me. One grazes my arm and another one goes through my calf, the rest misses me but not by much.

Eating dirt as I crash into the ground again, my Blades knock out of my hands. I go to stand up but something is holding me down. In the corner of my eye, I can see a barefoot holding me down.

How did Jayden get here so fast?

I look up to see the white-haired demon smirking at me.

I can hear Jayden running towards me again, loading his gun. I squirm, trying to get free; the demon starts laughing and pushing his foot down harder on my rib cage. I cringe as if I'm in pain but it doesn't hurt as bad as my cheek does. I move so I can reach for the dagger in my boot.

"You better wipe off my blood or it will eat away until there is nothing left," he informs me.

"Why did it become so much more gross now I know it's your blood?" I make eye contact with him but I don't freeze like last time.

I slash at his upper inner thigh, he moves just in time that I only nick it; his black blood is like acid and eats away at my dagger. I throw it at him before it's completely gone. The dagger goes right through him, he smiles at me and gives me a wink, then vanishes in a black smoke. The dagger doesn't hit the demon but it does pierce Jayden right in the middle of the chest. I scramble towards him and just get to him right before he tries to pull it out.

"Shit, don't pull it out, you idiot," I hiss at him.

He starts to squirm, "It's burning, Alex! Put out the fire!"

What? Confused, I rip his shirt open and there is black spreading, like the demon's blood is killing him.

Panic washes over me and I look into the crowd, searching for Jennifer. Once I spot her, I wave her to get in here. She vanishes into the crowd, pushing people out of her way.

Jayden starts to twitch, blood spilling out of his mouth and he is sweating so bad that I can see it dripping off his forehead. I am not great at healing people but I place both of my hands over him and whisper the Latin phrase, 'Be healed'.

"Consanesco," I whisper it about three more times.

Jayden stops moving and the black veins stop moving too, but they aren't retreating back so I am not healing him, I'm just holding it.

Mr. Daniel and Mr. Kim come up behind me; I'm sure within seconds of the knife striking Jayden, but it feels like forever.

Mr. Kim shoves me out of the way so hard that I'm about a foot away from them and Mr. Daniel sits on the other side of him. They both start their healing; they aren't doing any better than I was.

"Since when do you put poison on your daggers?" Mr. Daniel screams at me without taking his eyes off of Jayden.

"This isn't poison, this is demon's blood. Where did the demon blood come from?" Mr. Kim demands me to answer.

Opening my mouth to answer, Jennifer butts in, making the men move out of her way. She doesn't have to say consanesco. She places one hand on his forehead and the other one close to the wound. The light that escapes from under her hand is a light blue, and I can feel the heat from where I am standing.

The blackness slowly starts to shrink, and Jayden's breathing slows down.

Mr. Daniel grabs me by the shoulders. When I don't look at him right away, he gives me a firm shake.

"Where did you get the demon blood, Alexandra?" he demands me.

I've never seen his eyes so mad before—I can feel his anger in his grip.

I can hear Mr. Kim storming over to us. "You got it from your cheek… didn't you have demon's blood in you?"

I'm shocked that he even said that to me, I can't even find any words to explain what happened.

"Alex, come with me," Father Jack's voice booms over everyone's. Anna is standing right behind him.

Mr. Daniel drops his hands and turns to Father Jack—everyone stops what they are doing and looks at him.

"Mr. Kim and Mr. Daniel, once Jayden is in the hospital and the threat of losing him is gone, come to my office. I'll take care of Alex." Father Jack turns around and slowly walks out of the dome.

Anna notices that I am limping and doesn't even ask if I need help. She grabs my arm and puts it over her shoulder. We are staying close to Father Jack right now, but my leg is killing me and I need to slow down. I can feel Anna take more of my weight for me. I want to look back to make sure Jayden is okay, but the shame is making me keep my head down.

CHAPTER 12

I don't look at anyone or say anything to either of them. They don't try to speak to me either, at least until we get to Father Jack's office. Once we get to his office, I'm sure they'll start blowing me up with questions I don't even know how to answer.

I am dreading going up the three flights of stairs.

"Umm, can I fly to your office so I don't have to limp?" I ask.

Father Jack nods. Both Anna and I fly the rest of the way.

We enter his office and sit on the couch, waiting for Father Jack. Anna sits me down slowly on the couch which doesn't feel as comforting as it usually does. Resting my elbows on my knees, I hang my head. My hair falls out of my braid and acts like a wall for me.

Anna still hasn't said anything but she's resting a hand on my shoulder. I can feel the warmth of her hand and it's oddly soothing, but I will never tell her that.

Father Jack doesn't say anything as he walks in and I don't lift my head either. He goes straight to the washroom; I can hear the water running. A minute later, Father Jack comes back and kneels down in front of me. I look up at him. He has a washcloth and a bowl of hot water with him.

"Let's wash off that blood," Father Jack says, moving slowly and so gently that I can barely feel it.

"Father, I didn't know demons could bleed," I whisper.

He lets out a sigh, "Most don't, I've only seen about three demons that could bleed that black tar. In our history books, they are known as Caedes Sanguinem."

Trying to remember my Latin, I take a second for the words to come out, "Deaths blood?"

"Father, should we be telling her this?" Anna asks.

Father Jack nods, "Yes, she is obviously hunting one, so she has the right to know now." He looks back to me, "If a lot of it gets into our bloodstream, we can die in a matter of seconds… good thing you were there to start healing. But since you are so different from the rest of us, it's not spreading on you. Just the blood that made contact with your skin is eating it away like acid, which should be another nice scar for you."

"Great because I need a huge scar on my face… it's not like people don't look at me enough. I wish the consanesco worked on me."

He gives me a small smile, "Well, you do heal fast all on your own, unlike the rest of us."

We go quiet again. Once Father Jack finishes cleaning me up, it feels weird for him to do this, it's like I am a little child again and I need him to wipe my face. The water is a dark brown with some black floating on top of it.

"I must ask before the other two show up… where did you get the blood?" Father Jack's voice sounds so sad and worried.

I let out a sigh, "Last night, I was hunting that demon and we met up with him and got in a scrap, I nicked him with my dagger and I didn't know demons could bleed. If I did, I would have cleaned it." Not all of that is a lie.

Father Jack isn't taking his eyes off of me, "You're not lying, are you? I am surprised you didn't notice it before… it eats away anything it makes contact with."

I narrow my eyes, "Father, that's why I was so tired and didn't even leave my car this morning. And I am not sure how the blood works, I have never heard anything like it before."

He doesn't look convinced and I know that Anna knows for sure that I am lying—she always does.

"Father, can you tell me more about demons that can bleed? Why are they different? And why haven't I heard anything about them before now?" I try to ask the questions calmly, but the excitement in my voice is there.

Anna twitches a little, but we ignore her. I can feel her tensing up.

He sits at his desk with a sour face, "We do not tell students this until their last month of school because we do not want the younger students to know this information until they are ready.

"The demons who are able to bleed are direct descendants of Lucifer himself. We have a disadvantage to Lucifer, where demons are lost souls that we are able to save, but he also has Lucifens. They are like fallen angels and they can walk on this earth for as long as they want to. They do not have the fear of disease that took your mother."

"So, we are stronger than demons but weaker than Lucifens? Why did you wait so long to tell me?" my blood is beginning to boil.

"Because the last time a Lucifen showed up was about twenty years ago, I didn't think we would see another until you graduated. I also told the God creatures to warn me as soon as one shows up." He glares at Anna.

"I have never seen one or smelt one, so how was I supposed to know what he was? All I could tell that was different about him was he was stronger and had more of a death smell to him!" she yells at him.

"How dare you send me off fighting demons for the church without all of the information that I need to know! I would handle everything differently! Jayden wouldn't be in the state he is in now if I knew! You need to let everyone know and not just the seniors!" I demand.

Father Jack's face becomes tired and he looks like he just aged a few years.

"I've been talking to the high church for years to get this information out sooner, but they don't think younger students will understand."

I cross my arms. *There's no use fighting about this right now.* "That's not right or fair to us. But I need more information about this, where can I learn more?"

Father hesitates.

"You know I will just go to Eric with this if you don't tell me," I threaten him.

He shoots me a glare before he starts writing down something, then hands it to me, "Here, give this to Sister Autumn in the library. She'll show you where you can get more information about them."

I greedily take the note, "Thanks," and leave the room, with Anna hot on my heels.

Eric is sitting on the chairs, waiting for me. His hair has some major bedhead going on. I can see the bags under his eyes… he hasn't fallen asleep. His uniform is usually neat and all together, he even wears the jacket all the time and his tie is always perfect. But today, he only has his long-sleeve on and the dress pants—no tie or jacket.

"What are you doing here? You should still be resting. Are you feeling better?" I ask him harshly.

"I was but then they brought in Jayden and I got worried about you. You're not in trouble?"

I don't say anything, I just put my hand on his elbow and help him up.

Once we are a few feet away from Father's office, walking slowly, my leg is still killing me but the bleeding has stopped and my pant leg is drying to it and pulling at my skin. It's quite annoying.

"Anna, what can you tell me about Lucifens?" I whisper.

She doesn't say anything at first, "I know a bit, but like I said, I have never had to deal with one, but where we are going is a better place to talk in private."

"What is a Lucifen? And why have I never heard of them before?"

Anna sighs, "I'll tell you once we get to the library. We can't talk here."

He doesn't look impressed but nods anyway, "Do you want to know about Jayden?" he asks, changing the subject.

I shrug, "I'm sure no one will let me near him now. I honestly just want to go to the library where it's quiet and maybe fall asleep for a few hours without anyone waking me up."

"Yes, because the library is the best place to have a nap…" he says, laughing.

The library entrance is on the second floor; we don't fly down so we can walk with Eric. He doesn't like flying much but he does fly with me once in a while to stretch his wings.

Just walking into the library, smelling the books calms me down so much that the muscles in my shoulders relax. The library has thousands of stained glass windows from the floor to the roof. People who aren't even into books come in here just to watch the lights dance around the whole room. There are rows and rows of books, there are two stories of them. I'm sure if you had all the time in the world, you couldn't finish all of these books.

In the middle of the library is a larger round desk with unorganized stacks of books all around it. I can hear Sister working behind them but I still can't see her.

"Sister?" I call for her.

Her head pokes out with a huge smile on her face. She reminds me of a cute little mouse. Small nose that twitches all the time to keep her glasses up, her glasses make her eyes appear a lot larger than they actually are.

"Alex and Eric, nice to see you two on this lovely day. Why aren't you two outside?" she rushes up to us. She has to be about four-foot-nothing; she makes me feel like a giant.

I give a small smile and hand her the note. As soon she reads the note, her smile disappears.

"Oh, the Heavens," she looks at Anna, then to me with so much panic in her eyes, I almost want to hug her. "Does this mean you had to fight one?" she whispers so quietly, I can barely hear her.

I give a sharp nod.

She doesn't say anything but shakes her head and waves for us to follow her.

We follow her into her circled desk; she moves a rug to reveal a small trap door. She pulls out an old-looking key and opens up the door. There are stairs with a faint light at the very bottom.

"Everything you need is down there," she whispers. "Just ring the buzzer at the bottom of the stairs and I'll open it back up for you. If I don't open it up right away, that means someone is around and you'll just have to wait. I'm sure you remember how things work, Anna."

Anna nods.

"We'll be down there for a while... probably well after closing."

She smiles, "I have a lot of work to do after closing time, so I'll still be here."

I give her a nod and Eric and I help each other down the stairs. I'm expecting it to smell like old mouldy potatoes and dirt, but as we got closer to the light, you can tell that it is well-taken care of, but still really old. There are about five large bookshelves and a large table that can fit about twenty people. Where Sister's desk is messy and disorganized; down here, there is nothing out of place.

"Where should we start?" I ask.

"How about you start telling me what's going on?" Eric demand.

Sitting Eric down and taking off most of my armour that I still have on, I tell him and Anna everything, even the part about how attracted I am to him, how I am drawn to him. The longer I talk, the deeper their frowns become. I know I should keep it to myself but I have never been able to keep anything from these two before, so there is no reason I should start doing that now. And I am sure they'll find out eventually.

"They should be telling us way sooner about the Lucifen," that's all he says.

A smile twitches at my lips, "I agree. I am so underprepared for this. I want to see if there is any record of Lucifens walking on Holy ground before."

"We should tell someone that Lucifens can walk on Holy ground," Anna says. "To my understanding, the church does not know this."

"I told you they will kill Eric if I do. And like I said, if Eric wasn't here to control me a little, I would leash all my unholy powers onto the school."

I get him to smirk but Anna isn't laughing.

I sigh, "I know we should tell them but they keep secrets from us too, so just keeping this one for right now isn't so bad." Looking at her, I add, "Can you tell us more about them?"

She shrugs, "You know more than I do apparently. We don't know a great deal about them. They rarely come up here, and when they do, we can barely keep tabs on them. One Lucifen is as strong as three demi-angels. They have killed a lot of us apparently. I think Lucifer just sends them up here when he wants to remind us how strong he is."

I groan, "Why do I have to be dealing with one? And it's not like I can stop, he shows up whenever he wants to."

"Maybe somewhere in these books is something that can help us figure out how to track one down or maybe a spell to keep them off the school grounds," Eric says.

"Well, by the look of things down here, I'm sure there aren't any braille books, but I'll need your help with some translating because Anna and I suck with other languages," I add.

"Hey, I am fluent in French and Spanish," she squeaks.

Eric snickers, "I am almost positive that there aren't any French or Spanish books down here."

Anna looks annoyed but I start to walk in between the bookshelves, looking at each book carefully and grabbing the ones that I'll need. I make about three trips back to the table with an armful of books, there are even some scrolls. I only grab the scrolls that say 'Death's blood' on them. There is about half a bookshelf with them—most of them are so faded that I can't read them or in a language I have never seen before. The books are all shapes and sizes, and by the time I'm done, they almost take up the whole table.

Looking at the heap of books I have to read, "At a time like this, I really wish you could see."

"Sorry, maybe we can get someone to come down here and help us."

"No, they will ask too many questions on the information I'm looking for."

I sit down beside Eric and grab the closest book to me, "Might as well get comfortable… we are going to be here for a while."

CHAPTER 13

I read out loud for Eric, I figure that would be easier than trying to explain it later. Some of the Latin words I have to spell out for him so he can tell me what they mean, and there's no way I can pronounce them. Anna passes out by the time I reach the twentieth page.

I really need to work on my Latin words more—it takes us twice as long to read a paragraph because I can't understand it. I am lucky that God gave the gift of patience to him... if I was Eric, I would have told that person to leave a long time ago.

I look at my phone and realize we have been down here for about five hours now and all that we have learnt is pretty much what we already knew. And all that Anna has accomplished is making a lake with her drool—she might be really beautiful when she is awake, but she is not so hot while she sleeps.

Eric starts running his hands over the books.

"What are you doing?" I ask.

"Maybe we should be looking at the oldest book, people nowadays don't even read them anymore because the books get updated, especially if the book was written in Latin before or a language that is forgotten."

A groan vibrates my throat, "So, it will take us longer to finish it… why can't they be in braille? You could just read it and tell me what it's talking about."

He chuckles, "Just think about how well you'll do in Latin class now. Maybe eventually you'll be able to do this on your own and won't need my help."

I bounce my head off the table, "I'd rather you just do it."

Anna doesn't even twitch at the sound. I'm a little surprised that she is sleeping so hard.

I glance at Eric and he picks up an old scroll and runs his hands all around it, then licks it.

"Umm, what are you doing?" I ask, raising my head.

He smirks, "Tasting how old it is."

"You can tell that by tasting it?" I question.

He starts to laugh, "No."

I can't help but join him and I start laughing too.

After we calm down, Eric gives me the scroll, "This is the one you might want to look at."

I unroll it slowly, the language that it's written in looks like hieroglyphics. I scroll to the bottom to see if there are any words I can recognize, but there's nothing besides the church's crest and a crest I am not familiar with.

The crest has two swords that are right beside each other—one is pointing to the ground and looks like it's painted white at one point, and the other one is pointing to the sky and it might have been black at one point. There's a chain wrapped around both of them and something is holding the chain together but I can't make it out.

"Well, what does it say?" Eric asks, scooting closer to me.

"Do you know a lost language that uses hieroglyphics or a crest that has two swords?"

Scowling at the empty space, "This scroll is very old, older than most history. This history is before Jesus died for us.

"I'm sure that no one who can read this now. Not even God's Knowledge has the ability to go this far back. Most of us can't even go back to Jesus."

My hope is slowly slipping away. "What are we going to do? And why is this scroll here? Shouldn't this be in Rome or something?" I whisper more to myself than to him.

Who would be still alive then?

"I'm not sure why it's here but angels and demons don't die, and Lucifer has been here before the beginning of time. So, maybe his precious Lucifens will know too, or do you know any angels here right now?"

I shake my head, "Maybe Father will know. Do you think this scroll has the answer we need?" I ask. "Or does it have more questions?" I ask more to myself.

He answers my question with a question. "What are we looking for anyway?"

"I want to know more about them… when they started showing up, how they are taken care of, and if there is any past history of them being able to walk on Holy ground even if it's a projection of themselves. Maybe there is something we can use to make sure that they can't do it or they have a pattern that they always follow.

"There are so many things that we don't know, and if there is something I can do to give me an edge over them; even if it's a small chance of finding it, I still want to try. Especially if that means I can stop demons popping in and out of my life," I answer him.

"Okay, we should go and see Father then," he says, standing up.

I carefully roll up the scroll and hide it in the back of my pants and pull my shirt over it; doing it quietly as I don't want Anna to know I am taking it. I slam my fist right by her head to wake her up—she nearly jumps out of her skin.

She helps me pick up the rest of my armour and we start helping Eric up the stairs. I push the button as we pass it, and just as we get to the stop, the door opens up.

"That was perfect timing, I just finished my work for the night," Sister whispers. "I hope you found everything you need?"

I shake my head, "No, we have to go and ask Father some questions first."

She looks worried, "Oh, well maybe there is something I can help you with?"

I hesitate for a second, "Do you know if there are any angels here on Earth right now? And close by."

Her brows crease more, "Why do you need to know that?"

Eric shrugs, "Just more questions for them is all."

He answers so vaguely—he must have noticed that I don't want her to know what we are up to. The fewer people that know, the better because I have a feeling we are poking something we shouldn't be.

She shakes her head and only tells us that there are none nearby. We say our goodnights and leave the library.

The halls are empty again; the only sound is our feet echoing off the walls. When we round the corner to Father's office, we can hear men arguing. First, all we can hear is muffled but as we get closer, we can hear them and, of course, they are arguing about me.

I put my ear to the door, Mr. Kim is yelling, "You need to do something about her! What if she harms more God's Right Hands? She probably wants to win so badly that she is willing to poison everyone that gets in her way!"

Eric's hand tightens on my arm and Anna lets a small growl out.

Someone slams their fists onto something, making us jump.

"I did not teach that way! She would never do something like that!"

My eyebrows shoot up. *Wow, Mr. Daniel is sticking up for me?*

"She needs to be punished!" Mr. Kim demands.

Father Jack sighs—I know his sigh from anywhere.

"Okay, Mr. Kim, what would you have us do?" Father Jack asks.

Without hesitation, "Put her in the training dungeon until Jayden wakes up and see what he thinks her punishment should be."

The room goes quiet.

"You can't go back there," Eric hisses.

"You three, why don't you come in here?" Father Jack requests.

Before I open the door, I give the scroll to Eric. Anna looks shocked that I did something like that but I know she won't say anything. Then, I slowly push the door open to see all three men standing with their arms crossed, glaring at us.

I lock eyes with Father Jack. "So, Alex, what do you think of Mr. Kim's proposal?"

Narrowing my eyes at Mr. Kim, I say, "I will go willingly if Mr. Kim wears my doll," I challenge him.

Mr. Kim barks a laugh, "Why would I wear your disgusting soul?"

I give him a dark smile, "Because the last time I went there, someone died. So, if you send me there and someone dies, it will be your entire fault but I have a feeling that a G.R.H has enough energy that I can't drain them out completely."

Father Jack and Mr. Daniel nod in agreement with me.

"That is an excellent idea, and a God's Right Hand like yourself can handle it. Mr. Daniel, could you go and get her doll from Sister Katherina? Once you get back, we'll take Alex to the training dungeon."

Mr. Kim doesn't even have enough time to disagree to anything, but he is as pissed as I am about the whole situation.

Eric clears his throat, "Father, do you really think this is wise? It's not like it's her fault that she didn't know about the blood."

Father Jack looks disappointed, "I know, but the whole school is wondering what happened and something needs to be done about it. Alex has done things for the church that no one knows about, this secret is no different."

My lip curls, releasing a growl, "That's a piss-pour reason for punishing me so harshly."

Although, I'm excited for Mr. Kim to be wearing the doll. I don't say the last part out loud. I don't need people knowing the rush I get from having a new soul to feed off of.

Father glares at me, "You should have known that we need to do some sort of punishment."

My canines grow, stabbing into my gums, making me produce more saliva, "You wouldn't have to punish me if you told everyone about the Lucifens."

"Even you knowing about them is breaking the rules," Mr. Kim snarls at me.

I can feel the saliva dripping from my chin. I want to rip his throat out.

Father slams his hands on the desk, "Alex! Mr. Kim! That is enough!"

"I wish it was you in the dome, I would have pulled that dagger out of you just to watch you bleed."

I know I am the one who said those words, but the voice isn't mine, it became deeper and more satanic. Everyone in the room is looking at me. Father has a bit of concern, but there is some fear mixed in. Mr. Kim looks disgusted and terrified—two deadly mixtures. Anna and Eric just look scared and inch away from me.

I want to look down and look like a little puppy that needs help and not a beast that needs to be caged and beaten. But I stand my ground and keep my head held high. I am sure that everyone can hear my heart.

"Everyone needs to calm down, we don't need to make this a bigger problem than it is," Father Jack says through his teeth, trying to calm himself down.

The atmosphere is thick with tension, I'm sure I am not the only one getting choked out by it. I want to storm out of the office so badly; I want to go out to the fresh air. No one says anything or relaxes until Mr. Daniel comes back.

Mr. Daniel opens the door, cautiously peering in, already aware of the tension, "I guess I missed something?"

Father walks over to him holding his hand out, "Never mind that, we need to get this over with and, hopefully, Jayden wakes up soon."

Mr. Daniel ignores Father and walks straight up to Mr. Kim and thrusts the doll at him, "You protect this with your life, it's worth more alive than dead to all of us. And maybe if we are lucky, she won't kill you."

I look between the doll and Mr. Kim, my heart picks up with excitement. Just the idea of the rush that he'll give me is exciting me.

Oh, this might become a problem. I'm sounding like an addict.

Mr. Kim slowly puts the doll around his neck. I move to the couch before the doll hits his chest. Just in case it is all too much for me. The wave hits me before I get to the couch, the adrenaline is so much greater than Jayden's. Mr. Kim's soul is making me feel dizzy and a little bit nauseous. The pain in my cheek goes away and I can feel my skin slowly sewing itself back together. All the scrapes and bruises I got in the dome are fading or gone already. The bullet hole in my leg feels better too.

"Alex, are you okay?" Eric whispers.

The other three are talking about something that involves me but I can't really hear them with the ring in my ears.

I grab onto Eric and Anna so I don't fall, "Mr. Kim's... soul... it's almost too much," I say slowly. "It's a rush I'm not used to."

Before I can get my head cleared, Mr. Daniel is dragging me out of the room. I slump against him because my feet become useless.

"What is wrong with you? You're acting drunk," Mr. Daniel hisses in my ear, jerking me up to stand straight.

"Mr. Kim... he's too much for me right now," I mumble. "Just give me a minute to shake this off."

Mr. Daniel grumbles about dragging my sorry ass to the training dungeon, but he leaves me alone for a moment.

CHAPTER 14

We all follow Father Jack quietly towards the church, you might think that the training dungeon would be underground but it's not. The church has three towers—two are at the two front corners and the other is at the back of the church, it's twice the size of the other ones. This one has the training dungeon in it. The roof of the tower is all glass so angels can fly up and watch their comrades struggle in the dungeon.

As we climb the last step into the church, I send a small prayer that Jayden wakes up soon. Once we take our first steps through the doors, I push off Mr. Daniel so I can walk up the stairs alone.

Father turns around, "I think it will be best if Alex and I go up from here on out."

Anna grabs Father's arm, "Father, do you think this is such a great idea? What will happen to her if she kills the God's Right Hand? You don't have to put her in there, you can just tell people you did."

He shakes his head, "Come on, Alex."

Father Jack and I head up to the training dungeon. We walk to the door to the tower, which is the Jesus on the cross at the front of the church. It's so heavy that it takes both of us to move it.

Entering the base of the tower, the only light is a small flame in the middle of the floor. Right beside the fire is a chain rolled up nicely. The walls of the tower are smooth, cold marble—no cracks. It goes all the way up until it reaches the glass roof. The glass is the same thickness as the aquariums, I can't break it from in here… I've tried. When I first came here, I punched it so many times that I broke my knuckles.

I sit on the cold marble floor; there are pinkie-size holes in the floor so the water can drain down and the needle points blades to come out.

Father slowly takes off my boots and straps the chain to my ankles. We can't look at each other. He slowly walks to the door with my boots in hand—he doesn't have to explain to me what needs to happen or what I need to do. He turns around and looks at me, even though he is scared of me, I can see that there is also worry in his eyes.

He gives me a head nod and I push up with my wings. I fly up until I reach the end of the chain. I have to be about twenty feet off the ground. Father pulls up on the lever, and razor-sharp needles shoot through the ground.

They come at me so fast, I don't think they are going to stop. I panic, watching those needles come at me has to be the most terrifying thing in the world. I try to fly higher but the chain pulls me back down. The needles stop less than a foot away from me, my toes curl away from them; as if they remember the last time I was here and they got pierced.

Since the Sister who was caring for my doll at the time died because I became so drained, I drained more from her. I didn't really realize at the time what I was doing. Once my doll took the rest of her soul, I didn't have long before I started to fade. My feet touched the blades a few times, just enough to draw blood and to wake myself up.

Father came in time to drop the blades before I fell on them. I have never been so drained of life before. Father didn't tell me about what happened to the Sister until three days later. A part of me wishes that I died too, but deep down, I was happy that I didn't.

Looking at the needles. *I hate this room.*

The door shutting brings my attention back to the only way out of this place. The small fire in the room begins to slowly dim out. The moon is hiding behind a blanket of clouds, so the darkness closes around me.

I close my eyes and disappear to a different world. I never wanted to have a normal life but sometimes I let myself drift to where I was born with normal girl gifts, and my father didn't sell my soul to Lucifer.

On holidays, I get to go to my father's house, have a parent care about me. Have someone love me, without me worrying about him or her hating me because I can slowly kill him or her.

People don't realize that I am actually scared of them—mostly because they are so terrified of me. I am surprised that I don't get into more fights. I am sure if I were a guy with this type of power, I would get into a lot more fights.

Flapping my wings in a different world, when the sprinklers come on, dragging me back to reality. The training dungeon doesn't just have spikes and force us to fly nonstop, but they made it so we have to deal with different types of weather too. It will rain for about an hour, stop for an hour, then wind and freezing rain hits you, stops for an hour, then the temperature drops so much that the window starts frosting up. Most people get really sick after being in here from the change of weather and from the exhaustion.

The rain weighs me down, and the armour I still have on. I still have my chest protector and my long-sleeve shirt. Even though it's torn up, it's weighing me down that the spikes are licking at my toes, but the rain does feel good on my cheek. I am going to take my time in killing that demon, causing me more trouble than I need right now.

His green eyes flash into my mind... his white hair. My heart picks up and my cheeks turn warm. I'm not stupid, I know what these feelings mean. I am attracted to this Lucifen. Anger washes over me.

"I can't believe I am attracted to him! This is so frustrating." I look up, "You have a sick and twisted mind, God."

"I don't think he's the one to blame," his voice echoes off the tower walls.

I glare down, wiping the water from my eyes, and by the door... there he is. Mixed emotions run around through me. There is no way I can get to him without getting impaled. My canines and nails grow, I reach over my shoulder to grab my God's Blades but they aren't there.

He smirks, "Looks like you don't have your swords. Good."

I snarl at him.

He looks around the tower, "You know, this is totally messed up what they are doing to you. Do they do this all the time and to everyone?"

He's looking shocked or the rain is too much in my eyes.

"How long can you fly for?"

I don't answer his million questions, "Why are you here?"

He shrugs his shoulders, "To torment you, but it looks like your own kind is doing my job for me."

I bark a laugh, "I definitely don't need your help to get tormented. So, why don't you just let me have your heart so we can call it square for putting me in this room?"

He runs his hand through his hair, making it slick back. His eyes seem to be glowing in this dimly lit tower. The rain is making his shirt cling to his body and making him more defined. I can see everything, even with him wearing a black shirt and the dim light.

Thank God for my eyesight.

I narrow my eyes, "What is your name?"

"You could never pronounce it," he speaks some gibberish.

My tongue hurts at the thought of trying to pronounce it.

He laughs at my confusion. "I tell the humans my name is Drake, it's a lot easier to say."

I can't take my eyes off of him—I don't even see his hand pull on the lever. The spikes retract back into the little holes in the floor and the sprinklers stop too, but I'm staying in the air. I might be attracted to him and the pull to him is really strong, but that doesn't mean I am going to trust him.

He gives me a small smile and starts walking to the middle of the tower. He has to tilt his head all the way back to look at me.

"Does this make you feel more comfortable to come down?" he asks.

I scowl down at him, "I wouldn't trust you."

He sighs, "Fine." He twists his arm around the chain and pulls down on it hard.

I have no time to react to this and I crash to the floor. Having my wings out barely slows me down enough to do a three-point landing like a superhero. My palm cracks the marble floor and my knees scream in pain. But the pain is gone in an instant. I can feel Mr. Kim's soul flowing into mine. I rush to stand up and get ready to fight.

With his hand still wrapped around the chain, he pulls on it again, taking my feet from under me. The wind gets knocked out of me as I crash onto my back, he jumps on me before I can even move. I growl up at him, trying to get under him.

Why do I let myself get into these positions?

He pins my arms down and squeezes his legs tighter around me and makes sure that he sits forward so I can't wrap my legs around him.

"Will you stop fighting?" he snaps, his eyes are piercing mine.

"I will never stop fighting, no matter how hard you try to break me!" I spit.

I expect him to smile at the challenge, but he just looks down at me with a face made of stone.

"I just want to talk. I want to see why you are so special before I hand you over to my father." I stare up at him, hating everything in this moment.

Why isn't he a black shadow like the rest of the demons I fight?

123

I just realized that we are both soaking wet and he is sitting on me. My heart starts to pick up and my cheeks warm up. I'm hoping he just thinks it's because I am mad. I need to get this Lucifen off of me.

"If I promise not to fight you tonight, you have to answer some of my questions." *This will be easier than reading all those books.*

He smirks, "Making a deal with demons? Isn't that against everything you angels go for?"

I give him a dark smile, showing off my canines, "I'm not planning on going to Heaven." I look at his hands around my wrists, "Are you going to let me up?"

He raises an eyebrow, "Are you going to attack me?"

"I am still an angel… once I make a promise, I always keep it."

He slowly gets off of me, taking a few steps back. I pick up my head and look at him; he is watching me cautiously. He is standing, ready for me to fight. He is wearing a black long shirt and black jeans. He's barefoot and everything is clinging to him.

I sit up and put my wings away. I don't trust him and I don't want to become flightless again. I unbuckle the chains around my feet, even though the floor is still wet and very cold, I stay sitting and massage my ankles. The bruises are a deep purple, almost black… there's even some skin peeling off. I'm sure my ankle is even dislocated, but as I watch my ankles, the bruise disappears just as quickly.

Mr. Kim must be feeling like crap right about now.

"It's amazing that you can heal so nicely."

I tuck my feet away, "Healing this quickly comes with a price. Now, what are your questions?" I grumble.

"Why are you so different? Why does my father want you so badly? It can't be because of your healing abilities."

I scoff, "Looks like you won't be that much use to me after all."

He looks confused, "What do you mean?"

Annoyed with him already, I reach for the chain to put back on.

"You're asking the question I want to know too. I'm sure the only reason your father wants me, is what every man wants, whether he's human or not."

His brows knit together, "Stop talking in riddles, angel."

"It's power, you idiot," I answer annoyingly. "Not to toot my own horn and everything, but I am one of the most powerful demi-angels. And what I want to know is how your father figured that out before I was even born."

He shrugs his shoulders, "Well, that's easy… your father was a Lucifen."

My head snaps up, "What!"

"Really, you didn't know? What story did the church tell you?" he asks in amusement.

"Does this make you my brother?" I ask, disgusted.

He snorts, "No. Well, kind of… if you think we are all God's children and crap like that. Your father was one of Lucifer's followers. One of his best I was told and he was Lucifer's right-hand man."

What the hell? If he is telling the truth, that would explain a lot. But he is a demon, how can I trust him? No! No angel would ever be with a Lucifen! That's impossible! Why would the church even keep me? Maybe because I can walk on Holy ground.

I sit quietly, not sure what to do. He takes my silence as an invitation to continue his story.

"Well, your mother fell in love with your father, I think it was before the Great War. She, of course, thought she could change him, make his heart as white as hers again. Everyone shunned them; the church didn't accept it and we definitely didn't accept it. Well, in all honesty, we didn't even think we could have children with each other, but I guess since your father wasn't a dead human soul, it would work.

"So, once my father found out your mother was pregnant, he wanted the baby. Your father refused at first, but once your mother got sick and God wouldn't help, he came crawling to my father to cure her. Lucifer kept her well until you were born. And since your father didn't listen to my father's request at first; he let the sickness take your mother. I heard that she didn't even have time to hold you before she died."

"Stop!" I snarl, standing up.

He's causing more questions than answers at this point. I want to punch his smug little face.

He tilts his head, "You don't want to learn more?"

I glare at him with my clenched fists and my feet begin to freeze on the marble. I don't answer him again, so he continues.

"And since Lucifer wanted you so badly, the church thought it would be a bad idea for us to have you. So, they stole you away before we could get near you. I heard that there was a huge battle too—a lot of demons and demi-angels died for you. Both sides wanting you so bad… you must feel special."

Without thinking, I ask, "And what about my soul?"

He looks puzzled, "What do you mean about your soul?"

I bark a laugh, "Oh my God, I can't believe I believed you." The tightness in my chest eases, "You almost had me."

His lips curl, "I'm telling you the truth!"

"No you're not, you have your facts all wrong, bud." I slide my hand behind my back and reach for the hidden blade in my belt.

He throws his hands up in the air, frustrated with me, "Just because I don't know about your soul? You think I am wrong about everything… you should get your God's Knowledge to tell you I am right."

"Enough!" I snarl, throwing my dagger at him.

He dodges it just in time again to just cut his shoulder. He presses his hand over the cut and growls at me, showing his canines.

"That's the last time I try to help you, Alex, but you shouldn't trust the church just as much as you don't trust us."

He disappears after saying that.

"What the hell am I supposed to do with this!" I scream to the empty room. I slam my fist onto the floor, breaking a few knuckles. "What am I supposed to do?" I whisper.

I walk over to my dagger and the black blood is already eating away at most of it. I throw it into the fire and look over to the door. I want to leave but I know if I do, I'll have to stay in here longer. But there is no way I can pull the lever with the chain around my ankles without getting impaled. No matter what I do, they are going to know someone was in here.

I don't want to think about what Drake said. I want him to be wrong, so very wrong, but I have a feeling that there is some truth to what he said.

I moan, "I'm going to regret this—all of it. And he didn't clear anything up. Why did I think he could help me!" I start to pace, "And why did Father take my boots! My feet are freezing!"

I pace, thinking of my next move. I still want to talk to an angel, so hopefully, Eric is looking for one. I want to see if Eric can actually look back to my parents and see who is telling the truth. And of course, I don't really know what to do until after I speak with an angel.

And I have to worry about the Ultram, and the other God's Right Hands. If Drake is right and my father is a Lucifen, my chances of winning will be slimmer now. If I have Lucifen blood in me, I should almost step down.

My heart aches at the thought of just giving up on everything I've been training for and the fear of losing my wings. So, I'll still be in the Ultram just for my selfish reasons, but it will probably be a huge headache. And I have to find a way to find Drake and kill him and his twin bitches.

"Please, God, guide me to find an angel to answer these questions."

The floor around the small fire is the only dry spot. I sit down, tucking my knees under my chin, watching the small flames dance.

If he's right about my father, it would explain why I am so different and why I am so powerful. I push my wings out and look at them. They are so black that there are purple and blue highlights in them. Can something so beautiful be so evil? Maybe that's it… demons portray themselves as beautiful humans so they can get their prey—maybe I never had a choice.

If this is the truth, will I feel any different about God or the church? Am I meant to be the villain or the hero? People see me as evil and I am trying so hard to be good just to prove everyone wrong… or is it because I know they are right and I should just accept it?

I wrap my beautiful wings around me to keep somewhat warm and to keep myself cocooned. A tear slips down my cheek, I don't wipe it away, just let it dry. I fight the urge to let more spill out.

CHAPTER 15

I sit like this for hours until my butt becomes numb. Getting up, I look out the window and a faint light comes through. Morning slowly breaks upon the clouds, but it's not colourful—the light is still grey.

I sigh, "Another sleepless night, but thanks to Mr. Kim, I feel fine energy-wise."

A small knock on the door, "Alex?" It's Eric.

I slowly walk to the door, "What are you doing here? You know you'll get in trouble."

"Why does it sound like you are right beside the door?"

"You don't know?" I tease him, "The white-haired demon visited me last night and released me from my chains… before you think oh, great guy, he did it really harshly and my knee still hurts."

He doesn't say anything for a second, "What did he want?"

I rest my head on the door. "I'll tell you once I get out of here. How is Jayden?" I ask more for myself than his well-being.

"He should be walking soon, well, that's what Jennifer said."

"Well, let's hope it's sooner than later. Have you found anything else out or found out where an angel is?"

Eric might be blind but he is very sneaky, and if he wants to know something, there is no stopping him, he'll find it.

"Yes, but none of them are near us—one is in Calgary, two are in California. And the rest are overseas."

"Why do they have to be so far away all the time? It's beautiful here too."

"It's not like we have beaches or a huge city. The only reason our school is near Fort St. John is because it's not heavily populated and it's easier to blend in, and you shouldn't be too mad, a town like John brings a lot of different people who are here for just a short while, so that means the demons like it here more."

"You would think the angels would be here to help us out but now we have to travel to see one."

"Why can't you just call them? Wouldn't that be easier?"

My brows knit together, "They have cellphones?"

Eric's muffled laugh makes me smile a little, "Why would you think that they didn't?"

"I don't know, I think of angels as old beings that have no clue what technology is or how to use it."

Eric's laugh is turning into snorting, "You know that they watch us while they are up there, right?"

I shiver at the thought. "You know, that's really creepy and gross when you say that. Think they are watching us have a shower, taking massive dumps, even worse... they watch us have sex! We are their personal porn."

"Okay, you can stop now," Eric says, chuckling. "I'll be thinking twice about going to the washroom, and sex is differently something I don't have to worry about."

I can't help but smile, "You know it's true, but anyways, did you get the numbers?"

"Ha, the security here sucks. I went on one of the Sisters' computers and their password was 'God loves all', it's sad really. Also, why do they have all of the angels listed with numbers and locations? If someone bad got a hold of that, they can take them down without trying."

"Eric…" Once he starts talking, he doesn't stop, and then he gets mad at me because I stop listening to him after the first five seconds.

"Sorry," he mumbles. "I got the numbers of the people closest to us, but I can go back and get the rest of them. There's only one in Europe, two in Africa, and one in South America."

"No, that's fine, I don't want you to get caught. Even though I know you can just talk yourself out of it."

"Do you want me to call them or do you want to do it?" he asks.

"Call who?" Father Jack's voice comes through the door.

"Eric, I thought blind people have great hearing?" I say, mocking him.

I can only hear two people breathing, so I hope that means that Father is alone so I don't have to deal with Mr. Kim so early in the morning.

"I'm not Daredevil, you know," he shrieks.

"Help me push, Eric."

We open the door and Father looks around, glaring at me.

"How did you get out without scratching yourself?" he demands.

"I had a hidden knife in my belt and I was able to hit the lever with it." *So good at lying, it's scary.*

He lets out a sigh and slumps his shoulders, "You better be happy that it's just me and not Mr. Kim. He's out to get you—he wants you to be locked up in here until after the Ultram."

My lip curls a bit, "Let me go and do a job, I'll make him so exhausted, he'll regret everything. I've been trying not to absorb more than I need. But I can open the floodgates if he keeps pushing me."

Father Jack looks sad, "Just look to God for patience."

I can't help but roll my eyes. "I don't understand how a man like that became G.R.H. He is possibly the worse man I have ever met."

"Yes, he might be a horrible man, but God's Daughter has been the most excellent one we've ever had. She has saved more lives, demi-angels, and humans alike, and according to the angels, more humans have whitened their hearts and are in Heaven. So, he might be a grumpy man, but he makes her shine."

I can't argue with him there.

"So, what are we going to do about this?" I wave my hand around, gesturing to the training dungeon.

"Jayden is awake. So, you are free, but he wants to talk to you."

I can't help but smile, for my freedom and that Jayden is feeling better.

"Can I eat first?" I ask. "I don't remember the last time I had something to eat."

"If you didn't have anything while you were out with Jayden, you had breakfast two days ago," Eric pipes in.

My stomach growls at the thought of it.

Father smirks, "Yes, I'm sure that will be fine."

"Thank you!"

I don't wait for Father to change his mind—I grab Eric's hand and drag him to the cafeteria before anyone can stop me. The cafeteria is on the first floor but the little kids don't eat in there. They get their food delivered to their rooms.

It's still rather early, so the cafeteria isn't full. *Thank you, God.* The cafeteria isn't that big. It has about twenty round tables that fit about fifteen people. Where we get our food, during breakfast there is only one line open, but during lunch and dinner, there are about three different lines you can choose from that serve different meals. I usually go for the one with the most meat.

There is a small stage on the north side of the room, sometimes there are people who play music or have something to announce. When they have bands playing, I won't even come near the cafeteria, I don't understand why people like it when they play. It's always too loud, and I think it's really bad.

This morning, there are a few people in the line waiting for only white omelettes—all organic crap. I want to push these toothpicks out of my way but I hold back.

132

I go up to order, but the cook stops me. He's an older gentleman; he has hairnets for his head and for his beard. They both look like salt and pepper, that and the crow's feet on the corners of his eyes give away his age. He is also a God's Angel, so he doesn't have gifts like the rest of us—can't change forms or cast any spells, so they usually get jobs like this, some of them get jobs in the human world.

"Alex, you need to have shoes on. Those are the rules, and you need to have your school uniform on for us to give you food, you know this."

Trying not to glare at him, I give him my best puppy dog eyes, "Well, I just got out of the training dungeon, so I am extremely hungry, could you please just give me a pass today?" My stomach grumbles to make my point.

He lets out a sigh, shaking his head, "Just this once, Alex, and if anyone complains, I'll send them to you."

I beam a smile, "Thank you, I would like to have about five pieces of bacon, three breakfast sausages, a couple of slices of ham, four eggs, and a huge pile of hash browns, please."

I can feel the twigs staring at me, and the cooks in the back gawk at me.

"I'm hungry, if I don't finish it all, you can put me back in the training dungeon," I snap.

They flinch and get busy making my breakfast.

"Do you want anything, Eric?" I ask.

He laughs, "Why, so you can eat mine too when you are done scoffing down yours?"

I smile, "Awe, Eric, you know me so well."

"Is she off her bipolar pills?" one of the twigs hisses.

The smile flashes off my face.

"Just ignore them, Alex, you shouldn't let people who are beneath you bother you," Anna says coldly, walking up to us.

The girl tsks and storms off and I can't help but smile proudly at my friend for sticking up for me.

133

"Father Jack told me that you were in here. I wanted to see how you were. You didn't look so good when you went into the training dungeon. And to give you these." She hands me some slippers.

I give her a small smile as a thank you. "I'll be better once I get some food in me. But Mr. Kim's soul is making me feel great."

Anna and Eric order their food and I notice that they both get some extra food than normal. I might not have a lot of friends, but these two are all I need. I carry Eric's and my tray to our table. And yes, I declared it was ours a long time ago, I even carved our names into it—no one sits at our table. Jennifer's name is in the table too but she hasn't sat with us for a few years now, but I haven't had the heart to scratch her name out. We might not eat in the cafeteria all the time, but when we do, I don't want to look for a spot every time.

Our table is by a large stained window, the stains are green and blue and the morning sun is warming up my back and the colours are dancing on throughout the room. The table is also by an exit, so if we need to leave in a hurry, we can without people really noticing us.

The only time this room is full is usually during dinnertime, Father asks for everyone to be in here by six so he can lead everyone in prayer. I try to make it for dinner but most of the time I'm already in town working. Father doesn't seem to mind that I miss it, so I don't try that hard.

I scoff down my food and most of Eric's. Anna eats most of hers but I finish off hers too. The cafeteria is slowly filling up as the morning goes on. Still not as busy as a weekday—you have to love Saturdays. I can feel people sneaking glances at me, but I ignore them.

"Do you think I could grab a shower before I go and see Jayden?" I ask. "I really need one... I can smell myself, it's rather gross."

Anna wiggles her nose, "Oh, I know, I can smell you too. I'm sure Jayden would appreciate it if you showered too."

Eric laughs and agrees with her.

"Jeez, thanks," I smirk. "Would you mind calling those angels while I shower and visit Jayden? I don't know how long I will be and I need to find out what I'm dealing with as soon as possible."

"Why are you calling angels? They normally don't like to be bothered," Anna says.

He nods, "I'll explain to you later, Anna, but yeah, I don't have anything to do and I want to know as well," he frowns. "I don't like that I don't know something, it really bothers me."

I touch his hand, "Now you know how the rest of us feel."

"Not funny."

"All joking aside, I have a bigger favour to ask of you. How difficult is it for you to look into the past?"

He looks intrigued, "Not very difficult, I just get tired the further I look back."

"How tiring will it be to go back seventeen years?" I whisper.

"It doesn't get tiring until I go past my age, so not tiring at all. I might need an eight-hour sleep that night, so not that bad. Why?"

I look around to see who is watching—there are too many good ears in the room, so I don't feel comfortable asking here.

"I'll let you know more later today when we are alone. Text me when you are done calling the angels and we'll meet up in my room." I get up to leave.

"Umm, what am I asking them again?"

"About the crest of the black and white swords and to see about learning the ancient language that you don't even know."

"What are we going to do if they don't know?"

My shoulders drop. "I don't know, we'll figure it out if we come to that bridge."

I pick up our trays and clean them off, then go up to my room. Eric and Anna go to his dorm room. If I thought the stairs were hard yesterday, they are about a hundred times worse today. They are taking me about three minutes to climb one step. There are about thirty steps to my room, I can fly but it's really tight in here for that and I will end up damaging them again. The rush I got from Mr. Kim is definitely wearing off, and quickly.

"Did I drain him so much already?" I whisper to myself. *Maybe I should go and see if he is okay. Even though I think he should suffer a little, I don't want his death on my shoulders either.*

I fight against it and go straight for the shower. I've never wanted to take my armour off so badly before. My armour plates spill outside the bathroom and my shirt is so badly torn, I just throw it in the garbage. I need to wipe down my armour before putting it away properly and I still need to get my boots and my blades from Father. My shoulders slump and I have to replace all my daggers. I think that's what I spend most of my money on—replacing them—and I don't go cheap on them.

"Maybe I should learn to make my own? Blacksmith as a hobby." I laugh, "Yeah right… I barely have time to sharpen them, let alone become a blacksmith. It may be wise to befriend a blacksmith though."

I try to just skip the mirror, but in the corner of my eye, I see something on my cheek. My eyes widen at the gross burn scar on my cheek. There's something black embedded under my skin. I am sure the only way I can get it out now is if I reopen my skin and dig it out.

It reminds me of something, "Oh, God, I'm turning into Deadpool. And my hair is a rat's nest, I should just shave it all off."

I have grass and clumps of dirt tangled in it. Father Jack might have wiped my face, but it still looks like I'm five years old, wiping dirt on it. I look at my feet and they look like I've been jumping in mud puddles for fun.

I have to use the wall to help me step into the shower. My body absorbs the hot water as soon as it hits me. I don't realize how cold my feet are until I step into the hot water, it feels like stinging nettles. I have a dance trying to get my feet used to it. After a few minutes of that, the shower becomes more comfortable and relaxing.

I wash my body and my hair; I have to leave the conditioner in for a while to get all the tangles out. At least this time there's no blood in the mud water that I'm creating. I don't get out of the shower until my muscles don't hurt so much and I feel clean, also less frozen.

I'm trying really hard not to absorb more of Mr. Kim's soul to heal me, but it's becoming too hard not to think about with my muscles screaming at me. I'm also curious to see how much I can take from him before he loses his mind.

In the mirror, I run my fingers through my hair and call it good. I like letting my hair air-dry, it looks nicer that way. My cheek looks a little better but there are still black specks under the skin. The hot water brought some colour back to my skin. I brush my teeth and get dressed. I put on my school uniform so the teachers don't bother me but I leave the tie. It's the weekend… I think it's stupid that we still have to wear the uniform.

CHAPTER 16

I walk slowly to the first aid room, trying to avoid most people. It also helps that there is no one here too. I don't feel like having people staring at me right now.

I can hear a few people in the first aid room. A female, sounds like Jennifer, and three males—one is Jayden and one is definitely Mr. Kim. The other male's voice I am familiar with but can't place the voice with a face, I recognize his smell too. This is going to bother me. I can feel that my soul is still with Mr. Kim too. I debate on whether or not I should go in. I choose to wait. Call me a coward but I just don't feel like dealing with these people.

I stand in a doorway a few doors down from the first aid room, waiting. I don't have to wait long; the three people walk out of the room. The stranger is hidden behind Mr. Kim... I can't get a good look at him, just that he has light colour hair and towers over both of them. Once they round the corner, I make my way to the office doors.

I walk in, hoping Jayden went to sleep so I don't have to face him just yet. But my luck ran out a long time ago. He is lying in his medic bed, propped up with thousands of pillows, reading a book. His blonde curly hair is tangled and fuzzy, the colour of his skin almost looks normal now too.

He looks up when he hears me coming and a small smile tugs at his lips. I stop at the foot of his bed. I feel like I've been in this room way too much lately.

"I figured you would have waited until everyone left. I have not been alone since I got up, I've had about twenty visitors. Mr. Kim hasn't left my side and Jennifer has been taking care of me, Father Jack has been in here twice and Eric has been here too. I was surprised though to not see you when I woke up. I figured you would have been one of the first."

I can't look at him, "I was held up with something else. And if they didn't tell you, it's not my place to."

He shifts, "Eric told me," he whispers. "I don't blame you for what happened to me. I know you didn't poison your blades."

I look at him; the sympathy is flowing off of him. It's almost choking me. He looks so sad, I almost want to hug him and tell him it's okay. I've been through worse but I stand my ground, knowing how silly that is.

"What did Eric tell you?" *If Eric told him about Drake, that saves hiding it from him. And maybe he'll back off thinking he can be next on the Lucifen's hit list.*

"Mr. Kim demanded you get sent to the training dungeon until I wake up and get to decide what happens to you. I'm sorry you had to go in there." He looks so sad, it's pathetic.

I smirk, "Yeah, you could have woken up a lot sooner."

He gives me a goofy smile, "Well, I was having such a great sleep, you better be happy that I woke up when I did."

I become serious, "Is that all Eric told you?"

He looks concerned, "Yes, why? Is there more I should know about?"

I wave my hand, "No. How are you feeling?" I ask, changing the subject.

"A little better... whatever was on your blade has Jennifer stumped. She said the reason it took her so long to heal me was because she didn't know what it was or how to cure it."

Why didn't they just tell her the full truth! So many lies!

"I think the only reason I am awake now is because the God's Daughter is the one who figured it out, and two minutes later, I was awake."

"Well, thank God for his daughter," I mumble. *How are they going to cover this up?*

"So, is there a reason you called me down here?" I ask.

"Nope, I just wanted to see your beautiful face." He laughs, then pays the consequences.

The injury to his chest hasn't healed yet and I bet it's painful to breathe.

I walk so I'm closer to him, "Look, once you get out of here, I'll explain to you what happened since no one else is. I can't tell you here. I'm sure Mr. Kim would throw me back in the training dungeon."

He raises a brow, "Okay. Well, we can go now." He throws off his blanket and moves to put his legs over his bed.

"Where do you think you're going?"

The voice comes from behind me. I jump out of my skin. I whip around and go to grab my blades but just grab air. I relax once I see who it is.

Lana, the God's Daughter, is standing there with her hand over her mouth, trying to hold her laughter. Her hair is a pixie cut, which makes her look a lot younger. I can see some grey in there but not a lot. Her skin does not give away her age as it looks smooth with no wrinkles. She is dressed in comfy clothes—loose jeans and a baggy long-sleeve shirt and glasses around her neck.

I bow my head, "I'm sorry, I didn't hear you coming... you are very light on your feet."

Her smile is what I think a proud mother would give her child. I can't help but already love her.

"Well, I am amazed that I can sneak up on the famous Alexandra."

I smile at her. *Doesn't even bother me that she calls me by my full name.*

She turns her attention to Jayden. "You aren't leaving this bed until I say so." She has a hand on her hip and the other one pointing at him.

He starts to protest, but by the way she is looking at him, he is not going anywhere. He shuts his mouth and slumps back down into his bed.

"Now, what is so important that you need to risk opening up your stitching?" she demands.

I know I can't lie to her… it's one of the God's Daughter gifts. You can stretch the truth but if they ask an outright question like that, it's impossible to lie.

I sigh, "I was going to tell him the truth about what poisoned him."

Her face sinks a little and she starts to fidget with his blanket by his feet.

"So, you know that truth too?" She looks so sad, "This church has burdened you with so much, Alexandra, I am so sorry for that."

I give her a small smile; I listen to see if anyone else in the first aid room before I ask my questions.

"May I ask you some questions?"

I can see that she's thinking about it, "I see the church trusts you with their secrets, so I don't see why I should keep anything from you."

"I found a crest with two swords on it—"

She interrupts me, "I know of the crest, the crest is for the Followers. They believe that both sides, good and bad, are tied together. You can't have one without the other. So, to keep this balance, they believe to sacrifice one white heart and one black. I'm not sure what they did with the hearts but that is all I know of the Followers."

"More secrets… why aren't we taught about them too?"

"It's quite simple, it's a dark history and they were destroyed a long time ago. That's why Jesus came down—to help out the balance so people wouldn't get sacrificed anymore. Jesus and the God's Daughter at the time started the fight against them. The Followers were very dark and needed to be stopped."

"Well, how many times did they need to perform this?" Jayden asks.

I almost forgot that he's here.

"About every full moon," she answers him.

"I'm curious, but how did mere humans get these sacrifices?" I ask.

The God's Daughter's face darkens, "They weren't humans, they were demons, demi-angels. They were against Lucifer and God. The Followers thought it was their fault for making things out of balance. So, they thought they should kill Lucifens and angels."

"Why would God let the angels come down here to make more demi-angels then?" I ask.

She shrugs her shoulders, "Who knows what God is thinking… maybe it was a test to his angels to see if they could fight the temptation to come down here. And not all demi-angels or demons agreed to the Followers' ways, so maybe God didn't want to punish all of us for a few who did the crime.

"They also killed humans if they couldn't find an angel's heart. They would go for a pure human, one without any black in their hearts."

I start to pace, this is a lot of information that I don't understand completely.

"It's hard to believe that demons and demi-angels worked together at one point," I whisper to myself.

Lana sits on Jayden's bed, "Is it really though? We both come from the same place; demons have the blood of Lucifer in them, for them to walk on Earth, they have to drink his blood. Just because you have a dark heart doesn't make you a demon; it just gives you the chance to become one."

So many questions.

Before I can ask God's Daughter any more questions, Mr. Kim walks in with some food in his hands. He smiles so sweetly to Lana, it's rather cute but once he notices me, his mood changes. For a normal person, I would say my soul has affected him, but he already hates me and I already saw the dagger in his eye long before he ever put my doll on.

And just because Lana is standing right here, I put on a sweet smile and ask for my doll back. Mr. Kim rips it off his neck and throws it at me. The pain he causes me is too much, I can't hide it. I just barely catch it—I have to use the bed to hold myself up. My hair hides my face so no one can see how much pain I am in. If people knew how much they can control me with this doll, it would not be good for me.

As if Eric knows I need rescuing, he calls me, giving me an excuse to leave.

"Thank you for your help, God's Daughter, but I must go now."

"Oh, please call me Lana, and if you think of any more questions, just come and ask. I will not hide anything from you," she offers.

I don't wait around for any more conversation, it's almost hard to breathe. Eric says he's in his room, which isn't far, the males' dorm is closer on the west side of the school and the girls' is on the east. The church thought it would be harder for the students to meet up in the middle of the night.

I know I should find someone else to wear my doll, my body is getting too drained from the lack of sleep and the lack of healing periods. I've been getting beaten up too much lately. I also really hate depending on people to wear it. But if I want to live, I must, and I know I need to accept it.

As I pass the classrooms, I look in them to see if any teachers are around to hand it off to. Just as I get to the door to head outside, the door to the staircase opens and Mr. Daniel almost knocks into me.

"Oh, Alex, sorry but I can't stay and talk."

Before he rushes off, I say, "Mr. Daniel, can you take this?"

I put my hand out with the doll dangling at the end of it. I hate him wearing it but I have no other choice. He takes it without question and goes off down the hallway.

The path to the males' dorm isn't used often. The guys think it's better to fly everywhere once they get outside, showing off their flying skills. If you have smaller wings, you can take sharper turns, and the bigger the wings, the faster you can go. My wings are somewhere in the middle. I can take sharp corners easily enough but I am rather fast because I train my wings to be.

The dirt path has grass growing on it and the hedges don't look like they have been trimmed in a while. With fall well on its way, the leaves are turning yellow and starting to fall and crunch under my boots. The males' dorm is painted dark blue with green-stained windows. The girls' dorm is white with red-stained windows. Aside from the colour of the buildings, they are similar. There are three floors, with about forty rooms on each floor and a larger bathroom on each floor. Most rooms hold two people, so each dorm holds two hundred and forty students.

It might not seem like a lot of students but I think it's too much most of the time. And not even all of the rooms are full—Eric has his own room. We will be getting more students this year too because of the Ultram but they have their own housing. There is a smaller dorm by the church that visitors use and they are going to be staying in there.

CHAPTER 17

Eric's room is on the ground floor, so no stairs for me. And he is close to the door too. I don't knock as I walk in—the dorms themselves have two beds on either side of the room and two closets at the foot of each bed. A large desk that separate the beds, which can easily fit two normal students' homework on it, but Eric has his large desk full of his books. You can cut the room right down the middle and they would look the same.

Eric has the right side of his room—his bed is unmade with his blanket bunched up as if he's been having horrible nightmares. His clothes are in a pile by the closet. Beside his clothes and books, he doesn't have anything else in his room.

The left side of the room, I call my side. Even though it's forbidden for the opposite sex to sleep in the dorms, I have crashed on his extra bed more than once. I would stay over for late-night studies, talks, and other things. I am sure Father knows but doesn't say anything.

Eric is hunched over his desk—he doesn't even flinch as I walk in and flop down onto his extra bed, right next to Anna.

"So, what did Jayden want?" she asks.

I grunt, "Nothing, just to make sure I was okay."

Eric lets out a sigh, "So, a waste of time then."

"Not entirely," I prop myself on my elbow. "The G.D showed up and I asked her about the two swords. And she knew what they were. What do you know of the Followers?"

His eyebrows knit together... he doesn't know but he is intrigued to learn more. I tell him exactly what the G.D told me.

"Why aren't they in our history books? Why aren't we learning about them either?"

I shrug, "To hide the fact that we angels teamed up with demons and killed humans, Lucifens, and angels. We have a dark history, just like humans."

Anna grunts. "Yes, but the humans don't hide away from it, they learn from it."

Eric snorts. "Do you really think the humans tell the truth of their past? I don't think so, it's hard for me to trust even the bible because we might have written it but we are still half-humans and we can tell stories just as well as they can."

"I'm sure the only race that doesn't lie about their dark past are the demons themselves because they are proud of it," I add.

Eric smirks, "For someone who is failing most of your classes, you are quite smart."

"I'm just not interested in school. If school was just the Angel Saviours, I would be the top of the class."

"And I would be at the bottom," he smiles.

"I'm sure you would find a way to become the top dog in no time if that's how the school worked." I pause, "Did you call the angels?" I ask, getting back to business.

"Yes, but none of them would tell me about the crest, saying I haven't graduated. And they wouldn't tell me about the Lucifens either for the same reason. They even said that with me knowing as much as I do, it can get me in trouble. I just told them I had a vision about it and that I want to learn more. They still wouldn't tell me."

Annoyed, I get off the bed, "They wouldn't tell you anything, Anna?"

She shakes her head, "They know I am a G.C for a Saviour who hasn't graduated, and they said you're not allowed to know yet."

"Is there something even worse than what we found that they are so ashamed of? Why is this dark past so bad and scary that we can't find out earlier?" I mumble.

They don't say anything, knowing I'm just talking to myself.

After a while, Eric speaks up, "So, are we just going to wait until we graduate to find out?"

I run my hand through my hair, "At this point, we don't have a choice, but I really wanted to take care of this before the Ultram starts next month."

"Well, if the demon shows up again, refrain from stabbing him because obviously that's not working and ask him more questions... see if he will give anything about where he is and how he is doing."

"I'll try but he loves the sound of his own voice and he knows how to get under my skin. I don't think I will be getting a word in if he shows up." I lay back down.

The lack of sleep is finally catching up with me. Fighting to keep my eyes open, I stare up at the ceiling.

"Eric, for me not to stab him the next time I see him, can you do me a favour?"

I hear him move in his chair, "What can I do?"

"Can you look back to when I was born and see what happened? I need to know who is telling the truth." I turn my head and look at him.

"Are you sure that's not dangerous?" Anna asks.

"It's a piece of cake," Eric beams.

The setup for Eric isn't difficult. The lights need to be off and a few candles lit. He also has to write down the date he wants to go back to. He needs to hold the paper with the date on it and sit in a comfortable position.

"How long will this take?" Anna asks, shutting the curtains to shut out the afternoon sun.

147

He shrugs, "All depends on how long I need to see and if I need to fast forward or go back to make sure I understand everything. The date on the paper is just a starting point that I need."

"Well, I know for sure my mother put my soul in that doll and the church was there to help her. But what I want to know is if my father is a Lucifen."

Eric pauses for a second, "What difference does it make if he is?"

His question catches me off guard but the answer is simple.

"I want to know what I am made of and it would explain so much to me. To know that I am different because of him and not because God wanted me to be."

"Well, no matter what, I still will be your G.C," Anna says.

She makes me smile sometimes. She shapeshifts into a white cat and curls up on the end of my bed. Anna is normally a cat in the school and a bat when we are hunting. I always make rhymes about it to tease her.

G.Cs feel more comfortable as an animal—they are only human when they really need to be. I hear that if a G.C isn't chosen to be with a Saviour, they go and live in the woods, where they are free to do whatever they want. G.Cs are chosen the first year they graduate and Anna wasn't chosen, the other Saviours say she was too small.

That's why Father Jack forced us together; he didn't want her to disappear. The year we have been together, she has passed most G.Cs, I think she is better than most of them. Other Angel Saviours ask if they can switch G.C, I get mad at them for treating the G.Cs as if they are trading cards.

Eric gives me a nod and continues to set up. Once the candles are lit, he sits on his bed with his back against the wall. His hands are folded neatly in his lap with the date in his hands. He takes a deep breath and closes his eyes. I can feel the air change in the room—it becomes heavy and warm. It's making me sleepy. I sit on the extra bed and my head becomes heavy as well, I'm starting to do the head bob. I'm fighting to stay awake but the warm room is making me drowsier.

The next thing I know, I'm dreaming the same dream.

I'm flying through a dark cold night, no full moon this time. The dark doesn't bother me. I know there isn't anything to fear in the dark, but then something grabs my ankles and starts to pull me down. I fight; I kick and push my wings to carry me higher. But more hands grab on and weigh me down. I don't give up.

I can't see anything… whatever is grabbing me, they are blending in with the dark. The harder I fight, the more hands grab on. I look up, hoping to see someone there to help me, but all I see is Drake holding his hand out, wanting me to take it. I hesitate for a second, just as I reach out, the hands multiply. Drake looks scared and he tries to grab me as I crash to the ground.

My eyes fly open to see the candlelight dancing on the ceiling. I tilt my head to look at Eric, his head is limp, in an uncomfortable poison. His legs are still crossed and he's breathing softly like he is sleeping.

I move slowly to make sure I don't make any noise. I've never been around him when he goes back in time, so I am not sure what to do. I want to make him more comfortable but I don't know if that will cause another episode like a few days ago.

I want to be here when he wakes up, but my stomach is grumbling and I am sure he will be hungry when he wakes up.

Anna stretches with a huge yawn.

"Stay here and keep an eye on him," I whisper.

She nods and sits back down.

I leave the room and walk over to the cafeteria. The sun is setting; we've been sleeping for almost eight hours. I think I can still sleep for another six.

The cool autumn breeze is refreshing and helping me to wake up a little. I run my fingers through my hair to calm the tangles I get from sleeping and try to straighten out my clothes as much as possible. I'm sure no matter what I do, I'll look like I just woke up.

The cafeteria is empty… it's too early for dinner but there is a fridge with some sandwiches and other things and a long table with some veggies and fruit. I grab two brown paper bags and start to fill them up. I hear one of the cafeteria doors open and close but I don't pay it any mind. The only thing on my mind right now is food. By how heavy the steps are, I can say it's a guy and he's coming over to the food, too.

"You must be Alexandra," a deep, thick voice says with an accent I can barely understand.

The voice is unfamiliar and startles me a little. I turn to face him to give him a piece of my mind for calling me my full name, but when I turn around to make eye contact with a guy's chest, I tilt my head up to make eye contact. I have to tip my head all the way up.

The man is about the size of a house! He must have to duck and go sideways through doors. And his dark skin is like nothing I have ever seen. There is definitely no cream in his coffee. From what I can see, he has no hair as it looks like he shaves it clean. I have a strange urge to touch it—it's so shiny. His eyes are almost as dark as mine but I can see some light brown mixed in.

"Holy shit! Who did you eat to get that big?" I blurt the question without thinking.

I need to get better at holding my tongue with him around. He can eat me too!

Thinking I just offended him and that I am going to be in a world of hurt in a few seconds, but he bursts out laughing.

"My name is Luke. I'm here for the Ultram, I'm the G.R.H from the South African church." He sticks his hand out.

I take his hand and it engulfs mine, I'm sure he can crush my skull with those hands.

"Nice to meet you, and I go by Alex."

His smile is so big, I can see all of his pearly whites.

"Well, Alex, it's an honour to finally meet you. I've heard so much about you." He becomes serious, "If I am honest, I thought you would be bigger."

I smile at him; he's like a big friendly giant.

"Well, people underestimate me... always in my favour." I go back to stocking up, "I'm sorry, I would like to stick around and talk with you and size you up but I am needed elsewhere."

"Oh, of course. Well, maybe tomorrow we can spar and train?" he asks.

I think about it, "I don't see that being a problem. We can use my gym."

He whistles, "You have your own gym!"

I shrug, "It's not big but you can see that tomorrow... want to meet up after breakfast?"

He slaps my shoulder, making me stumble forward, "Sounds like a plan. I'll see you around then."

I wave bye and leave the cafeteria.

What the hell just happened? Since when am I nice to people? Let alone to a complete stranger? I think as I rush back to Eric's room.

Eric is still in the same position sleeping as I sneak back in and Anna is cleaning herself, not really paying attention to me until I pull out some cooked chicken slices for her. She eats all of the chicken I brought her and I eat until I can't fit anymore in my stomach. I begin looking through Eric's stack of books to see if there is anything that isn't braille and would interest me while I wait for him.

The thought of catching up on some homework pops in my head but I snicker and pick up a book that's about the Ultram. Maybe a history lesson on it wouldn't be such a bad idea.

I settle down onto the bed and Anna comes and curls up right beside me and starts to purr. About ten minutes later, my eyes become heavy again. Learning about the Ultram isn't as interesting as I thought it would be. Even the church can make a ritual that involves fighting and even death so dull it can put you to sleep.

I start to doze off again when Eric starts to mumble my name. I creep over to his bed. Anna stays on the bed, watching carefully.

"I'm here, Eric," I whisper.

I'm still worried that he'll have another episode. I don't need to know what happens between my mother and the church that bad to hurt Eric.

His head starts to sway back and forth. He inhales deeply, lifting his head up so fast, he cracks it against the wall. I flinch at the sound. His eyes open and I can see his milky eyes looking around.

I reach for his hand, "Hey, buddy, I am right here."

He fixes on me, "Alex, I have so much to tell you."

CHAPTER 18

By the look on Eric's face, it's not good news. The fear that I'm half-Lucifen puts a shiver down my back and that a Lucifen has told me the truth when the church didn't.

Anna jumps onto his bed and starts to rub her head on his arm, trying to soothe him.

I look Eric dead in the eye, "Tell me the truth. All of it."

He hesitates before telling me everything. Drake was telling me the truth. My mother fell in love with a Lucifen… his name is Zacharias. Eric went into great detail on what my father looked like. He was taller than Father Jack and I have his dark black hair but his was short. With a sharp jawline and his skin looked as if it never saw daylight. The presence he held demanded everyone's attention in the room. His eyes were black, too.

"I can see where you get your attitude from, I see a lot of you in him now."

My hands curl up into fists. Those words hurt more than I should let them. I move away from Eric and sit back on my bed.

"Can you tell me about my mother?" I whisper.

He smiles, "Did you know you have your mother's name?" he asks.

"I did, that's why I go by Alex. I don't deserve her name," I whisper my reasoning behind it.

"Alex, you should be proud to have your mother's name. From what I saw, she was a strong angel and brave. She went against even God because she wanted to follow her heart no matter what."

She still died, I think to myself. I smile softly, "What did she look like?"

She had long light brown hair with red highlights through it. Her eyes were chocolate brown with green specks. He said her smile could light up a room and she walked with such grace that it didn't look like her feet hit the ground. Her skin was lightly golden.

As he speaks, I paint the picture of her in my mind. She's different from what I thought. I was hoping I looked more like her, but I take after my father. So, that's a little disappointing.

"Can you tell me what happened the day I was born? Drake said that the church abandoned my mother and the demons abandoned my father."

"Well, from what I understand, the church wanted nothing to do with your mother until they found out that she was pregnant with you. Then both sides wanted her—they didn't care about your father. All they cared about was having you. So, I went back further to see what happened during her pregnancy with you.

And of course, your mother thought she could change your father's heart. He was going to take her to the church because he knew that you would be safe here too."

He takes a sip of water, "But when your mother was about six months pregnant, she became sick. She wouldn't have made it to the end of the month. So, your father prayed to God for weeks but no answer and no help ever came. Your mother was on the verge of dying. Your father waited until the last minute to go to Lucifer."

He fell silent for a few seconds, I'm trying not to rush him but I want to know more. He had to have seen more than that.

"When your father went to Lucifer," he fell silent again. "I-it was awful," he shivers. "I went with your father to Hell. It was terrifying, what I saw will haunt me for the rest of my life, Alex. I can't believe how many people end up there."

My heart breaks, "I'm sorry, I didn't know that would happen. I didn't know you would end up going there."

He shakes his head, "It had to be done because I know so much more now and not just about your father, but about Lucifer himself.

"When I saw your father with your mother, at first, I thought there was no way that he could be Lucifer because he was so sweet with her, so kind. After I hung around them, I could still sense his heart had some black in it, but when he entered the gates of Hell, he changed. He wasn't the same man I was watching before.

"His skin looked like there were black and silver flakes all over, making him look like an unbreakable marble. He grew too, he was taller and his muscles were bigger. He had his canines out and his eyes were completely red. His wings, Alex, were black like yours but they had silver feathers through them. They were beautiful to look at."

My wings are from him too. My heart sinks a little more.

Eric continues, "Demons bowed and backed out of his way. The ones that didn't look scared of him looked jealous. Your father had so much power that he was able to go back to the underworld, and as soon as he got back, it was like he never left. I'm sure your father could live off the fear they gave off. Even though I wasn't really there, but the air was so thick with fear, I could feel it weighing me down. I have never been so scared of someone before."

"What did my father do to give that much fear to fear itself?"

Eric shakes his head, "I honestly don't know, and you know what? I am okay with not knowing because I never want to know."

"I think I am in the same boat," I add. "What happened when he met with Lucifer?"

He dips his head, "To get to Lucifer's palace, which was an island of human bodies, we walked across an ocean of fire, it's not red like I thought. It's hot blue—it burned off your father's clothes, it was like fire itself feared your father. Humans, demons walked around naked. In the fiery ocean were mangled bodies and the wails and screams of something inhuman pierced my ears."

I can see a tear slide down his cheek. I rush to him and grab his hand. "You don't have to tell me any more, Eric, I am so sorry I caused you so much pain."

"I can still hear the screams, Alex," he whispers so softly, I can barely hear him and I'm so close to him. "We need to save more people from going down there. No one deserves that—no one."

I nod, "We will, we will save more humans."

He rests his head on mine, "I want to finish telling you what I saw."

"Eric, you don't have to."

He straightens, "I must… I want you to know what I know. The fiery ocean isn't the worse part."

I don't know what to say, I wish I had the power to wipe his memory of Hell.

He continues, "Once we got to the other side of the fiery ocean, there was a fortress made of brimstone and humans. The pathway that led up to the double-sided gates was made up of human teeth. Your father didn't flinch as he walked on the shattered teeth. As we got closer to the iron gates, I could see human heads on spikes with their eyes carved out. Human skulls and brimstone made up the large wall. We walked into a large room, inside human bones made up of the furniture and their skin was the floor—like animal rugs.

"I'm sure the smell of burning hair will never leave my nostrils."

Tears start to spill from his eyes, "At the end of the great hall was a throne, and you know how Game of Thrones has the iron throne, well, it looked like that at first, but as we got closer to it, it was burnt human bones. And Lucifer himself was sitting there; well, I didn't know at first because the man who was sitting on the throne was in a dark cloak and I didn't see his face. Lucifer was sitting there running his fingers through hair that was still attached to an old skull. There were five demons or Lucifens, I am not sure, standing beside him. The one on his right had white hair, his eyes were black but it looked like he smeared blood across his eyes from hairline to hairline. There were twins standing right behind him. If we were anywhere else but in Hell, it would be extremely awkward because the three demons that I could see were naked just like your father. And the two on the left side of Lucifer were just shadows of humans. Like what you see when you're looking at demons."

Can I only see Lucifens and demons are just shadows?

"Your father walked up to Lucifer as if he owned the place, but once he got to at least fifteen feet away, he got down to one knee and bowed his head to Lucifer. Lucifer laughed... I can't even explain how he sounded, it was low and it rumbled the whole room, it was terrifying and beautiful. Lucifer asked what your father wanted. Your father explained what was happening and asked Lucifer for his help. Lucifer agreed to help under the condition that he has to give you up in return for the life of his love. He hesitated for a long time. Or at least it felt like a long time until he agreed to Lucifer's request.

"Lucifer stood up and his hood fell to the ground. I have never seen anyone so breathtaking and terrifying. Long white hair down to his knees, taller than any man I have seen before. His skin was porcelain—so smooth with no imperfections. His eyes were bright green. His wings were gold, the fires in the room danced off of them; they looked so beautiful and unbreakable. They looked strong and powerful, I have never seen wings like his before, but then again, I have never seen an angel's wings before."

"So, Lucifer is nothing like the movies," I say, attempting to make a joke at a time like this.

"Not even close. But it's in the bible that he will appear to us for what we want most in the world. And watching him walking to your father was memorizing. He towered over both of us; I had to take a few steps back to see his face, your father didn't move. Lucifer stuck out his hand and your father took it. I didn't stick around to find out anything else. I'm sorry that I couldn't. I fast-forwarded to the day you were born.

"Your mother wasn't all the way better, she was still really weak and needed a lot of care, and she was confused all the time. She didn't know where she was or how she got there. Your father was able to sneak her out of the church's grounds. But it didn't take long for the church to be hot on their trail. Your father had your mother in an elementary school first aid room.

"Your mother came back from her daze and knew what was going on. She ran from your father but you weren't going to wait any longer and wanted to come out, she went into a classroom and gave birth to you."

"She was all alone?" I whisper.

He nods, "She didn't scream, not even a peep. She was so worried that your father would hear her. I have never felt so useless before—all I could do was watch, and even then, I looked away a lot. I won't go into details of giving birth. Even when you were born, you didn't make a sound... it's like you knew to be silent. Your mother was worried that you were stillborn though, but when you looked at her, I have never seen someone so happy.

"Father Jack came into the room then and there was a ruckus that was echoing behind him. There was a huge battle happening, I'm not sure about the numbers but I'm sure you don't care about that. She handed you to him and she grabbed the closest thing to her, which was the doll. She rested one hand on your heart and the other one on the doll. Healing light emanated from her hands. The hand that was on you, she lifted it up and brought it over to the doll. She cupped her hands around it and whispered something. I couldn't hear her and I put my ear right up to her.

"She collapsed, and even though I haven't seen many people die, I knew she was. Her light stayed on you and the doll, but once the light faded, she burst into a bright light and all that was left was her heart. That's when you started to scream. Father Jack grabbed the heart and the doll and jumped out the window and took off for the church with you still in his arms, screaming.

"That's when I came back."

What happened to my father? I think to myself.

We just sit there in silence for so long, I can't feel my legs anymore. I zone out on my hands. I'm hurt and I feel betrayed. I don't know how I'm supposed to react to this. I also didn't know demons could tell the truth.

"I don't know what you were wanting to get out of this, but I am sure what I just told you wasn't it," Eric whispers.

I don't answer him for a long time. I sit in a more comfortable position, resting the back of my head on the bed and stare up at the ceiling. Both Anna and Eric just sit there with me, quietly eating, but Anna does jump down and rub her body on my leg.

"How would you take that news?" I ask softly.

He lets out a sigh, "I honestly don't know, I am not even close to your position. I know what it's like to have a loving parent take care of me, but knowing that I am or will be the strongest being in the world, where both sides want you badly that I bet they are willing to lie, cheat, and even steal you…"

He pauses, "You know what, you have every right to be pissed, you have every right to go to the high church and rip them all a new one. But what do you want to do? How I look at it is that you have a few choices. Number one, pretend that you didn't just find out that you are half-Lucifen and technically a full angel. Live life as you always have. Two, break loose on the church and let the black heart take over. Or three, accept the fact that you are half and half and use your gifts how you want to, which I know is for sticking up for us little guys."

"They all sound so tempting. I can go crazy on the church and still be a good guy? It's not like the church is the weaker guy. And pretending that I am not half-Lucifen to everyone would be good…

159

everyone is scared of me enough. And I will always stick up for the little guy."

He gives a small chuckle, "If only we lived in a perfect world."

CHAPTER 19

I thank him for his help and for telling me the truth, then go back to my room. Anna is hot on my heels in her cat form still. No one is in the cafeteria or in the halls, or I'm just not paying attention. What Eric told me keeps going through my head. I feel bad for leaving him alone in his room, but he assured me that he was fine and just needed to sleep.

As I enter my room, it feels like I haven't been in here for a long time and I damn well know I was in here this morning. I crawl into bed with my comfy PJs and just stare at my mother's heart. I can feel Anna curl up beside me again—she doesn't purr this time. I'm tired and my bed is so comfy and warm, but some for reason, sleep hasn't taken over yet.

"What were you thinking, Mother? There must be more to the story than what I've learnt," I whisper out loud.

Sleep finally wins and I have the dream again… before I crash onto the ground, the church bells ringing wakes me up. I turn over to look at the clock—it's ten in the morning.

I jump out of bed, "SHIT! I'm late!"

If we don't show up for church on Sunday, we have to be stuck in the kitchen for the next week and I'd rather go to church than to the kitchen. Not going to lie, one of the cooks is a little too handsy for my liking, I had to threaten him a few times.

I shiver at the thought of working with him. I put on black jeans and a loose silver tank top with a long black overcoat. I just run my fingers through my hair and call it good. With the sun shining through the window, I decide to wear my blue flip-flops, there's only so many more warm days where we can have bare feet.

I don't really like socks, it feels like I'm trying to mummify them or something and they always get too warm.

Anna shifts into her human form and is ready for church. She is wearing a spaghetti-strap black dress with a floral pattern that ends just above her knee. Her shoes are black lace-up wedges. She puts her long red hair up in a ponytail.

Part of her gift is that she can picture the clothes she wants to wear and they appear on her. I've always wanted that gift, I would never have to go shopping again.

We run to the church and see no one. I can hear the choir singing the opening song before the first prayer. So, we make it just in time. I open the door with just enough to fit both of us through. Eric is already sitting in our spot. We sit in the last row closest to the door.

Anna goes in first and sits by Eric. I don't feel comfortable sitting in the middle... I want a clean exit if I need one.

As we slide beside him, "Cutting it close this morning, aren't you?" he whispers.

He doesn't look like he got any sleep last night. His curly hair doesn't look like it's seen a brush in ages and there are bags under his eyes.

I smirk, "Well, I don't think I have ever slept that much before. Father better be happy that I don't want to work in the kitchen or I wouldn't have shown up," I say, ignoring the fact that my friend looks horrible.

Shaking his head, "At least one of us could sleep," he mumbles.

He turns back to listen to Father with the morning prayer. I can see Jayden's blonde curly mop sitting at the front row, Jennifer is right beside him, and on the other side of her, I am guessing is Luke because, damn, that kid takes up about three seats. And the stained windows are shining on his bold head, making it look really cool.

I wonder if Luke wants to still fight? He must have heard by now about my fight with Jayden. I'm sure his trainer doesn't want me to fight him.

That reminds me… I still have to wash my gear and get my blades back from Father. Hoping I can at least postpone the fight until tomorrow. I should do a couple of laps today at least. Maybe do some homework too, freshen up on some math.

I zone out on the stained windows, not paying any attention to the lesson Father is trying to teach.

I feel the air change… something I have felt before, something I am getting used to. I don't turn to him—I don't need people looking at him if I acknowledge him.

"Wow, this is so boring! There are at least four kids asleep and more than half of them are zoning out like you are. How can you deal with this, love?"

I don't answer him, but my heart is picking up its pace.

"Why do you have to come to this? Don't humans have to go to church to show God that they believe in Him or something like that?"

Anna taps me with her elbow, "Are you okay? Why are you tensing up?"

"He's here," I mumble under my breath.

"Drake is here?" Eric squeals a little too loud, a few people look at us.

But I shoot them a glare and they turn back around.

"Keep your voice down," I hiss. "And yes."

"Awe, you told them about me… now this won't be as much fun."

I turn to Drake, "You're threatening his life, so I think it's only fair that he knows about it. And Anna is my G.C, so she would have found out sooner or later. No one else knows, so back off."

163

Drake shrugs his shoulders, "No matter to me, just more toys for me to play with."

He vanishes from my side and ends up on the other side of Eric.

"So, Eric, your God made you blind. If you turn your heart black, I'll give your eyesight back."

Eric is startled with hearing Drake's voice right beside him.

"Oh? Is that all that's going to cost me to get my sight back is to sell my soul? You know, I'm going to have to pass, God lets me see more than anyone in this room anyway."

Anna is blocking my view now so I can't see Drake.

"Wow, you are delicious… are you sure that you aren't an angel?"

I can just see Anna squeezing her boobs together to make them look bigger and her putting on her biggest smile that makes guys stumble over themselves.

I'm feeling jealous right now so much—I never really care that she can get any guy that she wants. I usually laugh at them, watching men drool and look like idiots it's really amusing, but now that Anna is flirting with Drake… I'm not okay with it.

"Put your tits away, will you? We are in church," Drake says coldly.

Both Eric and I choke down our laughter.

Anna growls, "Definitely a demon."

Drake spits, "Don't call me that. I am a Lucifen, not a disgusting demon."

"You two, stop it," I hiss.

Drake ignores me. "I can see what you desire, Anna, and if you keep acting like a whore, you will never get it."

She stands up and goes to slap him, but her hand goes right through him—he just smiles up at her. She shifts into a red wolf (she shifts into a wolf when she needs to fight) and snarls at him.

"Anna, leave at once!" Father Jack booms his voice from the front of the church.

She's not stopping growling at Drake.

"Anna, you need to get out of here and cool off. You are causing a scene," I holler at her.

She looks at me, whimpering, and as if she can feel everyone's eyes on her, she boots it for the door that someone already has open for her. I lift my legs up just in time for her to go by. The room goes quiet, but Father Jack brings everyone's attention back to him and carries on with his lesson. I make eye contact with Jayden before he turns back around.

Drake looks at me, "What about you? What would it take for your heart to turn black? I don't think it would be so hard, since you are already halfway there."

"Lucifens can see people's hearts too?" Eric asks. His curiosity always gets the better of him. He always has to know everything.

Drake's smile grows, "Only if they are black, but we can see people's desires before they even know themselves to help turn their hearts black."

Drake locks eyes with me, "Like I know Alexandra's desire is to have me."

I don't know if time is traveling fast or super slow, it feels like I am in a car accident where you open your eyes and you can see the glass flying in front of you but you know that you are moving fast.

I reach over Eric and grab Drake's throat. My canines are out and my nails grow longer and they dig into Drake's throat. I can see his black blood dripping down his neck. The surprise in his eyes flashes for a second but disappears, and amusement is the only thing that remains. I can hear the roaring around the church, I can feel people's eyes on me but I don't pay them any attention.

I want to rip his throat out.

"You should know by now that you can't kill me while I am in this form."

I draw his face to mine, "You know what? My desire is to have you… tell me where you are."

He winks, "Come and find me, my love."

165

He moves fast, grabbing my shirt and pressing his lips to mine, but as soon as his lips touch mine, he disappears.

I freeze—I can't move. I can hear my heart in my throat. I'm not sure if it has been two seconds or two minutes. Once I break from my frozen state, I let out a blood-curdling scream.

I run for the door and there are two students standing in my way. I shove them both so hard that they leave indents in the walls. As soon as I step outside, I take off to the sky.

I fly off the school grounds and start to scream, "Where the hell are you!"

I don't care who can hear me or who can see me. *I want Drake's heart in my hands, how dare he! How dare he steal that kiss from me!*

I know it's childish—a little girl's fantasy to have a perfect first kiss, but that was one of my only girly fantasies. And the nerve of him to say that crap out loud!

I pass over a small break in the trees and I see him standing there waiting, waving at me with a smug grin.

I land like a superhero and charge after him. I jump, flying through the air. I slam both of my knees into his chest. Knocking both of us to the ground, I pin him down. Both of my legs lock his arms into place so he can't move. I don't have my blades but my nails grow three more inches and become sharp. I stab all five nails into his shoulder, and with the other hand, I stop only centimetres from his green eyes.

Even with all of this, he is still smiling!

"Are you this mad because I kissed you or the fact that I told you what you desire most right now?"

I yell, "Shut up! I knew I was drawn to you, I'm not a fucking idiot! I am pissed because you thought you could touch me without permission. And you're a Lucifen, let's see if your heart is as black as a normal demon's."

I raise my arm to thrust into his head and scramble his brain.

"Wait! Do not do that... well, not yet."

Something in his emerald eyes makes me hesitate.

I place one fingernail under his chin, drawing blood, "What do you want from me?"

He tries to move under me, "Well, for starters, I would like you to slide down a little bit so I can breathe a bit easier."

I dig my nails further into his shoulders, his face twitches, but besides that, his face is like stone. With me sitting on him, I become well aware of his body heat and that we are really close.

I push off of him, using my wings so I end up being a few feet away from him.

I point at him, "Answer me this, why am I attracted to you?"

Dusting himself off, he says, "What, don't believe in love at first sight?"

"Demons, I mean, Lucifens believe in love? No, I don't think so… there has to be a reason that I am drawn to you."

He shrugs, "We believe in lust and desire, but love is only for stories."

"Well, I never thought I would agree with a demon before."

He glares at me, "Don't call me a pathetic demon. I am a Lucifen, get it right."

"Both beings are pathetic, so just drop it and tell me why I am drawn to you!" I snap.

Running his hand through his white hair, "Because you were meant to be mine."

"Pardon!" I blink.

"When my father, Lucifer, made the deal with your father, Zacharias, my father bounded your soul to mine."

"You have a soul? How did Zacharias not know?"

"I am half-human, stupid girl, and my father didn't need to tell him," Drake informs me.

"What do you mean you're half?" *I feel so dumb right now.*

A frustrated sigh escapes his nose, "Yes, Lucifens are angels and they can't have children with each other."

I point at myself, "Umm… yeah, they can…. if no one could then how in the world am I here?"

He shrugs, "One of those questions you're going to have to ask God."

"Why are you telling me all this?" I ask, confused.

"Take it as you will, make your life more miserable. Help you find the truth. Blah, blah, blah. In all honesty, I wanted to see what you would do once you found out. Would you turn on the church, would run away into my arms because, yes, I have played games with you but I have not lied to you."

"Why are you here now?"

"I wanted to warn you not to do the Ultram. It's not going to end well for you or anyone."

"I'll be needing more information than that please."

"We have what you guys call God's Knowledge, but ours feed off of the fear of humans. That's how they get their powers anyway; a few of them have foreseen the Ultram. And I am here to make sure you stay in the Ultram and wait for the end."

He takes a few steps closer to me, "My father is excited for what's to come, and he can't wait. He says it will be the show of a lifetime."

"Why are you warning me?"

He smiles, "I am a teen… I go against my father's wishes. I want to see what will happen if he doesn't get his way." His face becomes soft and far too human for me, "So, love, want to help me out and not go in the Ultram?"

I start to laugh, "You're nuts… you think I will give up my wings to mess with your father? Get bent, I'll compete in the Ultram and I will do my very best to win. And I will knock anyone down to win."

"What? I didn't ask you to lose your wings… they have nothing to do with this."

I stand tall, "If a God's Right Hand doesn't compete in the Ultram, they will be stripped of their wings and be lesser than God's Angels and will no longer be allowed on the church's ground."

He raises an eyebrow, "Now that's messed up. The church is just as bad as Hell. Well, just don't win then."

"It's not like I have a choice, God decides who becomes the next G.R.H."

He almost looks frustrated, "Why don't you just come with me then? If you come to Hell with me, you can keep your wings and you don't have to compete in the Ultram."

"Umm, let me think about that... no. I am not going to Hell with you. I might be half-Lucifen but I am also half-angel and I'm not going to give up on that."

He whips his head to the north as if he can hear something I can't.

"Look, I have to go, but just try and keep it in mind to lose the Ultram, okay?"

CHAPTER 20

He just disappears—he just left me standing here like a complete idiot. Few seconds go by and I can hear wings flapping. I look up to see Jayden, Father, and Mr. Daniel coming after me.

Jayden reaches me first, "What the hell was that all about?"

Glaring at him, "I don't have to answer to you."

"No, but you have to answer to me," Father Jack demands, crossing his arms as he lands.

"No, I don't have to answer to you either, God saw what happened and I think he'll be happy with how I handled it."

"Do you realize what happened back there? How many people you hurt?" Mr. Daniel grabs me by the shirt and starts to shake me.

Mr. Daniel's face is red and he looks so mad—I have never seen him this mad at me before. His whole body is shaking a little and I think his eyes are turning red, it looks like he wants to kill me.

"Get your hands off of me before I break them," I order calmly.

"Mr. Daniel, let her go. We don't need more people hurt today." Father Jack puts his hand on Mr. Daniel's shoulder.

Mr. Daniel shakes it off, "No, she's been acting weird and sneaking around. She's hiding something and needs to tell us."

My blood is starting to boil, "I'm hiding something, and you are such a hypocrite!" I look at Father Jack, "Did you know Lucifens can walk on Holy grounds? Did you know they can be invisible to people and they get to decide who can see them?"

Mr. Daniel shakes me again, "Don't lie, Alex."

I open my mouth to say I'm not, and he cracks me across my jaw, making me fall over. My jaw is hanging loose—he broke it.

"Mr. Daniel! That is enough! We do not strike students here! Go back to the school and I will deal with you later!" Father Jack yells at him.

Mr. Daniel doesn't listen to Father Jack. Instead, he reaches under his shirt and pulls out my doll. He squeezes the doll so tight that I can't breathe, and I can barely move. This is what a boa would feel like if it was wrapping around you.

Jayden rushes to me, "What the hell is wrong with you? Stop hurting her!"

Father Jack reaches for the doll but Mr. Daniel is too quick and moves out of the way. Mr. Daniel strikes Father in the back of his head, knocking him out.

"Does this hurt, Alexandra? I'm surprised you know what pain is. By the look on your face, you're in a lot of pain," Mr. Daniel snarls at me.

Jayden moves to go after Mr. Daniel but I grab his arm.

The cracking of my bones echoes, white spots blur my vision. I want to scream to release some of this pain but I don't even have enough air in my lungs to do so. Blood starts to gush out of my mouth and nose. The taste of iron is almost too much, I want to spit but that is difficult once your jaw is broken. I can feel hot tears running down my face. I can't see Mr. Daniel's hate anymore—everything is blurry and unclear.

Did Mr. Daniel have my doll for too long? Did I take his soul?

I can feel the dam walls breaking to his soul. His soul is flowing into me like a rushing river now. The more that pours into me, the harder he squeezes.

Another figure shows up and everything goes black after that. The next thing I remember is that it's easier to breathe but the pain is still here.

People are whispering for me to wake up. *Why is it that when people try to be quiet, they become more annoying?*

Keeping my eyes shut, I can hear about four people in the room, and by the smell, we are in the first aid room. Mr. Kim, Father Jack, Lana the G.D, and Jayden are very close to my bed.

I want them all to leave so I can sneak out of here.

I know they will never leave, and I kind of just want Jayden to stay so he can tell me what happened after I blacked out. I definitely don't want Mr. Kim here.

I must have fallen asleep again because when I wake up, the room is a lot quieter. There are only two heartbeats that I can hear, and for how slow they're breathing, I can tell they are asleep. If I wasn't in the first aid room, I would be able to smell who they are, but with all the smells in here, it's impossible.

I sit up slowly, making sure that the rickety bed doesn't tell people I am awake, and I am sure my body won't let me move fast right now. My whole body is hurting.

The sheets they use here are horrible, so itchy and stiff—at least they are clean. Once I stop squinting from the pain, I can see Anna curled at the foot of my bed as a white cat. I'm surprised that she didn't wake up when I moved. Looking around the room, I spot Jayden's blonde mop in the ugly pink waiting chair. I thought it would have been Eric waiting for me.

I wonder where he is. Although, I am sure he doesn't want to see me after finding out that I have a desire for a Lucifen. Like mother, like daughter.

My left leg is in a cast and so is my right arm. I've never had to be in a cast before since I've never broken a bone—the casts are so itchy!

"Jayden?" my voice comes out hoarsely, I notice my throat is very dry and my jaw pops.

I figure he will be easier to wake up than Anna, but he doesn't even stir, not even a twitch. I smile, only he can sleep that hard in a horrible position. I pull a pillow from under me and toss it at him lightly. My shoulders protest that movement.

Smacking him with the pillow doesn't get the reaction I want. He doesn't even jump, he just sits up a little straighter and hugs the pillow with one arm and rubs his eyes with his other hand. He looks like a cute little kid waking up from a nap.

He looks rough—his mop looks even worse than normal and the bags under his eyes are very large. And his clothes are wrinkled.

"Dude, you look horrible," I smile.

His eyebrows rise, "I look horrible? Have you seen yourself? You have a broken arm, a broken leg, four cracked ribs, your shoulders and back are messed up, and you have countless bruises and pulled muscles. And your jaw was broken, but since you are talking, it must have healed already."

"Is that it?" With me healing this slow, "Who has my doll?" I ask.

"Mr. Kim. Lana made him wear it. She was so worried because she couldn't heal you, not even a little bit. Father Jack asked Mr. Kim to wear it and, of course, he refused at first but he can't say no to Lana."

I rest my head back down. *At least that's one less thing I have to worry about; he already hates me.*

"What happened, Jayden? After I passed out. I remember you were right beside me and Mr. Daniel was slowly killing me, but I remember someone else coming into the mix."

He looks down and starts to fiddle with his hands, "Umm, once you blacked out, Father Jack woke up but Mr. Daniel knocked Father back down and started to kick him while he was down. I was just about to get up and go after him when something flashed in and took

Mr. Daniel down. Mr. Daniel dropped the doll to defend himself. I ran and picked it up and put it around my neck. I could feel you draining me quickly. Once I looked up, Mr. Daniel and the guy were gone just like that.

"I know I should have tracked them but I was more concerned about you and Father Jack, so I picked you up and brought you back here. The rest of the staff is freaking out. Father Jack has a few broken ribs." He runs his fingers through his hair. "I can't believe I didn't get to him fast enough, I was just so shocked to see an angel do that."

I sigh, "It wasn't his fault, my doll did this. If someone holds onto it for too long, they end up wanting to kill me and then they die soon after. But hopefully, Mr. Daniel let go of it soon enough and he's alright."

"Well, no one has found him yet, and for what he did to you, I hope whoever got him hurt him greatly. Father Jack has most of the Saviours looking for him. I took them back to where it all happened and they couldn't even find footprints leading away, so they definitely know that whoever took him had wings."

I look at Jayden from the corner of my eye, "Did you get a look at the guy?"

Shaking his mop, he says, "No, all I saw was white hair. I didn't even notice the wings."

Drake, what the hell are you doing?

"Alex, what happened at the church?" Jayden whispers the question so I can barely hear him.

"Did they explain anything to you?" I ask.

"No, I didn't really ask any questions. I had a feeling they weren't going to tell me and I knew you would." He's looking at me with such puppy dog eyes, I can't say no to him.

The air shifts to let me know he is here.

"Get me some water and I'll tell you everything."

He gives me a small smile and does as I ask.

"How are you, love?"

My lips curl but I keep my eyes shut, "What are you doing here?"

"I'm not allowed to check up on you? Make sure you're okay? You were in really bad shape when I left."

I glare at him—he looks so handsome right now. His white hair is a bit messy. I don't dare to look at his eyes, but his skin looks like it's been kissed by the sun, not so pale now. He has a black long-sleeve button-down shirt that is unbuttoned at the top. He's wearing dark jeans and has no shoes on.

"Hey, love, my eyes are up here." He laughs.

I don't acknowledge his comment, "What did you do to Mr. Daniel?"

"How many bones did he break? It's been four days... you should be healed by now, shouldn't you?"

I notice he avoided the question. "Answer my question and I'll answer yours."

He sits beside my broken leg, "He's in Hell."

"What!"

Anna jumps awake and hisses at Drake. She shifts into her red wolf and snarls at him. I put my hand on her back, mostly because I am worried she is going to step on my leg. She lays on her stomach but is still snarling at Drake, and Drake being childish, snarls back.

"Are you okay?" Jayden rushes back, eyeing Anna. "What's going on?"

Ignoring Jayden, I can't take my eyes off of Drake, and I know Jayden is confused.

"Why did you take Mr. Daniel to Hell? How can you do that? He had a white heart!"

Anna looks at me and whines as if asking if it's true.

Drake shakes his head, "No, he didn't, his heart was black."

"We are angels, we have the power to bring back anyone!" I yell. "You shouldn't have taken him!"

Jayden steps in my line of sight with Drake.

"Alex, who are you talking to? Mr. Daniel is in Hell?" His face is mixed with concern and anger.

I lean around him, "Can you please let him see you? Enough people in the school think I am a freak."

Drake gets up and walks over to Jayden and looks him up and down.

"Why should I let surfer dude see me? I'll get nothing out of it." I snarl.

Jayden looks worried. "Alex, no one is here. If you keep acting like this, they will put you in the psych ward."

Drake claps in front of Drake's face, Jayden's eyes look like they will pop out of his head. He stumbles a few steps back and lands on his butt. Anna jumps off the bed and puts her back to Jayden and snarls at Drake.

"That sounds like a great idea! How about both of you go there," Drake snickers, sitting back down on my bed, taking Anna's spot.

Jayden jumps up and storms around Anna. I have never seen him move so fast. He goes to shove Drake away from me, but he goes right through him as if Drake is a ghost. Jayden almost lands on my leg but misses and lands on the bed.

"Stupid angel, only other Lucifens can touch me in this form," Drake says mockingly.

Great. "Jayden and Anna, calm down. I will explain everything and please leave all your questions to the end."

And I did.

Jayden plops down back on his chair and Anna sits beside him. They both glare at Drake most of the time. And it sucks that I don't know everything, but I explained it the best I can. I even told him about my mother and father and what they are and what I am.

He sits in silence for a while and Drake is drawing something on my cast and humming. Anna's fur hasn't relaxed—it's still standing on end, and every time Drake moves too fast, she growls at him.

"So, he's half-human and half-Lucifen, and his father is Lucifer? And you are pretty much a full angel that is able to live on Earth? That explains a lot really." He turns his attention to Drake, "And why do you want her not to compete in the Ultram?"

Drake rolls his eyes, "Because my father wants her too. Something is going to happen, but I do not know what—he wouldn't tell me. All he told me is to make sure that the demons leave her alone so she can compete."

Jayden thrusts his hands in the air, "If your father wants it, won't it be something bad? So, why don't you want to see it? Isn't it in your blood to cause havoc?"

Drake smiles darkly, "Oh, I am causing havoc… for my father. If he doesn't get his way, he'll have a tantrum. That seems more fun than doing what he tells me to."

"What? That makes no sense. Why would you go against Lucifer?"

"Why not? Isn't that what you guys are doing every day, killing demons… or that's what you are training for. And what can my father do to me? I already live in Hell, I even grew up in it."

I shiver at the thought, just from what Eric told me about Hell. I definitely shouldn't be complaining about how I was raised.

And Mr. Daniel doesn't belong there, even if he tried to kill me.

"When are we going to get Mr. Daniel back?" I ask.

Drake raises an eyebrow. "You want him back after he almost killed you? Why would you want him back?"

I sigh. A headache is forming, "Because no one belongs down there, and Mr. Daniel was only trying to kill me because my doll was sucking him dry, it's a side effect from wearing my doll for too long."

"So, you want him out because you feel guilty?"

I don't blink. "Yes," I answer truthfully.

"Well, sorry, love, the only way a black heart can leave Hell is for him to drink Lucifer's blood to become a demon or a Lucifen." Drake shrugs, "I'm not entirely sure how it works for a half-angel."

"We can't just leave him there!" I shout.

Anna comes over and rests her head on my lap.

Jayden rests a hand on my shoulder, "He did try to kill you and it's not your fault. From what you told me, it's your parents. And his heart is black, so there is not much we can do for him."

"What are you talking about? That is literally our job to turn black hearts back to crystal."

Drake coughs, "Have you ever turned back a person's heart with barely any soul?"

I don't say anything, I don't see the point—they're both going to make sure I am not in the wrong. But, really, I am in the wrong, I must have been taking more of his soul than I realized.

I try to fight off a yawn but it is useless and my stomach is growling, "How long have I been sleeping again?" I ask.

"Almost four days," Jayden answers me.

I can't believe it's been four days and I am still this beat up. How much more damage did Mr. Daniel cause me?

Jayden snaps his fingers, "You must be hungry. I can run and grab you some food. I need to go and get Eric anyway. I promised I would once you woke up."

A small smile pulls at my lips, "That sounds great, thanks."

Jayden shoots a look at Drake, "Are you going to be okay with him here?"

Drake gasps, "How dare you think I would hurt her!" He snickers, "Don't worry, surfer boy, I won't hurt her today."

Jayden huffs, "Like I'll trust a demon."

Drake shoots him a deathly glare, "I am a Lucifen, you dumb wannabe angel. Don't you forget it."

"I'm dealing with children," I mumble to myself. "Jayden, don't worry, even in this condition, I can kick his ass and I have Anna."

She snarls in agreement.

Jayden gives me a sharp nod. "I'll be right back," he says, then walks out the door, still looking worried.

CHAPTER 21

As soon as Jayden shuts the door, I turn to Drake.

"Why didn't you take the doll?" I ask sharply. "What game are you playing at, Drake?"

He isn't looking at me but out the window, "I don't want your soul, Alex. At least not yet."

"Then what do you want?" I ask.

He looks over to me and smiles, "I want the world, Alex."

He vanishes after that.

"A bit dramatic, don't you think?" I mumble.

Anna scoffs in agreement and jumps onto the bed, and in midair, she shifts to a cat again.

I look down at what Drake drew on my cast—he wrote sorry with a rose under it. And there is also a doodle that looks like my doll with horns on it but he didn't colour in the heart, it's left white from the cast. I can't help but smile at it.

"For a Lucifen, he isn't that bad. Too bad I'm going to have to kill him one day," I whisper. *Not if you can change his heart.* I shake that thought right out of my head.

Anna hisses at me.

"You are just mad because he told you the truth."

I rest my head back down on the pillow and stare out the window while Anna gives me dirty looks. A raven flies by the window, I want to go for a fly.

I wonder if Drake has wings too

The door opens and I jolt a little.

Jayden laughs at me, "Calm down, it's just us... but I brought someone else too. He wanted to see you and, honestly, I'm too terrified to tell him no."

Jayden looks around the room to see if he can see Drake.

"He left," I answer the unasked question.

"Good," he grumbles.

Luke follows behind Eric. I still can't get over how large he is. He has to duck and turn sideways to get through the door. Picturing him and Jennifer together is funny—he can carry her on his shoulders and nothing would touch her.

"Hey, Alex, how are you feeling?" Eric asks.

"I've felt better, I definitely have never woken up in a cast before."

Eric pats the bed until he finds my broken leg, thinking he only wanted to make sure I'm actually in a cast, but he picks it up and lets it go. Even though it lands on the bed, it still hurts.

"What the hell, Eric!"

It doesn't just hurt my leg... I jerk forward, which hurts my whole body.

Anna hisses at him.

"That's what you get for running off like that."

"Jesus, couldn't you have used my other leg or something? That really hurt."

He shrugs, "I would say I'm sorry but I'm not."

Jayden is snickering in the corner, holding my food, and Luke looks confused.

"Stop that laughing and bring me my food," I grumble.

Jayden puts my food on a tray. He got me some sandwiches— one looks like a ham sandwich and the other one is peanut butter and jam. He also got me an apple and a banana and two bags of chips, a bottle of water, and grape juice.

"Are you really feeling better?" Luke asks.

His voice is so deep and thick, I can listen to it all day. I didn't know I liked that type of accent before I met him.

Around a mouth full of food, I say, "Yeah, don't like that I am still stuck in this bed. It smells funny in here, I would like to go back to my own bed."

He smiles so big that it shows his dimples.

"You're like the jolly giant, aren't you?" I don't mean to say that out loud.

His laugh bombs off the walls. "I haven't heard that one before. I like you, you've got some balls for such a tiny person."

"I'm going to take that as a compliment, thank you."

All three males chuckle.

"I'm sorry about not making it to our fight. Once I'm healed, I would really like to practice with you," I say, shoving more food in my mouth.

He waves his hand, "Don't worry, I knew you were held up. Jayden and I have been using your gym to practice anyway."

I almost choke on my banana, "You've been what?" I glare at Jayden.

He shrugs, "Well, it's not like you have been using it." He smiles at me, "Where did you come up with the idea for that anyway? And how did you get to build one for you? I want one back home. Also, how many laps can you do on your track? Luke and I made a beat."

"How many laps can you do?" I ask. "And I built it with my own money, so nothing better be broken in there."

Jayden and Luke both look surprised.

"That's impressive," Luke says.

I smile smugly, "Thank you."

"I can do about three laps, and Luke can do four and a half."

"Hmm, that's not bad."

"Oh, come on, and tell us how many you can do?" Jayden whines.

I smile, "Do you really want to know? I can do about—"

The door opens and we all turn our heads to see who it is. It's Lana with Mr. Kim hot on her heels. Mr. Kim has some huge bags under his eyes, it's making him look older than normal and his military haircut is a bit of a mess too. And his tight shirt looks a bit wrinkled as if he's been sleeping in it.

Lana looks so cheerful and happy to see everyone. Her hair is nicely spiked and her clothes look fresh.

Is my doll causing him to look like crap? Or is he normally like this?

Lana claps when she sees me, "Oh, how wonderful… you are finally awake. I was getting worried. I don't like it that I can't heal you." Her mood changes so quickly from extremely happy to worried and sad.

I smile at her, "No need to worry, thanks to Mr. Kim, I am healing quite nicely."

Her back is to Mr. Kim, so she can't see him glaring at me but my smile grows at seeing how much I piss him off.

"That's so nice of you, dear, Mr. Kim thought you would be ungrateful."

I gasp mockingly, "What? I am always grateful when someone does something against their will to help me out."

Jayden and Eric cough, trying to cover up a laugh.

Lana just smiles, pretending not to have heard that.

"Lana, can I move to my own bed now? I will be a lot more comfortable there."

"Well, I would like you to stay down here for a few more days, if that's okay? That way, I don't have to walk up those stairs to check on you."

I sink into my bed, "What if I come and see you? That way, I can get some exercise too."

I am so tempted to open the floodgates so I can absorb more of Mr. Kim and heal faster.

Lana is about to speak, "I'm sorry, Lana… but, Mr. Kim, how long have you had—" I stop myself short.

I look over to Luke, "Umm, Luke, if you don't mind, I have personal stuff I need to talk about."

Jayden picks up on my queue, "Oh, yeah, for sure. Luke, let's go and do a couple of laps and train. See you later, Alex, I do have a few more questions."

Luke waves as Jayden pretty much shoves him out the door.

"So, Mr. Kim, how long have you been wearing my doll?" I ask.

"Three days now," he grumbles.

"We should find someone else to wear it for a while." *I don't feel like sending someone else to Hell.*

"No one else wants to wear it," Lana whispers. "I offered but I am not allowed."

"What? Why?" I ask, a little shocked.

"People think you killed Mr. Daniel and they don't want anything to do with you now, even more so," Eric answers for me. "Teachers are trying to convince Father Jack to kick you out and they are even involving parents and the high church."

I know people don't like me but I didn't think they hated me this much. I start to panic, tears start to blur my vision. Just the thought of getting kicked out scares me so much. I know I've always wanted to leave and see more of the world, but this is also the only home I have ever known.

"They can't just do that! This is my home more than anyone's." My breath is coming out fast.

I must really look pathetic because Mr. Kim even looks sad for me.

Lana picks up my hand, "Honey, it's going to be okay. Father Jack wouldn't just kick you out, and you are a God's Right Hand, and it is our law that you compete and they won't go against that."

I draw my hand back from hers, "No, you don't understand… if my soul isn't by someone else, I will die, but you know who will die before me? Mr. Kim will if he doesn't trade off soon. I probably have already sucked him dry. That's why I'm taking so long to heal and that's why he looks so horrible."

She looks over to Mr. Kim and back to me.

"God's Daughter, I am slowly killing him. If he doesn't get that thing off his neck soon, his heart will turn black and try to kill me, and if he can't do that, he will die." I look at him, "I don't want anyone else to die because of me. So, just take it off, please, and give it to me."

"Alex," Eric whispers.

I shouldn't be alive anyway. I am a freak of nature; angels can't have children with each other, that's why they meet with humans.

"People want me gone, I don't want to hurt anyone anymore." *And this is why Lucifer doesn't get what he wants, too.* "So, it will work out."

I hold my hand out to Mr. Kim, "Give it to me."

He huffs, "Stupid child, do you think I'll be the one to cause you to die?"

I snarl at him, "Fine, I'll just wait until you kill me then, and should I mention that when that time comes, you are going to torture me first. You'll want to inflict so much pain on me and make me suffer because I am making you suffer right now."

I glare at him, not backing down. He looks away first, "And do you think you could live with yourself then? Do you think your heart can go back to being crystal after something like that? Giving me the doll is the best thing for all of us."

No one answers me. No one is even looking at me.

"Mr. Kim, if you don't give it back to me, I will start taking more of your soul."

He looks shocked, "You can control how much you take?"

"Most of the time, if I am really hurt. It's hard for me too, but I can. So, please, give it back."

Mr. Kim looks at Lana, "What would you like me to do?"

She looks at me, there are tears falling down her cheek, "Alex, a lot of people have died to keep you alive. Don't you think you should wait until you see what Father Jack does?"

I can't look at her. "Too many people have died for me or been really hurt. I most likely won't win the Ultram and Eric is always in pain because of me. The Angel Saviours don't want me and this whole school doesn't. I almost killed Jayden, but that one isn't totally my fault. Humans and demi-angels have died because of me. I think I have killed more demons than any other demi-angel, so I did my part."

"Alex! Stop talking like that! You know I still need you!" Eric yells at me.

I smile, "Eric, you know that's not true... once I leave, people will become your friend and Jayden will be here to help you out."

Anna hisses at me.

He slaps me. "What you are planning is suicide. Do you think God will let you go to Heaven just because you killed your fair share of demons?"

"I have a better chance of getting into Heaven now before I kill more people!" I scream back. "And I'm not going to Heaven anyway, I don't belong there."

Anna jumps on my chest.

"That's enough! No one belongs there," Lana yells. "I have decided that Mr. Kim will hold onto your doll for now and we'll look for someone else who can wear it." She stands up, "You need to see that there are more people who care about you, Alex. So, no more talking like this. We'll tell Father Jack that we are here to help you."

I still can't look at them once Lana and Mr. Kim leave. I can't even look at Eric or Anna; I can feel their anger rolling off of them. My cheek is stinging from when Eric slapped me. I look out the window again and zone out. They are allowed to be mad at me but I am not going to apologize.

I watch the sun change the sky from bright blue to navy with pink and purple clouds, to pitch black. Eric doesn't move once, besides his facial expression, his eyebrows crease together then relax. I can tell he's deep in thought and I don't want to know what he's thinking.

Eric has literally been through Hell for me. God gave him the gift to see into the future for me, and I never listen to him. It causes him pain and makes him exhausted and weak. And going into the past for me, and the memories of Hell will haunt him for the rest of his life. And kids look at him like they look at me—they are scared and disgusted with him for being friends with me.

I look at him… he is such a great friend, even if God forced us together.

"God doesn't want me gone yet, does he?" I whisper.

"No, if he did, you wouldn't be here right now. Father Jack wouldn't be trying so hard to keep you here. Jayden wouldn't be trying so hard to befriend you, I wouldn't still have visions of you in the future, living and happy."

"What makes me happy, Eric?"

He turns to me, "Life does, Alex, and the future I see of you will make you so happy and free. I don't know how you get there, but to have that future, you need to stop thinking these things."

I sigh, "I'm just tired of people getting hurt because of me. Mr. Daniel is in Hell right now. Drake took him there, Eric. He is there because of me."

He exhales, "Well, I can understand that, but it's not like Mr. Daniel didn't know what he was getting himself into when he agreed to wear your soul. You are a great person, Alex, you care about people. If this school went up in flames right now, you would be the first one charging into the blaze to save everyone and you would die trying."

I stay quiet.

"You know I am right, and a bad person would only think of themselves," I whisper.

He stands up, "Now, I have school in the morning but I will come and see you before then. I brought you some of your books; I picked the ones closest to your chair, I hope they are the ones you wanted to read." He hands me my phone too, "And, Alex, if you ever think about killing yourself again, I will go to Hell and drag you out."

I smile, "You are definitely the bravest one here, Eric."

I don't comment on the whole killing myself because, in all honesty, it's been on my mind for a long time. On the rough days, I tell myself to hold on until after the Ultram because if I don't end up God's Right Hand, this world doesn't need me to cause it more pain, but if I had something as important as protecting God's Daughter, I can do something right.

For the rest of the night, it is quiet in the first aid room. The night nurse passes out around midnight, her snores are the only thing that is making noise. Anna only moves once, she jumps from my bed to the chair that Jayden was in before. She stays there for the rest of the night.

The thought of getting kicked out of my home keeps me up. I don't want to leave like this. I want to leave with Jennifer and we can go and see the world. Do some Angel Saviours jobs when Jennifer is safe on the church's ground. Meet new people who aren't terrified of me, who know me like Eric does. That future seems to be getting further and further away.

"What's going to happen at the Ultram?" I shake my head, "I need to stop thinking like this, it's getting depressing. Mr. Daniel didn't just break me physically."

I move slowly off the bed to make no noise, there are crutches by my bed. I grab one… with my right arm broken, I can only use one. I slip my phone into the front pocket of the nightgown they put me in.

CHAPTER 22

I shuffle past the nurse as quietly as I can, she doesn't even stir. Her snores actually get louder. It still amazes me that people actually can sleep so deeply. I hobble to the door to the stairs to my room. Totally spacing that I need my keys, I still check it and, sure enough, it's locked. I move back down the stairs and look down the hallways.

"I don't want to stay in the first aid room anymore. Library? Or maybe Father Jack's couch?"

Father Jack's office is a lot closer than the library, but if it's locked, the library will be twice as far. But the privacy of Father Jack's office sounds more appealing. So, I limp my way to his office, praying for it to be unlocked.

As I walk past the classrooms, I realize I haven't been in any of the classrooms for about a week. At least everyone will have had a break from me, but all the homework I'll have to do... I'm sure Eric has done most of it, but I don't like the idea of him doing everything for me. Well, he can do my math for me no matter what.

Shouldn't really matter anyway. Even if I don't become the next G.R.H, I already have a job with the Angel Saviours. I'll still have my wings and strength... what else does an Angel Saviour need?

As I come up to Father's office, I can hear someone breathing inside. For the first time ever, I knock on his door. I can hear the rustling of papers and the chair being pushed back.

"Come in," his voice muffles.

I poke my head in, "Hey, Father, are you busy?"

He's shocked, "Alex! Since when do you knock?" He comes over to the door and helps me to the couch.

I smile at him, "Since it's way past curfew."

He looks ashamed, "I'm sorry that I didn't come and see you. Lana came and told me you were awake but I figured Eric and Jayden were with you, and by the time I looked at the clock, I figured you would be asleep." A small smile shows on his lips. "But I should have known better."

I hiccup, "Father, are you kicking me out?" I hiccup again and tears start to pour down my cheeks, "Damn, shark week must be coming soon."

Father laughs, "No, you are not going anywhere unless you want to. You are a God's Right Hand, you must compete—that is one of our top rules."

I sink into the couch, "I don't want to leave yet. Especially like that. I didn't think people were that scared of me."

He sighs, "A group of people who are scared of the same thing is never a good thing. But it's not like you made it easy for people to like you."

"I know, but they started it, they knew I was different and would start picking on me and it got worse when I started the Angel Saviours."

"And that was my fault, but you needed to get control of your gift… you were developing it fast than anyone has ever seen." Father pats me on my shoulder.

"You know, that's why I want to win the Ultram so people can finally accept me, and if I am Jennifer's G.R.H, people won't be so scared of me. Because why would God choose a beast to be her protector?"

He shrugs, "Maybe Jennifer needs a beast to look after her."

I don't know if he is saying that to make me feel better or make me realize that I am a beast and I should just accept it. But with the weight of me moving out off my shoulders, I become tired and my eyelids feel heavy.

"Is it okay if I stay here? The couch is more comfortable than those hospital beds," I ask.

He chuckles, "Almost like you are three again, I still have some work to do or will that bother you?"

"No, that's fine," I yawn, taking the knitted blanket off the back of the couch, and as soon as I lay my head down, I'm out.

The dream starts out the same, *I'm flying through the night air but there are stairs out this time. I start to fly towards them; I have a strange urge to become one of them. I reach out, and just as I'm about to touch one, the hands start to grab onto my leg and pull me down.*

I look down to see black shadows reaching out to pull me down. I fight them off but more of them show up and I can't fight them off anymore.

As we get close to the earth, it opens up and Mr. Daniel is there, with a creepy grin and blood dripping from it, and I can see his heart is as black as Drake's. I fight harder to get away but nothing is working.

Mr. Daniel jumps up and grabs onto my wings and starts to steer them. I can't keep myself up and start to fall fast, and somehow, Mr. Daniel gets on top of me. His eyes are crazy and he's laughing.

He flips me around and grabs me by the throat, and as his fist comes down to my face, I wake up.

I sit up fast—too fast, my body is still screaming at me. I groan, looking around the room. The stained window in Father's office looks beautiful in the morning sun. Father isn't in his office right now; he's probably dealing with my mess. I just sit here and stare at the angel standing over the demon, it still gives me the creeps, but right now, I'm finding something peaceful about it.

Would Mr. Daniel come back as a Lucifen?

The ticking of the clock brings my attention to it, and it's only six in the morning. I stand up slowly, feeling a little better now, but I know I need to make my way back to the first aid room before Lana gets too mad at me.

My leg isn't hurting as much. I can step on it now but I can't put my full weight on it yet. And I think my arm isn't broken anymore. It also doesn't hurt to take a deep breath or move my shoulders.

Worry washes over me—the thought that I absorbed too much from Mr. Kim. Moving as fast as I can to the first aid room now. Being in such great shape, this hobbling around is taking a toll on me. By the time I make it to the first aid room, I can feel the sweat dripping down my forehead.

I'm too busy trying to catch my breath, I don't think to listen to see how many people are in the first aid room. I open the door to see a small group of people standing by the bed I should be in right now. Mr. Kim is standing really close to Lana by the foot of the bed, Father Jack is standing by the window, and Eric is sitting on the chair that Jayden was sleeping on; Anna is sitting on Eric's lap. Even as a cat, I can tell she is upset. And Jayden is leaning against the wall with his arms crossed, looking pissed.

"Don't you think it's a little early to be so upset?" I ask.

Everyone looks at me; their faces are mixed with surprise and worry.

My body sinks, "What's wrong now?" I groan.

Father Jack comes up and wraps me up in a hug.

I'm not sure what to do, "Okay, I am definitely worried now."

He pulls back a little, and he's upset. "I'm sorry, Alex, but the church reconsidered you staying here. They think it will be safer for everyone that you stay off the grounds until the Ultram starts. Your teachers have already begun putting packages together for you to do."

Don't break down... you knew this would happen. Don't break down. Don't break down. I keep on repeating it.

My heart keeps on jumping, I need to take several deep breaths. I need to get out of here.

My mouth becomes dry and my throat becomes tight. "Well, I should start packing, how long do I have until I have to leave?" I can't look anyone in the eyes.

Father Jack sighs, "By Sunday."

My throat tightens more and it's harder to fight off the tears. *I need to get out of here.* "Well, if someone can get me some boxes, I'll meet them in my room." I turn around to leave.

"Alex, I know you want to be left alone, but let me look over your wounds and then I'll leave you alone," Lana's voice is so soft and quiet.

I just nod.

Lana ushers everyone out while I go over to the bed I was on before. I can't look at anyone, I can feel their eyes and know they want to say something to me, but I just want to be alone. Anna doesn't leave, she sits on the chair looking at me. Her green cat eyes feel like daggers. I really don't like people feeling sorry for me.

I lay down on the bed and put my left arm over my eyes and start to cry, the tears are hot and my body starts to shake. My chest feels so tight; it's hard to draw in a proper breath. I have never felt this before, I feel like I have failed. I feel like I have done everything wrong without realizing it. I have a mixture of feelings right now—shame, anger, confusion, hate... I didn't know you could actually feel your heart break.

"You're going to be just fine, Alex," Lana whispers.

Keeping my arm over my eyes. "But this is my home, I—" My voice breaks and the tears continue to spill out.

Lana doesn't say anything else to me until she's done looking me over.

"Your arm is healed, so I'll remove your cast, but your leg isn't ready to come out yet, but at this rate, you can be out of it before you—" she doesn't finish her sentence.

She removes the cast on my arm and takes off some of the bandages.

When she finishes, her phone goes off, "Hello... yeah, okay, I will." She hangs up.

"Umm, Father Jack found you a place to live. He says he'll drive you there tomorrow and said for you to just get some rest today." She lays her hand on my shoulder. "You won't be there forever, I'm sure of it. You will be back before you know it. And I'll get Jennifer to drive Eric over for you."

I want to tell her not to bother, and to just forget about me. But I know it will be a waste of breath.

I sit up on the bed. My eyes feel puffy and wet and the salt from my tears are making my arm and cheeks itchy. The tears have stopped though, but the self-pity is still here, like a black cloud hanging over me.

Lana finally lets me go after I get dressed. Eric brought down sweats and a baggy sweater for me when I ended up in here. She offers to take me up to my room but I decline, saying I just want to be alone. She whispers, "Sorry," before I leave.

I look at Anna. "I want to be alone for a while. Please stay down here."

I leave the two of them in the first aid room. Looking down the hallway, I can see Jennifer leaning against the wall, holding some books. She looks like she is deep in thought. She looks up once she hears the door of the first aid room shut.

There is pity in her eyes and I hate it. I have enough pity for myself, I don't need other people.

"Umm," she stumbles with her words, tucking some of her hair behind her ear.

"Lana is free now, sorry you had to stand out here," I walk past her.

She grabs my wrist, "I'm sorry, Alex."

I glare at her over my shoulder, "Don't be... everyone will be happy that I'm gone."

I pull my hand away from hers.

"Alex, please don't be like this."

I don't answer her. *What's the point of acknowledging me now?*

She whispers an apology again as I walk away.

My shoulders tense up. *Stop feeling sorry for me!*

The closer I get to my room, the less sad I become but anger fills my body. I don't bother with the key to the doorway to the stairs. I break the door off its hinges. Ignoring the pain in my leg, I rush up the stairs. I burst through the door to my room, my chest is heavy again and my eyes are blurry.

I let out a frustrating scream and start smashing everything. I rip my movies and books off the shelves, breaking and ripping them up. Knocking my dishes off the counter. Watching them smash on the floor and punching fists through the cupboard doors. I shove the shelf over with all the hearts on it with a large crash. The demons' hearts don't break, but they clank as they bounce and slide all over the floor, which is satisfying enough.

I'm sure someone will be coming up soon. I sit on my bed with my knees to my chest and my arms wrap around them. I'm not sure how long I just stare at my mother's heart, but no more tears spill from my eyes.

I'm so zoned out that I don't hear people coming up the stairs.

"Alex, are you okay?"

I look up to see Jayden, Eric, and Anna. I don't answer them, I just set my head back on my knees and continue to stare at the crystal heart.

"What the hell happened in here? Did you get hurt?" Jayden asks.

My knuckles throb at him asking if I was hurt.

"I'm fine," I mumble.

"Watch your step, Eric. Alex decided to redecorate and there is glass everywhere."

Jayden makes it to my bed, "Hey, it looks like you had a twister come through here. Are your hands okay?"

I stay quiet.

"We think it's bullshit what they are doing to you," Jayden says.

"Do you not want to bring anything?" Eric asks.

"Is your human parent still here, Jayden?" I ask, not taking my eyes off my mother's heart.

He sighs, "Yes, my mom is still here."

"Is she a good mom?"

"I think so. Why are you asking these questions?"

I don't answer his question. "How often do you get to go home to see her?"

"She lives close to the school, so I go to eat dinner every night."

"When that home gets taken away from you... you get thrown out saying you're not allowed to come back and no one loves you enough to keep you there... when that happens, that's when you can come to and ask me if I am okay. Until then, you can have a nice fuck off. And get out of my room, it's still mine until Sunday," I snarl at them.

"Alex, you don't have to be so harsh!" Eric yells. "We are your friends, and we are here to help you."

"Can't I just be left alone!" I yell like a little teenage girl.

Jayden exhales, "You can push all you want, Alex, but you're not going to get rid of me, but I will leave you alone for tonight. I will be back tomorrow and help you clean up."

"Stubborn asshole," I mumble.

The bell rings for class to start. Jayden leads Eric out. After they hit the last step of the stairs, the silence engulfs me. Anna doesn't move from her spot, I always forget that she is here. I become really tired from my hissy fit and crying is really exhausting.

With the sun still shining through my window, I climb under my blankets. I pat the bed for Anna to join me. She jumps up and nudges my hand. She loves her head being rubbed, and petting her is rather soothing. After a few minutes, I shut my eyes and start to drift off when I feel the air change.

"Rough day, love?" his voice is surprisingly soft and gentle.

My eyes slowly open to be looking directly into his eyes. He is so close right now, I can see myself in his eyes. My heart doesn't jump like it usually does; it actually is calm right now. Anna doesn't even hiss but she goes to the other side of me to stay away from Drake.

"You can say that again," I whisper. I am even too tired to fight with him.

"Want to tell me about it?"

"What's the point? I have no say in what happens to me. I should just live with it and this decision that was made for me I wasn't happy about, so I acted as a little kid and had a tantrum."

"What was decided for you?"

His questions are getting annoying. "I'm tired. Can I tell you later?" I close my eyes.

I feel something on my cheek; I open my eyes to see his hand moving my hair off of it and tucking it behind my ear. He keeps repeating it, running his hand from the side of my head into my hair, almost like he is petting me.

Just before I can ask him what he's doing, I pass out.

CHAPTER 23

I didn't dream as I slept. Not having that dream makes me wake in a startle. I have had that dream for years now, I'm not used to sleeping without it.

I stretch, "Ahhhh, that's a bit pathetic."

"What's pathetic?"

I jump out of my bed so fast that my foot gets tangled on my sheet and I land on my back. Anna gets scared too and takes off under the bed.

Drake bursts out laughing. "Oh, I am sorry… I thought you knew I was here."

He leans over the bed, and once he looks at me, his laughing fit continues.

"You look so funny! Haha, your hair is all crazy and your face looks so lost right now."

I start to laugh too; I get up a little more graceful this time, rubbing my butt.

Then something clicks, "Wait… have you been here the whole time?"

He stops laughing but there is still a smile on his face, "What are you going to do if I say yes?"

"Why?"

He shrugs, "I honestly have no clue why. I am sure the twins are hating me right now. I've been ignoring them. But once you fell asleep, I had full intentions to leave. But when you're not yelling at me or trying to stab me, you're kind of beautiful, so I stayed and watched you sleep."

I feel weird, "Are you the reason?"

"Am I the reason for what?"

I wave him off, "Never mind, and why are you being so creepy that you needed to watch me sleep?"

He smiles; his smile is really making me weak in the knees. The only time I feel weak in the knees is when I go too hard on leg day and it's hard for me to walk. But Drake's smile is so cheerful and full and his teeth are so white and straight.

My cheeks heat up, "Stop smiling like an idiot already."

I grab my crutch and make my way to the door. Drake rushes over and helps me through the maze of clutter on the floor.

I really made a mess. I'm a little ashamed of how I acted, such a little child.

"Where are we going?" he asks.

And on cue, my stomach grumbles, "I'm starving and I only have a few more days of free food, so I want to stock up."

He cocks his head to the side, "What do you mean?"

"I have to leave the grounds by Sunday. Father Jack is taking me to my new place tomorrow, so I will be packing for the rest of the weekend." It still hurts thinking of leaving.

He looks worried, "You shouldn't leave... this school is protecting you. Why don't they want you here anymore?"

I smile at him, "They think I killed Mr. Daniel and they don't think it's safe for me to be here around the other students."

"That's not right, you had two other people there with you... they know that you didn't do it," he says angrily.

I exhale, "I don't want to talk about it, the church makes all the rules here and I don't have a say. In all honesty, I am surprised that they didn't just cut my wings and throw me to the dogs, but they are still letting me compete in the Ultram."

"Don't you control whether you show your wings or not? Can't you just keep them hidden?" he asks, following me down the stairs.

I shake my head. "For a demi-angel to get their wings cut off, we have to go to the Pope. He can force our wings out," I shiver at the thought. "I'm not sure how he can do that, I stopped listening to the teacher because I just stared at the picture of the demi-angel getting their wings cut off."

"It's hard to believe that there is a God with that type of thing happening."

I take my arm off his shoulders once we reach the bottom of the stairs.

I shrug, "Everyone, good or bad, has punishments for breaking their laws. I heard some people choose to have their wings cut to be more human. It's really our choice if we want them or not. Some people are more in love with their wings than anything in this world, and I am one of them."

"Same, I don't think I could live without mine. But my father doesn't even de-wing someone because they go against him, he just kills them."

I laugh awkwardly. "Well, you should recommend it to him because I'd rather die than lose my wings."

He smirks, "Maybe after the Ultram. I don't want him to de-wing me for going against him."

I roll my eyes and smile at him, realizing that I am talking to him and no one else can see him as we walk down the hallway of the school. Anna is walking behind us, but she's still a cat, so even talking to a G.C like this is weird. The hallway isn't packed but there are a few students and they are all staring. And I can hear them whispering.

"Father Jack is kicking her out for killing Mr. Daniel."

"Really? Mr. Daniel was so nice and handsome."

"Who is she talking to? She's finally gone crazy."

More and more whispers. My fist balls up. Ignoring them is getting harder and harder.

"Aren't you going to do anything? They shouldn't be talking about you like this! How dare they. In Hell, if you have a greater gift than anyone, people don't talk about you like this! The fear that is flowing off them right now is amazing." He keeps taking deep breaths.

Now I have to ignore him too?

I get my phone out and put it to my ear to act like I am making a call.

"People talk about me like this all the time, their whispers are getting louder. They know that I can't make a move on them now that I am not in the church's good graces."

"Do something about it then," he snarls.

"No, they are all bark and no bite… what's the point in wasting time dealing with them? They all know my name and I know none of theirs. If they want me to take up space in their minds, they can."

Entering into the cafeteria, there is a lot more people in here. The noise and chatter stops as soon as I walk in.

"Damn, you can put fear into people just by entering the room. You remind me of your father. We are definitely going to hang out more. I wonder what you would be like in Hell."

I snarl at his comment, giving him a death glare.

"You sure know how to get a room's attention," Jayden says as he walks up to us.

Jayden looks a lot better today—his curls look taken care of and his bags are gone.

Anna goes over to him and starts to rub against his leg, and I can hear her purring from here and she shifts to her human form before she gets into trouble. She's wearing tight yoga pants with a long bright blue shirt. Her hair is in a high ponytail. G.Cs aren't allowed in the kitchen in their animal form.

"Are you feeling better? Your eyes are still red," Jayden whispers.

"I had a nap and I'm feeling better now, I'm sorry for being so harsh," I say.

"You shouldn't be sorry for anything, Alex, you don't deserve this. And people butting into your life is nothing for you to be sorry about," Drake says, putting his arm around me.

Anna growls at Drake.

Jayden glances at him and Jayden's whole body tenses up, "Why are you hanging around her?" he hisses.

I roll my eyes, shaking Drake off of me, "More like he is hanging around me. And no one else can see him, so just ignore him."

Jayden opens his mouth to say something but a few girls flock over. I think they are in the grade under us because they don't look familiar. They all have blonde hair—it's obvious that they dye it and they definitely have lip injections too.

"Barbie is calling and wants her look back," Anna mumbles.

We all snicker.

The three girls glare at me, then the middle one grabs Jayden's hand.

"Jayden, you've not finished your lunch, you don't want it to get cold, do you?"

He smiles at them, but it's that fake smile he uses. He used it when we first met each other but that wall is down now.

"I'm sorry, ladies, but I need to talk about G.R.H stuff with Alex."

They all frown, "Awe, okay. But you shouldn't hang out with her too much or you might disappear too." Before turning around, they all shoot their glares at me.

I sneer at them and they scatter like little rodents.

Drake laughs, "Man, you're childish. I can just eat them if you guys want me to get rid of them."

Both Jayden and I can't help but stare at him with disgust.

He throws up his arms, "What? I was joking."

201

"You have a sick sense of humour. And I am definitely not hungry anymore." Jayden grumbles.

"Well, I still am," I say, heading to the line.

And everyone follows me. I look back at them like they are a bit crazy. I am not sure why so many people follow me… maybe Eric and Anna, but the two new additions acting like this is weird.

I take a grilled cheese sandwich and some mushroom soup to go. Anna grabs the same thing and Jayden grabs some sandwiches and snack stuff. Drake points out how full the room is with fear because of me and how it's feeding him. We look at him with disgust again.

"Have you seen Eric?" I ask Jayden.

He nods, "He went to the library first thing this morning. I was going to bring him some lunch when I was done. I think Luke is with him too."

I raise an eyebrow, "Luke is his friend now?"

Drake nudges me, "Are you jealous that the nerd has a new friend?"

I smile, "No, quite the opposite, I don't have to worry about him once I leave."

"Don't worry about Eric. Luke and I will look after him. Probably by the time you get back, he'll have a girlfriend," Jayden laughs.

I laugh so hard that I almost spill my soup. I'm laughing because Eric is gay—he told me a few years ago. He isn't attracted to females, he'd rather listen to a male's voice than a high-pitched annoying airhead girl's. The sad part is that Eric can't be open about who he really is. He'll have to wait to be himself until he gets off the school grounds.

I am laughing at the thought of the two guys turning Eric straight. Both Drake and Jayden look at me weirdly.

I wipe a tear away. "I'm sorry, good luck with that," I say, leaving the cafeteria.

I dunk my grilled cheese into the soup and eat it as we slowly walk because I'm limping and Jayden is holding my crutch for me. I don't remember the last time I was this hungry, and this comfort food is hitting the right spot.

"So, surfer boy, why do you desire to lose the Ultram?" Drake asks out of the blue.

His question catches me off guard. I almost choke and so does Anna.

Jayden glares at me, "Why did you tell him that?"

"She didn't. I can see what you desire the most. So, I am curious about why you want to lose."

"It's none of your business, demon." Jayden snarls.

Drake barks, "Don't call me that."

"Then don't call me surfer boy and mind your own business." Jayden turns to me, "I can't believe you let him just hang around... why haven't you killed him yet?"

"I've tried," I snarl at him.

"She's tried a few times, but I can't be killed in this form. She has to find my real body, then she can kill me, but good luck with that."

They don't stop bickering with each other, not even when we are in the library. People are looking at Jayden like he is the weird one, or they think he is yelling at me.

When Eric comes to the library, he likes to sit in the far corner of it. He says that it's where it smells the most of old books and there are less people too.

I love the smell of books but the library smells more of dust and a hint of old an lady's B.O. Why do all old ladies smell the same?

We find Eric in his usual spot, sitting in a beanbag chair running his fingers over the pages. The library here has a printing machine that copies a book and prints it out in brail for him. He gives them the book he wants done and the Sisters print it off for him. They even made this corner of the library his—he has about two rows of books and more are added almost every day.

"Are you feeling better?" he asks.

I feel ashamed. "Yes, and I am sorry for how I acted this morning."

He smiles, "You have every right to freak out. I'm working on getting you to stay or at least to come back."

The rest of us sit down with him and Jayden hands Eric his food.

"Well, explain more, bat," Drake orders.

Eric frowns, "Why are you here? And why bat?"

I try not to smile at Drake's nickname for Eric. *Blind as a bat.*

Drake looks at me. I wipe the smirk off my face. I don't need him to know I think he is funny.

"Jeez, no one wants me around. You know, for right now, we are all on the same team. I want Alex to stay in the school grounds too," Drake says.

"Until you don't want her to be. I've seen you lead her to Hell, so stay away from her."

I look at Drake.

"Maybe one day, but as of right now, I do not want her in Hell," he answers truthfully.

"I think you should leave," I snarl.

He smiles, "Only if you really want me gone, love."

"Leave!" I bark.

He vanishes without another word.

"Did he just call you love?" Jayden asks.

"Yeah, I think I'd rather be called surfer boy."

Jayden grumbles. Eric hasn't found anything that could get me to stay. I can ask for sanctuary, but once I leave the church's ground, I will never be able to leave it. And there is no freedom to it. So, if something happens out there and I need to get back on Holy ground, that will be my last card I use.

I have until Easter for the Ultram to be finished, and if I win or lose, they'll let me back. If I lose, I lose all my gifts, so I'll be less threatening, and if I win, they can't separate me and Jennifer.

I get comfy in a beanbag and stare up at the ceiling.

"What do you guys normally do on days like this?" Jayden asks.

Eric stops moving his fingers, "What do you mean?"

"You know… a normal day. What do you guys do?"

"What's a normal day, guys?" I say mockingly.

"I'm not sure, I don't think we have had one," Eric goes along with me.

Jayden looks annoyed. "Come on. I am being serious."

I shrug, "We go to class, I am normally late or we both are when Eric needs to come and stitch me up. Eric gets straights As and he helps me out a lot. We hang out in here for most lunches, sometimes we hang out in my room. Anna is normally out scouting for me during the day. After school, Eric helps me with more homework, and afterwards, I work out with Anna and go on jobs when everyone is asleep."

Jayden's face sinks.

"He's disappointed, isn't he?" Eric snickers.

I laugh, "What did you think we did?"

"I don't know… thought it would be more exciting than that," Jayden mumbles.

I smile, "Well, my days are going to get a whole lot more boring now that I can't come to school."

"Well, I'm coming to live with you, so you won't be too bored," Anna says, sitting down.

I roll my eyes, "Yay, a babysitter."

"I thought it would be fun, it will be a slumber party." She looks excited.

I shiver at the thought of being so girly.

"Well, let me have your car and I will bring Eric to come and visit you."

I bark a laugh, "Get bent! No one drives my car."

Jayden continues to bag for me to let him drive it at least once. And Eric sits there with a huge smile on his face. I haven't seen him so happy in a long time. Anna keeps on listing off things we can do together to keep each other entertained, but all of them sound less entertaining than watching paint dry.

"You know, Eric, you have a good right hook... maybe we should teach you how to fight," I say, interrupting Anna and Jayden.

Eric looks down. "I'm sorry that I did that, I got really mad that you were talking like that."

Jayden straightens up, "What? You punched Alex? Man, I would love to have seen that." He looks at me, "You must have really pissed him off."

"I deserved it, but I wasn't joking, Eric. We should start training you. That way, I won't be so worried about you being here with this surfer boy."

Jayden groans, "Not you as well!"

I stick my tongue out.

"I will agree to it if you get your booklets done every day."

"Okay, I will do as much as I possibly can before you get there, and then you can help me for an hour with the questions I don't understand. And then we'll train for two."

Eric sticks out his hand and I take it.

"Can I come and train too?" a deep voice asks.

There is only one person in this school with that type of voice. I look at Luke and almost fall over.

"Umm, sure, I'm not sure if my new place is going to be big enough though, and it's mostly training for Eric," I say.

He plops down. The whole floor shakes and the book in Eric's lap falls off.

"I'm fine with that. So, they are really kicking you out?" Luke asks.

I nod, "Yup. I leave on Sunday." It still stings.

"Damn, that sucks. But after school, do you want to meet and train?"

"Umm, sure. You guys finish classes and I'll finish packing."

Luke pulls out a book from his coat and starts to read it. It has a guy and a girl on it—they are holding each other and are pretty much naked. The title is something cheesy I can only see half of it, but it looks like 'True Loves Bites'... something along those lines. For some reason, he reminds me of Ferdinand the bull—so big but really gentle. I still don't want to piss him off though.

I snicker to myself and pull my phone out and put an earbud in. I go on YouTube to get some training tips on how to train other people, and to see if there is a beginner video for blind people and training. Just to make sure there are more tricks that I can use for Eric.

We get fifty minutes for lunch, so we have a while to kill. Jayden takes the opportunity to sleep—he is so out, he is lightly snoring. Anna just plays on her phone, probably texting all her boyfriends. She told me once about all of her boyfriends, but after the third one, I quit listing. The bell rings and we all go our separate ways. The boys go back to class and Anna says she has to go and pack, so I head back to my room.

CHAPTER 24

Even though my doors are all broken, people still avoid it, but as I walk up the stairs, I can smell someone's perfume. She hasn't been up here in a long time. I step through the doorway to my room and most of my mess is already cleaned up.

"Umm," I look around… all the glass is gone and the books and movies are back on my shelves.

She didn't touch any of the black hearts though.

"You've killed a lot of demons," Jennifer says as she picks up some garbage.

"You don't have to do that, Jennifer."

She smiles at me, "I was getting bored waiting for you."

"Why are you here?" my tone is a little harsh.

She looks so small and even a little scared, "I wanted to see you before you left and to see if you need any help."

I lean against the counter, crossing my arms, "Why are you caring about me now? I don't need your help."

"I'm sorry that I haven't been your friend lately."

"Lately?" I laugh. "This is the most we have talked in three years, Jennifer."

I step closer to her, "Why are you here? I can smell the fear rolling off you. If I make you so uncomfortable, you should just leave."

She looks hurt and her eyes have some tears starting.

"I am scared of you, that's why I stopped being friends with you. Everyone is terrified of you."

I clench my fist, "But you weren't everyone... you knew me. You know I wouldn't hurt anyone, especially you—you were my best friend," I spit. "I don't know what hurt the most, you leaving me or you believing everyone and what they say about me."

She doesn't meet my gaze. "I know," she wraps her arms around her. "But with the Ultram coming up and the G.R.H starting to show up." Tears start to spill to the ground. "With men showing up and looking at me like I am a prize. And the realization that I don't really get to pick who I get to have with me for the rest of my life. You were the only one who looked at me as a friend to protect and not a prize, and I am so sorry that I took you for granted."

I freeze—I don't do well when people start crying. I don't know what to do.

"The other three G.R.Hs showed up while you were sleeping. And two are all touchy, and out of all of them, I want my friend to be my protector. Now the only person that actually cared about me is leaving." She's becoming really hard to understand with her hiccups. "And I know that I am realizing it really late, but I hope you can forgive me one day. And when you win the Ultram, Alex, I'll make it up to you, I promise."

My body relaxes, "You know, I've always had the intention of winning the Ultram. And at first, it was just to protect you because I believed that no one could do a better job, but now I want to win the Ultram to prove that I am right for the job and, hopefully, people won't be that terrified of me."

She rushes over and hugs me. She's a few inches shorter than me, so her cheek is on my chest and I get a face full of her hair that smells like vanilla. She's hugging me so tight, it's hard to breathe. My ribs are apparently still bruised and it's well past the normal hugging limit, but she's not letting go.

I probably stink, why is she still hugging me? This is so awkward.

"Umm, Jennifer, I need to start packing."

She still isn't letting go and her tears are soaking my sweater.

The air changes, "Wow, that's hot," Drake says.

I push Jennifer to arm's length. "Umm, you're really late for class, you probably should go."

She nods, wiping the tears away. "Thanks for this."

I give her an awkward smile and wave her goodbye.

"Awe, you didn't need to stop on my account. You guys should have kissed too." Drake smiles.

"Oh, shut up. Why are you back, your bodyguards let you?" I ask, picking up a box.

"So, you are really leaving?" he asks.

"Yes, it's not going to be that bad. Anna is going to live with me and Eric says he'll come and visit me and help me with my homework. And I won't have to deal with everyone staring at me all the time."

He vanishes again without a word—I look at where he was standing. I feel my heart pull a little. I don't really want to be alone right now, and even having Drake here would have been nice.

I packed for a good two hours. I have everything I want to bring with me and everything else can stay. My bed will come with me but it can wait. I still have two more nights here.

The final bell finally rings and I make my way to my gym. My body is still a little stiff but my leg feels fine. That nap this morning was really great. I put my earbuds in so I don't have to listen to people whispering about me. I don't even have the strength to keep my head up. They can think that I am beaten and weak now because I am getting kicked out.

I don't see Eric or Jayden as I walk to the gym, but as I enter my gym, there are smells I'm not familiar with. There is a small group of people in my gym.

"What the hell? Why the hell are you all in here? This is a private gym," I snarl at them.

The other students are all scared to come in here, so I never put a lock on it, but I'm thinking that I need to start to.

The group of people look over to me and Jayden comes over.

"Who are all these people?" I snarl.

Eric, Luke, Jennifer, and Mr. Kim are in the group, and eight other people are among them.

"Umm, these are the rest of the G.R.Hs and their trainers. Mr. Kim was telling them how awesome this gym was and thought it would be a great idea to show them. And once they found out you were coming, they wanted to meet you."

I growl, "This is my private gym!"

"Well, do you want to kick them out?" Jayden asks. "Because, honestly, I don't like some of the newcomers."

Yes, I want them gone.

I sigh, "No, you don't need to kick them out yet. But I should start charging people to use my gym. This place cost me a lot of money."

Jayden smiles, "That's the spirit. Well, you might as well come and meet everyone else."

Luke introduces his trainer, Krag. His trainer is just as tall as Luke but not as wide. He's bald too; I still want to touch it. He isn't dressed up like the other trainers, he is just wearing a blue tracksuit and gold and blue sneakers. His smile is taking up half of his face and his teeth are so white, it's almost blinding.

"It is really nice to finally meet you, I was really excited to see how someone so tiny would do up against Luke."

I give him a half smile, "Well, I would have loved to go a few rounds with him."

Mr. Kim points to the next man in line. "This is Travis, he's from the U.S church in New York and his trainer, Mark."

Travis looks familiar, he has blonde hair that is cut the same as all the boys have now—really short on the sides and long on top. Light brown eyes with thick lashes that make all the girls jealous. And his skin is tan. His clothes are all brand names and look expensive; he has one of those knitted sweaters with two large buttons on the side and his jeans are dark with rips in the knees. I'm not much of a shoe person, but I remember seeing the shoes he's wearing online… they are over a thousand dollars; they are white Sneakers Buscemi Men. I can tell that he is really lengthy and lean, most likely fast, but not strong.

His trainer, Mark, is well dressed too and his nose is in the air, looking down at the rest of us. His hair is black and looks like Travis's. His eyes are covered with Gucci sunglasses.

Rich douchebags.

Travis is eyeing me up and down with a smug little smile, which I want to smack off.

"You're the church's top Angel Saviour? Not much," Travis's voice even sounds stuck up.

I smile at him, "Well, remove that stick up your ass and I'll show you why I am at the top."

Besides the rich douchebags, everyone snickers.

Travis bares his teeth and takes a step forward, but his trainer puts his hand on his shoulder. Travis doesn't fight it and moves back. I just keep on smiling.

Good little puppy.

"Alex, be nice," it almost sounds like Mr. Kim is asking, not ordering me.

His kindness is a little shocking but I give him a nod.

"Next is Dunken from Finland, and his trainer, Armo."

Dunken looks nice, he's not making eye contact with me but he is sneaking glances at Eric. Dunken has brown wavy hair, and his skin is pale. He might be our age but he already has a nice beard growing. His shoulders look too big for his legs, he's really top-heavy. He has an oversized white shirt on and his jeans look like they are worn. He's put some miles in those jeans.

Armo is almost as big as Luke but he has some Thor hair going on. And a long beard with some braids and beads in it. It's totally awesome. He is wearing a nice suit though, but I have a feeling it's just to look good, it's a little wrinkled and I can tell there is a stain on his tie and he is standing a bit awkwardly.

"Wow, you're like a real Viking!" I blurt out.

Both Dunken and Armo look proud that I say that.

Armo taps Dunken.

Dunken finally looks at me but only for a second, and he starts to stumble over his words. "Umm… best of… umm… luck."

Travis snickers at him, but everyone ignores him.

"Best of luck to you too." I stick my hand out and we shake.

"And next is Sunni Li and his trainer, Li Jun. They are from the Asian church."

They both bow to me, and I feel awkward, so I bow too.

Sunni Li is really short; I am looking down at him. He has his black hair split down the middle and gelled down. He's wearing glasses that make his dark brown eyes bigger. He doesn't look happy to be here, almost annoyed that he has to talk to us. Even though I have to look down at him, I have a feeling he looks down at all of us, that he is better than all of us. He's wearing our school uniform, which looks like it's in perfect condition—not a single wrinkle in sight. He also has a book under his arm; it looks thick with numbers and symbols on the front of it.

His trainer, Li Jun, is about the same size as me. His dark hair is short, it almost looks like Mr. Kim's military style. His eyes are dark brown. And he is really well dressed; his suit is so sharp, it looks like it can cut someone. And he is standing so straight, probably to look as tall as possible. He has the same look as Sunni—he thinks he is better than all of us too.

I look back to Mr. Kim, "Now, are you going to tell me why I am meeting people in my gym?"

"Your gym? Where is your name?" Travis snickers, he sounds like a snake.

I snarl. "My name? Instead of wasting all my money on branded clothes, I spend it in here and make sure I can beat people like you."

"Alex, I asked for you to be nice," Mr. Kim grumbles.

"What? I was! I didn't break his jaw for speaking to me like that."

"Control your God's Right Hand," Mark snaps.

I smile at Mark. "Come over here and make me, asshole."

"That's enough!" Father Jack says, coming into the gym. "This is not how God's Right Hands act. Alex, you shouldn't talk to your elders like that. Show more respect."

I don't answer him.

"With everyone here, I have some things to say. Number one: no fighting unless it's in the dome, or just sparring. If you are caught fighting or stirring up trouble, you will be sent to the training dungeon for three days. Number two: this is Alex's gym and she has worked hard to build it, so respect it. Number three: I am sure that you have all heard that Alex is no longer welcome to stay on the church's ground, but once a day for three hours, she is allowed to come and train with everyone."

Father Jack looks over at me, I am not sure if I am grateful or would rather just stay away until the Ultram. I can see Eric and Jennifer looking happy with that, even Jayden and Luke look thrilled.

"We can finally spar!" Luke shouts, pulling me under his huge arm.

"And that brings me to the last thing I need to say; once a month, we will pair two of you up to fight in the dome. And that will be counted as one of the trials for the Ultram."

I look over at Travis and smile. *I can't wait to fight that prick.*

"Alex," Father Jack takes me to the side, "Mr. Kim has agreed to be your trainer, too. I know you two don't get along but he asked."

I look over to Mr. Kim and he's whispering to Jayden.

"Is he still wearing my doll?" I ask.

He nods.

"He shouldn't be wearing it and he won't let me wear it. If I am to work with him, I don't want him wearing it. I can wear it for a few days until we find something else to do," I say.

Father rubs the back of his neck, thinking about it, "On Sunday, we need to find someone. I don't want it off the school grounds but you can wear it until then."

Father calls over Mr. Kim, "Alex will wear the doll until Sunday and we'll look for someone else to wear it."

Mr. Kim looks at me. "You promise you'll give it back to me if we can't find someone?"

"No, you've had it for too long already and I don't want to get blamed for killing the God's Right Hand. Just the thought of Lana's face is enough for me to worry about killing you."

Both of them know I am right, if people are already freaking out about Mr. Daniel, what will happen if I kill a G.R.H? I would definitely be hunted down. And they would kill me. My soul isn't worth a G.R.H.

Mr. Kim hands me my doll and puts it around my neck. I can feel the draining already. The doll feels heavy around my neck and I want to take another nap. I'm still not completely healed from the fight with Mr. Daniel; I can feel it even more now.

Father Jack says he needs to speak to Mr. Kim alone for a minute, so I head over to the group of people. The trainers are talking among themselves and the other G.R.H, Jennifer, and Eric are standing together.

215

CHAPTER 25

As I walk up to them, I get dirty looks from Travis and Sunni, but everyone else is smiling at me.

"So, how many black hearts do you have?" Travis asks.

"That's none of your business, brat," I snarl.

He takes a few steps to me so he can tower over me. I hate that I have to look up to him.

"Watch your mouth, girly," he spits.

I don't hesitate as I drive my fist into his gut. He doubles over; Jayden and Luke block the view from the adults.

"Listen here, you spoiled little asshole, you are nothing in this school. I might not be around to always remind you, but I am the top Angel Saviour the church has, no matter what country you're from. I am above you, so if you disrespect me or anyone I care about, I will destroy you." I squeeze the pressure point in his shoulder. "Got it?"

He doesn't answer me at first, so I squeeze harder.

"Yeah, I got it," he gasps out.

I help him to stand up, and as childish as I am, I step on his nice white shoes.

He curls his lip at me but doesn't say anything.

I smile, "Good, now does any new G.R.H have an issue with me? Or can we work out because I have a lot of tension in my shoulders right now."

They mumble no, so I point to the changing room. There is only one because I did not on planning on sharing my gym with anyone. I'm already in my workout clothes, but I really don't feel like working out, I don't think I can work out with my leg. I really just want to go back to bed, but I also want to see what that spoilt brat can do... as well as the rest of them.

"Alex, are you sure you want to work out with us? Your leg is still bandaged up and I'm sure you're still tired," Jennifer says, coming up to me but glaring at Travis.

Travis is waiting in line with his arms around Sunni, acting so smug about something and Sunni almost looks irritated, pushing his glasses up his nose.

"Was it Travis who was being a dick to you?" I ask.

She crosses her arms, feeling uncomfortable, "Yeah, so was Sunni, but Travis is definitely worse. Luke was a little too friendly at first but has eased off a bit and Dunken hasn't said one word to me." She looks back over to the group of guys, "Out of all of them, I hope God picks you or Jayden."

Too bad he doesn't.

"Well, it's up to both of you, right? And maybe some of them will warm up to you. It's hard to believe that Mr. Kim and Lana were a good pair when they were younger."

Jennifer chuckles, "No, she didn't want him at first either, she thought he was too full of himself to be her protector and way too strict. Her human parent was way too strict on her and she didn't want to live like that for the rest of her life. But apparently, once they become a full G.R.H, they are totally different people."

I shiver at the thought of her ending up with Travis.

"See, you might get Travis and he'll change for you and make you the happiest person in the world," I say that more as a joke than anything.

But she doesn't take it as a joke, she just glares at me.

217

"Alex does have a point, Jennifer. It might work in your favour more if you have an open mind about all of this," Eric says, involving himself in the conversion.

She sighs, "Yeah, you're right, but all of this is really difficult sometimes."

"Well, it's difficult for all of us involved with this," I whisper.

The boys are taking forever to get changed; I'm not sure what they are doing. I can only stretch for so long. My body feels so stiff and heavy. I almost don't want to work out with them.

"Alex!" Mr. Kim calls me over to him.

"Lana says you are not to work out, you are still healing and need to rest."

Thank you! "What? Can I at least stay and watch my competition? I promise that I will just sit with Eric."

He narrows his brow at me, "If you stay with him, but if you so much as lift up your blades... I'll kick you out."

"I can't even sharpen them?" I ask, being more of a pain in his ass than anything.

He grunts, "Fine, you can sharpen them, but that's it. If you get hurt more, Lana is going to kick both of our butts."

As I walk over to Eric, I can feel a smile twitching at my lips. I'm trying not to smile about not working out.

Plopping down beside him, I say, "You should walk the track so you can get used to it and maybe one day we can run it together."

He doesn't look impressed, "Do I really have to start training with all these people here?"

A picture of Travis laughing at Eric and me having to kill him flashes through my mind. Probably not the best idea to kill him just yet, killing newcomers is day two stuff.

Mr. Kim gathers the boys together to start the laps. They have to run four laps and see who has the shortest time. The boys stretch their muscles out and I'm having a strange urge to join them. Even though I can see them better at this viewpoint, and see who my real completion is.

Jennifer is standing by Mr. Kim looking awkward and like she doesn't want to be here. I feel sorry for her; I don't understand why she is so uncomfortable.

"So, who do you think is going to win?" Eric asks.

I think about looking over every guy. Luke and Dunken seem to be too heavy to be fast and Jayden is the third biggest. But from experience, that's not always the case. Travis does have running legs, or he just skips leg day. And then Sunni might be the smallest guy, but that could mean he's the fastest.

"You know, for shits and giggles, I am going to say Sunni," I say. "What about you?"

"Jayden for sure. Luke might have the stamina to do a lot of laps, but Jayden is a sprinter. I came with them once to listen to them work out. And Jayden did four laps in fifteen minutes and it took Luke twenty."

With my added adjustments to the track, it's really difficult to run a mile in less than ten minutes. The first fifty meters is just running… monkey bars are next; they have a slight incline to them, by the end, you are at a height of fifteen feet. The monkey bars are only five meters and the bars themselves are about two meters long; you need to have a good swing or you won't make it. From the monkey bars, you have to drop onto the balance beam, which goes for ten meters. You are still fifteen feet in the air.

There are posts in the ground that act as steps to get down. Once you get to the ground, you run for fifty meters to a tunnel where you have to crawl for thirty meters, get up, and run for another fifty meters.

After running that, you get to climb blocks that are stacked like a tower. Each block is a meter high and a meter long. The bottom row is five blocks long. I jump it without using my hands, and once you get to the top, you need to climb down. The next thing is over and under. I set up long logs where I need to jump over and slide under but I put them all at different heights so it's not the same thing.

The last log you need to go under. As you stand up, you need to start climbing a rope ladder that's only ten feet off the ground to a small platform where you get to do the pegboard. I have a box of pegs up there, so I don't have to waste time grabbing the pegs I just used. It's only eight meters long, so not that difficult. You just jump down when you get to the end.

The last bit isn't difficult but once you come to it for the fourth time, you really don't want to do it. All you need to do to finish the lap is drag three hundred pounds to the finish line. You have to do all of this four times, just to remind you.

When I do this by myself, I just drag it once so I don't have to reset it every time I finish a lap. But looking at my track, I can see that they have changed it a little. Normally, this track is only for two people to do at a time, not five.

They add more harnesses for pulling the weight and more pegs, but that seems like that's all they have changed. So, the only time really to pass someone is during the short running stretches.

"I really wish I was in this with them," I grumble.

"Well, you'll be healed in no time and I am sure they will be doing this every day," Eric mentions.

"True, if they get practice now, they might be somewhat of a competition then."

The boys line up, for some reason, I am really excited. My heart is racing and my leg is bouncing. I can tell the trainers are anxious to see the outcome too—they aren't talking anymore but are solely focused on the race.

"Get ready… set!" Mr. Kim blows on a whistle.

The boys take off.

"Travis is taking the lead right off the bat, Sunni is right on his heels. Dunken is a few paces behind them, and Jayden and Luke are taking up the rear," I explain what's going on for Eric.

Now that I think about it, I think it's unfair to let them all race at the same time. The newcomers don't know how exhausting my track is and don't know how to pace themselves. Jayden and Luke are in the right mind because they have done this before.

Travis is so lengthy that he's doing really good on the monkey bars and can skip one. This is where Sunni falls behind; Dunken is able to pass him. Sunni needs to almost jump to reach the next bar. I didn't think of that when I picked him to win. Jayden and Luke catch up to Sunni but don't get the chance to pass him.

Travis is fast and lengthy but doesn't have a sense of balance or doesn't really like heights, but I doubt it—who's ever heard of an angel that's scared of heights? He's slowing right down now and everyone catches up to him.

With the steps going down (a bunch of logs of all different sizes), the boys are able to pass Travis. His trainer is tsking. Mark's lips are curled in a sneer.

Jeez, the race just started.

Sunni is taking the lead, and Travis is bringing up the rear, for the short run to the tunnel. Sunni makes it through the tunnel in record time, I have never seen someone move so fast. The bigger boys slow down. You can hear Travis cursing at the guys to hurry up. After the tunnel, I can tell that Jayden is picking up his pace, he's closing the gap between him and Sunni, but there is still a big gap. Sunni definitely knows where he needs to increase his speed.

With the tower coming up, it will be difficult for Sunni to move up it easily. Sunni is at the top of the tower by the time Jayden reaches it, but Jayden moves up it gracefully. Travis is hot on Jayden's heels now. Dunken is a few paces behind Travis, and Luke is keeping his same pace. Luke seems to be enjoying himself instead of wanting to win.

Jayden and Travis are able to pass Sunni during the over and under logs. Sunni has to jump up, grab onto the log, and pull himself over, and that's slowing him down a lot.

The air shifts and I can feel him sitting next to me.

"He's here, isn't he?" Eric whispers.

"Uh-huh."

"Hello, love. Why aren't you racing?"

"Still too injured," I answer. Trying to stay focused on the race is getting hard.

"Just sitting here must be hard for you. Why don't you leave? Or are you checking all the boys out? Maybe I should be jealous or maybe I should go and race too."

I look over at him but he is already at the starting line. He looks at me and gives me a thumb up with a huge smile. He turns his attention to the track and his face changes, he looks serious, and the focus in his green eyes is amazing. But he doesn't take off right away.

"What is he waiting for?" I mumble.

"What is he doing?" Eric asks.

"He's at the starting line, waiting for something."

I look to see where the other boys are. Travis and Jayden are head to head right now, dragging the three hundred pounds. Luke and Sunni are just finishing up the pegboard, and Dunken is halfway down it. Just as Jayden finishes taking off his harness (Jennifer is using her gift to put the weights back to the start to be ready to use again), he passes the finish line and Drake is jogging beside him. Jayden notices Drake and almost trips over his own feet.

"Smarten up, Jayden! Watch where you are going!" Mr. Kim yells from the sidelines.

Jayden looks pissed while Drake looks amused—now a real race is starting. Jayden isn't holding back, he's taking off. There is a dust cloud following both of them, but by Drake's face, he isn't taking this as seriously as Jayden is.

I want to yell that Drake is still a lap behind, but I remember not everyone can see him.

Eric nudges me. "What's happening?"

"Umm, Jayden and Drake are head to head right now," I whisper. "Travis and Sunni are falling behind fast and Luke is keeping the same pace by the looks of it, he might be catching up to them. And Dunken is really far behind."

"What do you think he's going to get out of his?"

I know he's talking about Drake.

"I have no clue, all he's doing right now is getting under Jayden's skin. Jayden is not happy and Drake is just toying with him," I hiss.

Once those two boys touch down from the log steps, Drake takes off. He's so fast, I have to say I'm impressed. Jayden, on the other hand, does not look so impressed—he tries picking up his pace. That's not smart of him. Drake still has a lap to do and Jayden is so far ahead that I don't see any of the other G.R.Hs catching up to him.

"Jayden, pace yourself, you still have two and a half laps!" I holler.

Surprisingly, he listens to me and slows down a little.

"Love! I thought you were on my team!" Drake calls from the top of the tower.

My jaw drops, "He's already on the tower."

Jayden isn't listening to me now, he's picking up his pace again.

CHAPTER 26

The rest of the G.R.Hs are no longer in the race, this race is just Jayden and Drake and I think the only reason Jayden is still in the race is because Drake is a lap behind. If Drake started with the rest of them, they would have been left in the dust.

I want Jayden to win now, "Come on, Jayden!"

Eric starts to cheer for him too. Jennifer looks confused—well, everyone looks confused. To them, it looks like Jayden is just racing himself at this point. The other G.R.Hs are not looking impressed. They all pick up their paces too, even Luke.

"Drake is coming up on Dunken," I whisper to Eric.

"What! Already?"

I can't believe how fast he's going through the track. I'm having doubts that I will be able to beat Drake. Jayden is on his third lap now and starting to look a little tired. Drake doesn't look like he's even broken a sweat yet and he's already halfway through his second lap, he's caught up to the other G.R.H.

Travis is losing steam too, he's no longer keeping pace with Sunni and Luke.

"Pick up the pace, Jayden!" I roar.

He does. He's at the tower now, halfway through his third lap, and Drake is passing the finish line to his second lap.

"Don't you think you are pushing him too hard?" Mr. Kim asks, coming up to me.

I raise an eyebrow, "He's not puking, so he can run harder." *You would be pushing him harder if you knew what he's running up against.*

"Mr. Kim, I am sure Jayden is appreciating that Alex is pushing him to win and to do his best," Eric says.

Mr. Kim grunts.

Even though I am cheering for Jayden to go fast and he is, it seems like Drake is moving faster too. Drake is taking the race seriously now. Jayden runs two steps and Drake runs three. Drake is slowly catching up but in the last lap, Drake is coming up behind Jayden. By the tower, they are head to head. This is making Jayden push himself harder.

"Does he push himself this hard all the time?" one of the trainers asks.

"How much I would like to say yes, but no, he doesn't. I've never seen him push so hard," Mr. Kim answers.

The rest of the G.R.Hs are about to be lapped by those two. Luke is at the front of the group and picking up his pace, Sunni is behind him, looking worn out but still pushing himself. Travis is no longer running on the sprint sections and Dunken looks like he is just walking through all of it.

Jayden and Drake are head to head for the rest of the lap, but once they get to the pulling the weight part, Jayden starts to pull ahead.

I'm screaming my head off now, I'm so into this. "Come on, Jayden! Push!"

Eric is cheering alongside me.

The sweat is dripping off of both of them, and their faces are beet red. I can see their muscles working hard; they are both starting to yell as if that will give them some extra power. As they close into the finish line, it seems like everything is moving in slow motion.

Words escape me—I can no longer cheer. I hold my breath as I watch them cross the finish line. And Drake's foot steps over the line first. Jayden collapses on all fours and pukes his guts out. I would be a little disgusted if that was the first time this floor had seen vomit, but it's definitely not.

Mr. Kim rushes to him, "Way to go. If you had been working this hard all along, you would be better than Alex."

Jayden ignores Mr. Kim and locks eyes with me. I can see that he is asking if he won. I look down and shake my head. Jayden snarls and punches the ground.

"He didn't win, did he?" Eric whispers.

"No," I answer.

"Was it close?"

I sigh, "It doesn't matter."

I look around to see if Drake is still around, and to my surprise, he is. He's off to the side with his hands on his knees, still trying to catch his breath. The sweat is just pouring off him and his legs are shaking as if they can barely hold him up. His white hair isn't so neat and tight now, all sweaty and there is a bit of fuzziness to it.

I walk over to him, "Did you cheat?" I snarl.

He straightens slightly, "No, I didn't," he rasps, wiping his forehead.

I open my mouth to ask him something else but he disappears.

"That's getting annoying," I grumble.

The other G.R.Hs cross the finish line. Luke, Sunni, and Travis, then after fifteen minutes, Dunken. Besides Luke's trainer, Krag, all the other trainers are furious with their G.R.H. The other trainers take their G.R.H and leave the gym. The other G.R.Hs look ashamed and pissed and they are all glaring at Jayden as they pass him.

The group in the gym now is a lot smaller. Mr. Kim is helping Jayden over to a bench where Jennifer is starting to heal him. Krag is praising Luke for finishing second and for passing everyone. And Eric and I are standing off to the side, watching.

Jayden skinned his knees badly in the tunnel, blood and sweat is running down his shin. His hands are in bad shape because of the monkey bars and the pegboard. And his calf muscles are torn from pushing himself so hard. You can see his muscles twitch and spasm.

"I can take him to Lana, she asked me to go and see her later today," I offer.

Mr. Kim nods and goes back to his conversation with Krag. It's amusing that Mr. Kim has to look up to him.

I put Jayden's arm over my shoulder.

"I don't need to go to her. Jennifer did a good enough job," Jayden complains and is still really pissed off.

I can tell that he wants to be alone too but I want to talk to him. Jennifer starts to come with us but I want to be alone with Jayden.

"Umm, Jennifer, would you mind cleaning up the mess? I know it's a lot to ask but I don't do well with throw-up." Just the thought of cleaning it up makes my stomach turn.

Her face turns up, but she's used to it with being in the first aid room most of the time.

"Yeah, I'll do it. Tell Lana that I will be there as soon as I am done here."

I smile and nod.

Eric says that he will stay behind and help Jennifer out.

Jayden says that he is fine, but he's putting a lot of his weight on me as we shuffle to the first aid room. It would be so much easier if I could just carry him but I don't even want to ask.

"You'll get him next time," I whisper.

Jayden groans, "What else is he great at? Is he so much more powerful than us? He didn't even look that winded."

I notice how much Drake put into the race and how much it took out of him. But I know if I say this to Jayden, he will think I'm siding with Drake.

"I'm sure he cheated somehow. He is a Lucifen after all," I say. "Can't really trust him to run a race fairly."

He grunts in agreement, "Damn demon."

I chuckle. "We look like a pair right now, two G.R.Hs limping to the first aid room."

A chuckle rumbles in his chest and he gives me a smile.

As we enter the first aid room, Lana starts yelling at us. She reminds me of how a mother should be, scolding us for hurting ourselves and always being in the first aid room. I help Jayden to an empty bed. Lana made me stay too so she can look at the cast on my leg. Even though I'm holding my doll, it does feel better, I did walk all the way over without any crutches.

Lana works on Jayden first, getting him an ice bath ready.

"Lana, I don't think I need an ice bath, please don't make me go in there," Jayden complains.

"Jayden, get in the tub or I won't heal your muscles and you won't be moving at all tomorrow," Lana threatens.

I snicker at them.

I have to help Jayden into the tub.

He's breathing like he's giving birth, "Cold. So cold," he whines.

"Come here, Alex," Lana orders me to my bed.

I limp over, trying to walk as straight as possible. I want the cast off. I lay down on the bed and she removes the cast and checks everything out.

She narrows her eyes at me, "It should be healed more than this, Alexandra. You need to try to stay off it more. So, tonight, go straight to your room and get some rest. No more running around."

I smile at her, "I was planning on it."

"Can I get out now?" Jayden asks.

Still smiling, "See ya, Jayden. Don't whine too much."

I leave the first aid room with Lana telling Jayden to man up and stop being such a big baby.

In the hallway, I can see Anna is in her cat form walking towards my room.

"Hey, Anna, done packing already?" I ask her as I catch up to her.

She takes a paw and points to her mouth.

I glare, "You know I pay for the food in my room, right? Why don't you go to the cafeteria?"

She meows and rubs against my leg.

I groan, if a G.C wants to eat in the cafeteria, they have to be in human form. On most occasions, I feed Anna. I should be used to it by now but she eats so much. Sometimes I get food from the cafeteria for both of us, but today, I don't feel like having dinner in there.

I pick her up from under her shoulders and hold her at arm's length.

"I will feed you if you get me new boots," I say, looking in her eyes.

She hisses at me and tries to scratch my arm. I let her go, laughing.

"Hey, I don't think I am asking so much, I feed you all the time... a pair of new boots would be nice."

She meows at me and continues down the hall to my room.

"It's going to be a huge pain actually living with you."

She sticks out her tongue at me.

The thought of seeing my new house tomorrow kind of worries me. Here, the only way Drake can visit me is in his spirit form. But once I leave the school grounds, he can come and visit me in his full Lucifen form. If he does that, I will have to kill him. I don't think I want to now.

I go up to my room with Anna and cook us a small meal. Canned clam chowder... I would have cooked us something else but most of the things in my fridge need to be thrown out. The clam chowder is good anyway and Anna loves it too. She devoured a bowl of it, you can see her tiny little stomach sticking out.

I put a blanket over the doorway to give me some privacy.

"I can't believe I busted another door and Father Jack hasn't said anything yet."

Anna doesn't even meow back, she's too busy cleaning herself. In the bathroom, I change into my short shorts and baggy t-shirt. I didn't do much today but I feel exhausted—it does not help that I have my doll with me.

I crawl into bed and nestle in. The sun hasn't even set yet, I don't remember the last time that the sun stayed up longer than me, but I am definitely not going to hunt tonight. Anna jumps onto my bed and starts to knead the blanket.

I poke my head over the covers, "You have your own room."

She doesn't sleep over often, it's actually really rare for her to.

I narrow my eyes. "You packed up your bed already, didn't you?"

She glares at me and turns her back to me.

I smirk. "Dummy."

I settle back into my pillow. I stare at my mother's heart until my eyes become heavy.

I had the same nightmare where Mr. Daniel is the one dragging me to Hell. I wake up when the walls of Hell close around me.

The black hearts that are still scattered over the floor sound like they are clapping again. Anna looks at me a little worried.

"They started to do that a few weeks ago. I don't really get it either," I whisper.

I look out my window and the sun hasn't even started to light up the sky yet.

Anna shifts. She's in comfy clothes—a long baggy sweater and yoga pants, and her hair is in a perfect ponytail. "Does Father know about them doing this? It's really creepy."

I sigh, "They act up when I get mad and when I have my dream." *I wonder why they don't act up when Drake is here?*

I slowly move out of bed. My body is stiff and not wanting to get out of bed yet.

I get up and start a pot of coffee. My leg feels a lot better, I think I need to have a small workout to loosen up. But I know better… if I start to work out, I won't stop until I'm hurting. It would also be nice if I had a new soul to connect with, that would definitely help a great deal.

"You should start breakfast while I have a shower," I say to Anna as I go into the bathroom.

CHAPTER 27

The hot water feels so nice and I stand under it for a long time. Today is the day that I will be seeing my new home. I really don't want to go but it might be better to give people a break from me.

I get out and dry off. I put on some skinny jeans with some holes throughout them; I need to point my toes so they don't go in them. I don't have many real bras… I wear sports bras more than anything. I pick a grey sports bra with a dark blue tank top with a baggy grey sweater. I throw my hair up in a ponytail—I decide to wear my high tops today instead of my flip-flops. We are going into town so you never know when you might need to run away.

I come out of the bathroom, feeling refreshed. And the smell of coffee fills the room, it smells so good first thing in the morning.

Anna smiles, handing me a cup of coffee, "Coffee is good enough for breakfast, right?"

I roll my eyes, smiling at her, and just grab a bowl of cereal.

"Anna, did Father Jack mention when we were going to see our new place?" I ask, putting more cream and sugar than coffee in my huge mug.

"Umm, no, he didn't. I'm sure he would like to do it first thing."

I'm not going to call Father or text him to let him know I am awake. I want to delay going to town as much as possible. I walk over to my movies and pick one out. I want to watch something that makes me feel good about my life. So, I pick supernatural, then pop down into my chair and sip on my coffee while waiting for my cereal to get soggy.

I zone out on the TV and didn't notice that the sun is starting to shine through the window.

"We should go and see Father now. Might as well get this over with," Anna says, heading toward my blank door.

I follow her with my hands deep in my sweater pockets, "I can't believe that was the last time I'll be sleeping in my room. I have been living here since I was five."

I lived with Father Jack for the first five years of my life, but the church thought it would be better if I lived up here when I turned five. I was excited and scared to live on my own. The first few nights, I didn't sleep up here—I would sneak down to Father Jack's office and sleep there. But by the time I turned six, I stopped doing that and was able to take care of myself.

You would think that a little girl of five would be scared walking through the bigger kids' hall, but it wasn't that bad. They stayed out of my way and I stayed out of theirs. And the staircase isn't far from my door, so I didn't have to walk through the older kids' hall for long.

As I follow Anna, I pull out my phone to see three missed calls, all with voicemails from Father Jack.

I groan, putting the phone up to my ear.

The first voicemail came through at seven-thirty, "You better be up by now and getting ready, that's why you're not answering your phone."

Second one at seven forty-two, "You have until eight to get down here or I'll be dragging you down."

Third one at seven-fifty, "Alex, answer your phone!"

We walk into Father Jack's office just as he begins calling me again.

He shuts his dinosaur of a phone, "Why don't you answer your phone? I was calling both of you. You two are always on it."

I look over at the clock; "It's eight right now, so we aren't late. Let's go and get this over with," I grumble.

Father sighs. "I know this isn't ideal for you, but I am sure that you will love your new place."

I answer with a grunt and lead the way to the garage.

Father Jack drives a red old Volkswagen Golf Cabriolet. I keep telling him to upgrade a little bit—a soft top in the winter isn't the greatest thing. But he says it's a classic and it still runs great and there is no reason to trade it in. His hair brushes the top of the roof too. He needs a bigger car as he can barely fit in it.

I have to crawl into the back because, out of the three of us, I am the shortest and there is less legroom in the back. My knees are still touching my chest. Father Jack does take really good care of his car though, almost as much as I take care of mine.

As soon as Father Jack starts up his car, he starts to play gospel music. Both Anna and I let out a groan; Father has had the same cassette tape in there for as long as I can remember—he never changes it. Every song on there, I am sure that Anna and I can sing in our sleep, but I am smart because, today, I remembered to bring my headphones.

To rebel a little bit, I listen to metal music and not Christian metal either. I love European metal the most, even with some of it being hardcore, I find something relaxing about it. I know, I am weird.

We don't talk the whole way into town—I enjoy being the passenger sometimes. I just get to look out the window and zone out and get lost in my mind. I don't even know what I am thinking half the time.

We drive through town and pull up to an apartment building.

"Really, an apartment? You think I wouldn't be happy with living here, why? I have never had to share walls with someone before," I sneer, glaring at the building.

The apartment building is five stories, it looks like each apartment has its own balcony, so that's cool. But besides that, the building looks old and needs some work. The siding is a dark brown colour and very unflattering.

"Don't judge a book by its cover, Alex," Father Jack says as he tosses me the keys.

On the keychain, there are more than twenty keys; they are all numbered.

Raising an eyebrow, "Why are there so many keys?"

Father grins, "The building is yours."

My jaw falls, I can't think of anything to say.

Father Jack laughs, "Your face is priceless! I knew you wouldn't do well with neighbours, so Lana and I were able to get this for you and Anna. You can do whatever you want with it, you can rent some of the rooms if you wish to make extra money, or you can leave them empty."

"What about the people who lived here before?" I ask, looking at all the empty windows.

"The person who was selling it kicked them all out a long time ago and it has been empty for about a year now. The old owner thought it would be easier to sell if no one was in them. He did renovate the whole inside." He puts a hand on my shoulder, "Let's go in and see it."

As we enter through the doors, you can smell the dust, but everything looks so new. The floors are marble-looking and the wall has this sparkly black glass on it, it's so clear, you can see your reflection in it. The trim around the room is gold, making everything appear more extravagant. The lobby has a little office on the left side, and beside the lobby is a black door, and on the top, it says one hundred to one hundred and five. On the right side are all the mailboxes for each room. In front of us is a staircase and an elevator.

"Each floor has five apartments, in each apartment, there are three rooms, a laundry room, one and a half bathrooms, a living room, and a full kitchen with a dishwasher."

We go through every room on every floor and each floor is a little different. On the first floor, the hallway to the apartments is painted a warm brown, and the lights are in the floor so nothing is hanging and the trim is a dark green. The carpet is a cream colour, which doesn't seem like a smart idea but it all works together.

The rooms on this floor enter straight into a hallway where the three rooms and bathroom are. The kitchen and living room is just one large space, nothing is separating them. The floor is all hard word, even the kitchen. Everything is painted white, it's so bright that it almost hurts my eyes.

The second floor's hallway is painted a dark red with dark brown trimming and the carpet matches the trimming. The lights down the hallway are little chandeliers.

As you walk into the apartments on this floor, the door opens up to the living room/dining room. On the left side of it is the hallway with the rooms, and to the right is the kitchen. This floor seems to be a little more separated. The walls are painted a light brown colour and the living room has an off-white colour. And the rest of the flooring is hardwood.

On the third floor, it's a lot brighter—the hallway is painted a bright blue and yellow. The lights aren't on the ceiling like the other two; the lights are on the side of the walls.

The apartments look almost the same as the second floor, but the bedrooms are on the opposite side. The paint inside is a light blue.

The fourth floor is probably the most boring out of all of them. The hallway is painted white and the trim is a bash colour. The flooring is a dark hardwood. The light fixtures are those half-dome ones that always seem to get bugs in them.

The apartments on this floor, you enter through a small hallway between the main bathroom and laundry room. As you pass those rooms, you walk into an open-concept living room and kitchen. The living room has a shelving unit that is built into the wall, which is the only thing I love about this apartment.

Two bedrooms are on one side of the living room and the master bedroom is on the side of the kitchen. I didn't like that setup at all.

The fifth floor is definitely my favourite. As soon as the elevator opens up, I know this is the floor I'm going to be staying on. The hallway is painted gold with black trim all around it, there are twice as many doors on this floor. The floor looks like the walls in the lobby— black glass with gold dust through it. The lights on the ceiling are perfect little circles; they are very interesting. They almost look like they are just floating up here. It looks like if you touch them, they might pop.

"That's odd. Sister June didn't mention that it was this colour, I thought she said that the fifth floor was more of a brown colour," Father Jack says.

I shrug my shoulders, not really caring, "Maybe you misunderstood her."

The apartments on this floor are amazing just like the hall is. You walk in and there is a large closet to the left of us, and to the right is the kitchen and the whole floor is a dark grey marble. There is an island with a stove in the middle of it. The countertops are a whiter marble and everything looks brand-new stainless steel. The walls are painted a light grey.

The wall that is separating the kitchen and the living room isn't a wall but a bookshelf like the one I have back at the school. It looks like it's made from a dark cherry wood.

The living room walls are what grab my attention first. They are painted gold with some orange mixed in, and with the light hitting it from the full-wall window, it makes it look magical. The full-wall window is amazing, too. There are sliding doors. The view on this side is nice, there are no new builds on this side, so all we see are trees and hills.

So, I am able to walk around naked and no one can see me, unless they are flying up. Then that will be awkward.

The master bedroom has its own sliding door to the balcony, so that's a plus, and the room is definitely big enough to fit all my weapons and armour. The paint in here is so me... it's a little scary. One wall is turquoise and the other one is black. It almost matches my Angel Saviour armour, it just needs to have some feathers around it. The half-bathroom seems a little bigger than the ones on the other floors.

The rest of the apartment looks the same as the other one, but the spare bathroom that is on the side with the main bathroom has a door that leads to the hallway. I think that it's a little odd but it doesn't bother me because I will not be having people in my apartment.

"By the look on your face, you like it," Father Jack chuckles a little. "But this isn't the best part. I knew you would be picking this floor, I also know that you are going to love the next part."

Anna and I look at each other—I'm excited. Father Jack leads us to the staircase and we head up to the roof.

The roof is a yard pretty much—there are grass and trees growing up here. There is a glass gazebo in the middle of it with chairs and a table. It looks amazing... all it needs up here is to be dark and some twinkling lights.

"So, yeah, the fifth floor and roof is off limits for everyone but me and the people I choose to be up here," I say. Still looking around amazed.

"Hey, I am staying on the fifth floor too!" Anna squeals.

Father Jack laughs again, "I figured as much. So, are you planning on renting the other apartments?"

"Umm, I'll think about it. Wouldn't hurt to have extra money. And if it's people who don't know me, even better."

Father nods. "Okay, well, let's get back to the school. You know your way here now so you can leave after church tomorrow."

Father leaves us up on the roof.

"So, a lot better than you thought?" Anna asks, smiling while looking around.

I smile, "So much better, I can't believe Father Jack was able to get this for me. It must be a lot more than he is telling me."

Sadness flashes in Anna's eyes, "Well, there is a lot of us who don't think it is right that they are kicking you out. A lot of us helped out."

I owe a lot then and I don't like it… or am I just not used to people doing things for me?

We leave the roof and follow Father Jack back to the car.

CHAPTER 28

Anna and I didn't sleep a wink last night—I'm only taking a few boxes of stuff, mostly movies and books, my chair, TV, and bed. With Jayden's help, I have all my stuff downstairs in the parking lot in four trips.

Jayden is mostly healed. It isn't really fair that the God's Daughter is able to heal him just fine and not me, but I am happy that he is feeling better from his run the other day. He does look a little tired still, and I can see that his muscles pull and haven't relaxed to their normal state.

His blonde hair is tamed back into a ponytail, I didn't think his hair was that long, but when I first saw it this morning, I burst out laughing at him. Anna said he looks more handsome, showing off his high cheekbones more and his sharp jawline. There are some bags under his eyes still but one more good night's rest should fix that right up.

He has some light blue wranglers on, which make his butt look yummy (girls look too), and a dark blue t-shirt with a V-neck that is a little on the small side.

First thing this morning, Jayden and Luke came up to my room to see if we needed some help. They drew straws to see who had to help Anna because, unlike me, Anna has twice as much as I do and doesn't pack light.

"What are in these?" Luke grunts, putting one of her many boxes down. He pulled the short straw and had to go and help her.

Even though Luke has some sweat starting to form on his forehead, he still has a huge smile on his face. Big friendly giant comes to mind whenever I look up at him. He's wearing dark track pants and a baggy long-sleeve shirt. I am surprised that they make clothes that are baggy for him.

Anna shrugs like it's no big deal, "Most of it is gifts from some of my admirers."

I roll my eyes, "You know you are allowed to throw some of that stuff out, right? And there is no way you can remember where each gift came from."

She takes offence to that, "I do so! Each one of them is special to me."

"Maybe if you took more time remembering your homework than what gift each boy got you, you might be more ahead in life," Father Jack says, coming up behind her.

She turns, smiling at him, "That doesn't sound nearly as fun."

Father shakes his head in disappointment, "Hurry up and get to church, we'll finish loading up the rest of your stuff after."

Eric is already in our normal seat at the back but Jennifer is sitting on the other side of him. Jennifer smiles and says good morning to all of us. I don't say anything and sit down beside Anna. Jayden and Luke push me down, causing all of us to slide down.

"Since when do we have to share this bench?" I grumble.

I don't like being too far from the exit, and as it stands, now I have two people to the right of me and three to the left.

"The better question is… since when did you get so many friends?" Anna snickers.

Church is even more boring this week, especially with no visit from Drake. It's hard to believe that it's only been a week from when Mr. Daniel tried to kill me and Drake dragged him to Hell. And now I am going to be kicked out and sent to live somewhere else. Although my apartment building is totally awesome and I still get to come back every day to practice with the rest of the G.R.Hs, and there are only two more weeks before the Ultram starts on October first.

I didn't dress up for church today, I'm just wearing my old comfy jeans where the knees have holes from wearing out, not because I bought them like that, and a black baggy t-shirt and a grey sweater. The air outside is a bit chilly and the clouds in the distance are hinting at some fresh snow soon.

I start to doze off when Mr. Daniel's face flashes through my mind. It startles me so much that everyone on the bench is looking at me.

Is his face going to be in my dreams from now on?

Church is finally over. The seven of us start loading everything up in the trailer that Father Jack rented for us. It doesn't take us long either, Father Jack and Eric go in the moving truck, and Jayden rides in my car with me. Anna and Luke get stuck driving Father Jack's car to the apartment building.

Jayden and I reach the apartment first.

"Wow, they kind of went cheap for you, hey?" Jayden says, looking at the outside of it.

I can't help but smile, "The whole building is ours, no one will be living here besides Anna and I until I decide to rent out the rest of the rooms."

Jayden's blue eyes almost pop out of his head. "What! Really? That is so awesome."

"I know, it's really hard to believe. Come on, I'll show you where I want my stuff."

I open the doors to the lobby and see Drake sitting on the steps. My heart flutters a little but I am able to frown at him. He's wearing dark jeans and a white t-shirt, and no shoes. His white hair is styled how all the guys have it nowadays—all slicked back and off to the side a little. I still have an urge to mess up his hair though. I need to stab my fingernails into the palm of my hands so I can fight the pull that's happening between us.

Is the no-shoe thing a Lucifen thing? I want to ask but don't.

He smirks at us, "Love the new place, the top floor definitely suits you."

Both Jayden and I snarl at him.

He puts up his hands, "Hey now, I come in peace... just wanting to help you move in."

"We don't need your help," Jayden answers for me.

My eyebrows twitch—that annoyed me greatly. "I don't want your help, there are enough people coming to help."

"Why don't you leave us alone, or show up in your real body so we can kill you and get this over with?" Jayden spits the words out.

Why can't I have that much hate for Drake? I know I should. What's wrong with me?

Seeing how irritated Jayden is, Drake can't help but smile, "Still sore about losing to me?"

Jayden snarls. Drake sends him an air kiss and disappears.

"He's such a prick!" Jayden yells.

I shake my head at both of them, "I'm surrounded by children," I mumble to myself.

I'm not sure if it's a good or bad thing that I'm so used to Drake showing up out of nowhere and then vanishing. I am getting more upset to see him disappear. He is what I am trained to hate and even kill but I don't know if I can do any of those things to him now.

Those thoughts put me in a horrible mood now, and I'm barely talking to Jayden as I show him my new place. His mood changes as soon as we get into the elevator—he's back to his normal cheery self, talking my ear off.

I'm picking the apartment that is closest to the staircase so I can go up to the roof easier. As soon as I open the door to my own apartment, I can hear the others showing up.

"Just put the boxes in the living room, I'll organize everything once you all leave," I mumble.

Jayden needs to use the washroom before he gets busy. I rush down to get to work. Just as I open the door to the lobby, Eric is rushing toward me. He's looking scared and worried. By how Father Jack is acting, he doesn't know what's up.

"What's wrong?" I ask, rushing Eric into the hallway of the first-floor apartments.

He's shaking. His mouth opens and closes like a fish out of water for a few seconds, "I saw Mr. Daniel... he's coming." He runs a hand through his curly hair. "He wants you, Alex. The hunger I felt rolling off of him... oh, my!" he shivers.

"The only way for him to come up here is if he drank the blood of Lucifer." I pause, "He wouldn't do that... he wouldn't be so desperate, would he? And does that make him a Lucifen? I need to ask Drake."

Eric reaches out to me, "He has! I saw him do it. I was in Hell again!" the tears drip from his eyes. "And there is something about Drake... I don't really understand it, but you'll be needing him."

"Needing him? You know what you're saying, right?"

He looks like he's in pain, "I know what I am saying and I'm saying you won't make it out alive without Drake."

I rub the back of my neck, "Do you know when this is going to happen?" I ask.

Eric snorts a laugh, "Of course not! I just get stupid glimpses of the future most of the time. Sometimes I know, but with God and his jokes, I only know that it will be soon. But that could mean tomorrow or a month from now."

"Damn it," I snarl.

"You are easier to reach if you aren't on church grounds, you should come back home. We need to tell Father Jack," Eric says, turning towards the door.

I grab his shoulder, "Wait, let me talk to Drake first. It might be easier for Mr. Daniel to reach me here, but it's also easier for Drake to reach me here too."

He looks like a scared little puppy, "Alex, I don't think we should wait."

"If I don't hear from Drake by tomorrow, we'll tell Father Jack, okay?"

He still doesn't like waiting but agrees to it.

"I'll take you up to my room so you can relax a bit, I'll bring up my chair so you can sit down. Okay?"

He nods.

How in the world am I going to find Drake? Does he even have a cell phone? Did he know this was going to happen, that sending Mr. Daniel to Hell is actually causing more problems?

I do as promised and bring up my chair first for Eric, and with Jayden's help again, all my stuff is in my room in no time. I don't feel like being around the rest of them while they help Anna with her stuff. She is moving across the hall from me. If Eric didn't say goodbye, I would not have known they left. The plan was to go and have lunch after we dropped everything off, but I told them to go without me, saying I just want to get everything settled.

With the whole building quiet, I feel like I can breathe now that I am alone. I don't look at any of my boxes in the living room or kitchen—I'm going straight to my room. I think having your room organized first is the smarter thing to do.

My bed frame is in pieces and my bed and box springs are leaning against the wall. Building my bed is not an easy thing to do alone—this would be so much easier if I had monkey feet though. Having to prop one of the rails on my foot while I hold one under my arm, the other hand is falling asleep trying to work the bolts in. One of the bolts is stripped and the Allen key isn't working properly.

"Ugh! Whoever made these things is an evil man!" I scream in frustration.

The air changes with laughter. "Is my love having problems?"

I snarl, whipping the Allen key at him. He catches it with no problem and it just makes him laugh harder.

My lips curl, "You're spending too much time with me, I know what your fake laugh is and your real one is now."

His smile widens.

My heart starts to beat faster. *Get your shit together, Alex,* I snarl at myself.

"Did you bring Mr. Daniel to Hell just so he can come back as a Lucifen to make my life more difficult?" I ask before I get distracted by him.

His smile is gone, "No, I didn't think that would happen. How did you find out before me?" he asks. "The blind bat," he answers it himself.

"It might not have happened yet, but it's going to and he's going to come for me soon," I inform him.

A growl rumbles in his chest, "I thought sending him to Hell would have been more of a punishment than taking his heart, but Lucifens have no use for black hearts."

He starts to pace my room, "I can go to Hell and try and stop it, but my father would suspect something. And where God sees everything on Earth and Heaven, my father sees everything in Hell. No one moves without him knowing. So, there is no sneaking down there."

My brows knit together, "What did he think when you put Mr. Daniel down there?"

His lips curl up into a smile, "I told him the truth, that Mr. Daniel went mad and wanted to kill you and I saw that his heart was black, so I gave Mr. Daniel to my father as a gift. I thought that my father would use him as a slave. Not turn him into a Lucifen!"

The doll feels warm against my chest as if it's reminding me that I still have it.

"Damn it! How in the Hell did we forget?" I snarl at myself.

Drake narrows his eyes at me, "What else is wrong now?"

"Nothing," I snarl at him. "I just forgot something at the school."

Without thinking, I rush to leave, grabbing my keys. As soon as the air in the hallway hits me, I can smell it—the smell of death with a mixture of fear. My heart freezes, the hair on my neck rises. My hand goes to grab my blades but they aren't there.

CHAPTER 29

Mr. Daniel is standing at the end of the hallway—or a demon that looks like him. He's smiling at us. His smile is so long, it's inhuman. His lips and teeth look like he brushes his teeth with that charcoal toothpaste and doesn't rinse it out. His teeth look like mine when I get mad. His body looks a little taller but he is also hunching over. His hands are dangling by his knees and his nails are black and long, almost halfway down his calf. His chocolate brown hair is standing up as if there is hairspray and someone took a hair dryer to it.

The only reason I know this demon standing in front of me is Mr. Daniel is because of his eyes—his dark blue eyes are the same even if they are looking wide and crazy now, with red around them. There is a dark shadow that is surrounding him. I have never seen this type of thing before.

Drake snarling snaps me out of my thoughts.

Mr. Daniel shakes his head and tsks at us, "Your father will be disappointed, you were supposed to just keep watch of her, not interact with her."

"What are you doing here, demon?" Drake snaps.

I glance at Drake; he's taller somehow. He must be a foot taller now! And his skin looks like it's made of silver and black stone. His teeth have grown—they are larger than mine and he can't shut his mouth. His eyes are all black, there is no white in them, and most of his upper face is dark red, showing how hungry he is. And his hair! His white hair is longer, I'm not sure how much longer because it's standing straight up too. It reminds me of the anime character—mental note to make fun of him later. His nails are black and long too, with the black tar dripping onto my floor, burning holes into it. His shirt looks like it has shrunk because his muscles have grown.

Mr. Daniel cocks his head to the side, "Lord Lucifer sent me to play with Alex some more and to see if I can bring Him back something." He licks his lips in a disgusting manner.

Wanting to gag, but I don't, I hide my disgust for him. Making my lip twitch into a smile.

"Want to play?" I ask. "Mr. Daniel, I hope you know I play rough and when we are done, I'll be taking your heart."

Amusement flashes in his eyes.

Drake's body is vibrating and he lets out a snarl. "Alex, his desire is not just to torture you or to have your soul."

Mr. Daniel eyes me up and down, "Yes, I would like to play, but some of my new friends want to play too."

I can feel something coming in all directions—I can't count how many are coming. It doesn't matter if I can beat one, I can beat them all. Taking a deep breath to center myself and get ready for whatever is coming. My wings jolt out of my back as if they know I'll need them. My teeth and nails grow; my nails aren't as long as either of theirs but they're better than nothing.

"Get him to the roof, I'll join you guys soon," I whisper to Drake.

He gives me a sharp nod without taking his eyes off Mr. Daniel.

I hope I can trust him with this.

It's almost like we are in sync with each other because as soon as I move to go back into my room, he moves for Mr. Daniel. I can hear the two of them snarling and growling at each other, crashing through the hallway. I don't turn to see what's happening, I rush to my bedroom to get to the box with all of my weapons in them. I can't open this box fast enough.

Just as I wrap my fingers around the hilt of a blade, a tap echoes off my window. I look over my shoulder to see not one pair of red eyes looking at me, but more than I have time to count. There are so many of them that they are blocking out the afternoon light. I can see that all of the demons are smiling at me right now, showing off their canines.

I grab a dagger along with my blade, slowly turning as I stand up, "You bastards are going to trash my new place, aren't you?"

Their muffled snickers come through the cracks. I was hoping to avoid causing damage in here, but I don't see that happening.

Tossing my dagger into the air, snatching it by the blade, doing a 360 and wiping the dagger at my sliding door. The dagger smashes through the glass and pierces one of the demons in the temple. I don't pause for the dagger to hit the glass. As soon as the dagger left my fingertips, I ran after it.

It's amazing how things move in slow motion in these situations, but I am moving so fast that none of the demons are able to set foot in my house. I burst through the demons easily, jumping into the sky and taking them up into the sky.

The sun is no longer showing itself, it's hiding behind dark clouds. A mixture of snow and rain comes in sidewise. The wind is freezing, finding its way down into my bones, and the rain and snow are not helping. The freezing rain is stinging my eyes and the wind is making it hard to keep my wings steady. At least with this weather, there aren't going to be many humans out and about.

Demons don't have angel wings or bat wings (this isn't Hollywood), but they do have ghost-like ones. Just like their shadowy selves, they have wings to match. They almost look like angel wings but there isn't an actual feather on their wings. The best I can describe them is if Peter Pan had wings and so did Peter Pan's shadow, they'd look like Peter Pan's shadow wings.

I'm not fast enough and a demon grabs onto my ankle and holds onto it. The déjà vu of my dream hits me and I panic. I start to swing stupidly and unorganized. I am able to still pull the demon and myself up with each thrust of my wings.

Hearing a roar from the top of the roof shakes me out of my frantic state. I don't know who is in pain but I hope it's Mr. Daniel. But if it's Drake, I need to get up there and fast.

The demon digs his claws in more, this pain is nothing to having Drake's blood burning away at my skin. The other demons scramble to get a hold of me but I'm not letting them. Looking up, I can see more demons coming from the sky. I have never seen so many demons all together before.

"Okay, this is enough!" I scream.

Swinging my leg up with the demon still attach to it, at this angle, I am able to slice the demon in half. His death grip on my ankle isn't letting go. I need to reach down and rip it out, but I don't have time with the other demons on my tail. I cut his arm off as close to my leg as I possibly can.

Looking all around me with demons coming in every direction, I wish they made God bombs or something so I can be done with this already. With the weight of the demon gone, I am a lot faster now, and since I need to get to the roof, I push up.

With demons falling like black rain, it's almost easier to cut them down. I don't leave without a mark though. Each one is able to reach me with their claws, scratching at my wings, back, and face. I am not healing fast enough. I can feel the blood and sweat dripping down my body and my wings are getting torn to shreds, it's getting hard to hold myself up.

I am getting drained. The doll is acting like a weight around my neck. My blade is getting heavy and so are my eyes. Being stupid, I take my eyes off the demons. I look down to see how high I am. I am well above the roof now, I can see Drake and Mr. Daniel fighting, but demons are also attacking Drake.

As I look back up, a demon clocks me right in the jaw. I know I am falling but I can't stop, my vision is becoming blurry and my hair is whipping my face. I am not in as much pain as when Mr. Daniel got a hold of my doll, but it feels like I need to sleep. I know that once I fall asleep, I won't be waking up.

"Alex!" Drake roars.

I'm not sure if Drake is screaming my name or if I'm starting to hallucinate from exhaustion.

I'm waiting for the hard impact of the roof, but something hard and soft at the same time smashes into me. I am no longer falling but going up again. I can feel something warm and strong wrapping around my torso.

Drake yells in my face, "Hey, Alex!"

Barely able to hold my head up, I mumble, "Sorry, I can't fight anymore."

"Hold on!" He sounds like he's panicking.

He's moving so fast that I am getting pushed into him. I can feel his heartbeat through his shirt and I can smell a hint of fear coming off him.

What are you so scared of? How are we moving so fast? I want to ask him these questions but my mouth isn't working.

I can hear the flapping of wings as if they are slowing down to land. The crunching of fresh snow makes my eyes open slightly. There are trees with ice hanging from them surrounding us and there is no sign of any demons. The wind and snow has stopped—it's so quiet now besides Drake's heart and fast breathing.

Looking at Drake, I can see his wings. I thought mine were beautiful but his are breathtaking. They are black... so black that there is no other highlight; like I have blue and purple but there are flecks of silver in his. The silver is making it look like there are diamonds embedded in his black wings. I want to touch it to see if the silver will flake off onto my fingertips.

"Hey, love, stay awake. Tell me what's wrong?"

The worry in his voice makes me look into his eyes, they aren't black anymore. The emerald in his eyes is so beautiful.

Not a bad last view.

I can feel my lip twitching at my thoughts, "Well, it looks like I won't be in the Ultram after all. So, you get your wish."

I start to cough and the taste of blood fills my mouth.

"You dying was not my wish. I thought you healed quickly! Why aren't you healing?"

He lays me down on the cold forest floor. The wet snow sends chills down my back. He starts removing my already shredded clothes. His large warm hands feel good on my bare skin. I'm not sure but I think a moan rumbles in my throat. His fingertips graze my upper chest and lift up the weight on my chest that was making breathing difficult.

Something cracks inside me. What spews from behind the floodgates is a gold liquid, the liquid is burning hot and it pours throughout my body.

A blood-curdling scream is ringing in the woods, sounding inhuman. Tears spill from my eyes and they are burning. I arch my back and can feel things cracking and popping. The molten gold starts to cool off as it reached my toes. My body hurts so much but not from what the demons did to me.

I'm not exhausted anymore but I feel like I have been thrown in a meat grinder. The tears are becoming itchy and annoying. I slowly lift my hand, but the hand that is coming into view isn't mine. The hand I am looking at is shimmering with gold and the fingernails are long as a small dagger.

Flinching away from it and sitting up, my body screams in protest and I start freaking out. My eyes are almost popping out of my head.

"How is this possible?" I say. Well, I think it's me… the voice sounds different somehow.

The voice that came out of me is smoother and warmer.

The only thing that is covering my chest is my sports bra, and my ripped jeans are even more ripped now but that is not the reason why I am so shocked right now. My whole body looks like it's been painted with gold dust. But I also look like I have grown taller too! My ankles are way past my jeans—they are almost capris now. I can tell that my arms are longer too.

I turn my head to see what my wings look like. They are gorgeous, my throat tightens at the sight of them. They are still black but the tips of the feathers look like they have been dipped in gold paint. There are three claws that are on the forearm part of the wing, which are gold too. I give them a few flaps, they feel stronger and longer, and the urge to go flying courses through me.

Slowly getting up, my new body is strong but a little wobbly at first, like a newborn gazelle.

"I'm surprised you're not freaking out more," his voice is soft and quiet. It's as if he's worried that if he speaks any louder, he will scare me.

I don't want to look at him, so I choose to stare at the snow instead.

He swallows hard, "You look... breathtaking, Alex." His voice is still soft.

My floodgates are still open and I can feel the doll drinking him up. He's still holding my doll.

"How are you feeling?" I whisper, still not ready to look at him.

"Umm, okay, I guess. I haven't had to fight like that in a very long time; I don't get challenged much in Hell being Lucifer's son. So, I am sore and tired."

Taking a deep breath, I turn to look at him—he's a couple of feet away, giving me some space, maybe? He still has this silver and black dusted skin. He has his wings tucked in behind him, but I can see the black and silver of them. His canines are forcing his mouth open—to normal people, that might look terrifying, but to me, it's normal. I can feel his eyes travel over my new body. His white hair is up like he put a lot of hairspray into it and backcombed the shit out of it.

A snort escapes my lips. I cover my mouth but it's too late. The snort just opens another floodgate and I can't stop laughing at him or at the situation and how crazy all of this is. Drake smiles and laughs with me.

"What is up with your hair?" I wheeze out.

"Hey! Don't make fun of my hair!" he's still laughing. "You should see yours."

"You look like an anime character." I'm laughing so hard that my stomach is hurting.

Once the laughing stops, we don't talk for a minute. A chill breeze blows through the trees, causing me to shiver. I wrap my long arms around my body and that reminds me that I'm half-naked. Drake rushes over, pulling off his t-shirt that has its own rips in it but it's better than just a sports bra.

I grab it. "Thank you," I mumble, pulling his shirt over my head.

My skin keeps catching my eye, "This is really amazing but is there a way of hiding it? Because you don't look like that all the time." I wave my hand at him.

He grins, "No, I don't."

He shifts back to his normal form... or the one I am used to. I'm standing above him now; I can't help but smirk at that.

"I just think about how humans look normally, so I take away all of the things that make me amazing. It's the same idea as hiding your wings," he offers his advice.

"Okay, I don't really ever remember the training on putting my wings away or bringing them forward. They just do what I want now," I say truthfully.

He scratches his chin, "Okay, well, I'm starting to really freeze now so we should hurry back."

My wings start to push me off the ground without me thinking about flying. "Well, I do want to try these new wings out, and I am sure the humans are still hiding indoors." I raise an eyebrow.

"What about your friends seeing you?"

I shrug my shoulders, "It's not a big deal. I have a feeling this is part of me now, so why should I hide it from them? If they don't like it, they don't need to be my friend."

I grab his arm before he starts to take off. "Before we go though, can you tell me what happened to Mr. Daniel?"

Anger floods his emerald eyes, "I wasn't able to take his heart before saving you, I am sorry."

"He's still going to haunt my dreams then."

"What do you mean haunt your dreams?" he asks.

Shaking my head, "Not your problem, so don't worry about it."

I take off for the sky before he can ask me any more questions. These wings are amazing though. They are more powerful than my other ones. Drake falls behind quickly, even though the air is freezing and making my eyes water, I don't feel like slowing down until I see my apartment building.

CHAPTER 30

Before landing on my balcony, I circle the building a few times. There are no demons anywhere, they are all gone, even the ones I was able to cut down, but now without doing the exorcism on them, they can come back. The only thing that is left as proof that they were here is my shattered sliding door and a few scratches and scuffmarks on the roof.

I don't hear anyone in the building, so they must still be out for lunch, which isn't a bad thing, I don't mind explaining my new appearance but I don't feel like explaining Mr. Daniel.

Landing without a sound on my balcony, glass is still everywhere. I need to duck my head to get through the doorway; I can't believe how tall I am now! I was expecting my place to be trashed too, but everything is where I left it. Some snow got into my room… I'm not sure what I am going to do about the window, but before I deal with that, I go to the bathroom in my room.

Taking a deep breath before looking in the mirror, I turn to face it and I chuckle because all I see is my chest, I run a hand along my arm to see if the gold will wipe off but it's still there. I crouch down and the woman in the mirror is barely recognisable. My whole face is gold like my body, but I look skinnier, my cheekbones look sharper, and so does my jawline.

My eyes look larger but a bit sunken in—they aren't black anymore, they are all gold, even the sclera. My eyelashes are still black but they are so long, it's ridiculous.

I have to go on to my knees to see my hair. I can see why Drake was laughing at it. Of course, it's gold, but it's standing on its end, like how Drake's looked but the tips of my hair is black. I touch it—it feels gross like those little troll dolls' hair.

A cold breeze hits my bare skin, reminding me that I have more important things to do besides admiring myself. I go over to my box of clothes and pull out the baggiest clothes I own and some nice thick socks.

Drake lands on the balcony just as I finish getting dressed. My clothes aren't really baggy anymore, my sweater is a little too short in the arms and if I lift my arms up, the bottom of my shirt goes to my belly button and my sweats are capris.

Drake pauses before entering, just staring at me, I can't help but stare too. He is shirtless and his jeans are torn. His bare torso is so defined, I am sure you can wash clothes with his abs.

I smile, looking away from him, "What took you so long?" I ask, bugging him.

He huffs, "I did a couple of laps around the building to make sure no one was around."

"What, you don't think I did that too?" I ask the question a little more harshly than I need to.

"Doesn't hurt," he answers calmly.

I pick out some clothes that I'm sure will fit him—an old pair of basketball shorts and a large shirt. I toss them to him and he stumbles back with a grunt.

My hand flies to my mouth. "Sorry," I mumble.

He wiggles his eyebrows at me, "I'll forgive you if you change me."

I snarl at him, showing off my canines. He just smiles and goes into my bathroom.

Shaking my head, I start to tinker with my window. Surprisingly, I find some tape and garbage bags, dumping out a few of my boxes so I can use them. I slide the garbage bags over the pieces of cardboard and start to tape them to the window.

Drake steps out of the bathroom with just the shorts that are sitting a little too low and the t-shirt is in his hand by the look of his skin I would say he should have a shower.

"Why don't you go back home?" I ask. "I'm surprised that you didn't disappear while you were in the bathroom."

"In my real body, it's harder to vanish, so I don't do it often. And why would I run away just like that?" he asks.

Giving him a sidewise glance, "Really, you still have my soul, don't you? I can still feel it on you."

He's looking confused, "I remember touching it in the woods, but when I did, there was a bright flash... it was so bright that I couldn't see anything for a minute. You started to scream so loudly, and watching your body transform into your angelic body, I totally forgot about your soul to be honest."

Standing up and towing over him, I say, "You're lying. I can feel it on you. When you touched her, you forced my floodgates open and I'm not able to close them."

He's standing his ground, "What do you mean floodgates? You can search me if you want."

Drake drops his shorts, showing everything.

Covering my eyes, "Oh my God! Put your shorts back on!" I order, shoving his shoulder.

As my hand touches his shoulder, pain rushes up my arm to every part of my body. Molten gold isn't what I'm seeing this time, it's like a cloud of ash cooling everything. I bite my toughing so I won't scream, but the pain isn't as bad as the gold. The world became smaller too and I'm starting to swim in my clothes.

When the pain eases, my normal skin-coloured hand is still clutching Drake's shoulder. Black blood trickles down his chest. I detach myself from him—his blood isn't burning me this time. We are both kneeling on the floor looking at each other; I know I am normal now.

Narrowing my eyes at him, I say, "What the hell is going on, Drake? What did you do?"

He's matching my glare, "Me? How is this my fault? It's your soul."

"Well, where is it?"

As I ask the question, the doll appears on his arm... not in 4D, but as a tattoo on his arm.

What a horrible tattoo.

"Oh, this can't be good," Drake growls.

He places his hand on the doll, and as soon as he touches it, wind picks up in my room and a light is glowing from one of my boxes—the box that I put my mother's heart in. Rushing over and ripping the box open, I carefully pick up the crystal heart and the light shining from it is so bright, I can't look at it directly. The heart starts to vibrate a little and feels warm in my hands.

"Look at you," a woman's voice gasps.

I look around to see where it came from. "Did you hear that, Drake?"

"Yes," he says quietly.

"My little angel is all grown up now," the heart says.

My throat tightens. "Mom?" That word is difficult to get out.

A musical chuckle comes out of the heart, "Yes. I see that my binding is taking effect now."

Drake growls. "What binding?" he spits the question out.

He's standing in front of me... I didn't even notice him move.

A red light flashes in the heart, "Do not talk to me like that, Lucifen! I knew your father would have scammed Zacharias, Alex's father. So, I came up with my own to protect my precious angel."

"Umm, care to elaborate?" I ask.

"I wasn't really sure what Lucifer had planned for wanting you, but I knew he had a son, so if and when Lucifer's son touched that doll, he would become bound to it and become the protector of your soul. If something happens to you, Alex, in any way, something will happen to Lucifer's son."

"Mom, did you know that without my soul in me, I will need to absorb others and they will go crazy and die?"

"Yes, I did, but without your soul, Lucifer had no use for your shell." Her voice has so much sadness in it.

"I figured the church would protect your soul while you were free to leave the school grounds. I thought you would have more freedom. And now that Lucifer's son has your soul, you will never have to worry about that again," she explains.

"What do you mean?" Drake demands.

"Your heart is already black, Lucifen, therefore, she can't make it any more black than it is," she says angrily at him.

"I can't stay any longer, Alex, but I want to let you know that I can always hear you. And I am so sorry for everything—I thought I could change him. I thought I did, please forgive me. I love you and the woman you have become." As she speaks, the light and warmth starts to fade.

I know calling for her to come back will be useless, "I do forgive you," I whisper.

"What the hell! This makes no sense! You were supposed to be bonded to me, not the other way around!"

Glaring at him, "Do you think I want to be bonded to you at all?"

"Your dear mother is missing a small detail. Lucifer will kill me just to get what he wants! And if that kills you in the process, he'll be pleased that the church can't use you either." He shoves his hands through his hair.

"Just don't tell him," I say.

He barks out a laugh, "Don't you remember that as soon as I go to Hell, my father will know everything! He's like God but just for Hell. I will never be able to go back home!"

"Well, what do you want me to do about it?" I scream at him. I grab one of my daggers, "Here, let's cut off your arm, maybe that will work… or better yet," I point the dagger at my soul on his arm, "Kill me, then this whole mess will be over!"

His eyes soften a little, "I don't want to kill you, but I don't want to die either, and I definitely don't want to lose this arm." The corner of his lip twitches.

"Well, at least I don't have to worry about killing anyone anymore. And I have an endless supply for my soul but how am I going to explain this to everyone? I can't hide it from them and the church will want to get involved."

He groans and flops onto the floor, "Well, you can tell them but I will not get involved in the church. They won't be able to contain me anyway… the twins will come for me and then they will be in trouble. And once the church knows, I am sure my father will know too."

"I can't keep it a secret. Father Jack will be wanting to know where my soul is."

He sighs, "Can't you tell him your protector has it and you are forbidden to tell?"

I flip my bed down so I can sit on it. I'm exhausted and don't feel like finishing setting up my bed today.

"I'm sure that won't be good enough, but I will think of something and won't say anything until he asks."

I can hear him rummaging through my bags. As I pick up my head to see what he's doing, a pillow comes flying at my head.

"You're great at labelling stuff," he says, putting a blanket over me.

I prop myself on my elbows, "I need to fix my window before I can go to bed anyway."

"I'll do it."

I throw off the blanket and go to help him; all we need to do is tape up the window. Once we do that, I can still feel the cold air coming through the cracks.

"Great time to be breaking windows," Drake snickers.

I shrug, "I like sleeping in a cold room anyway, so it doesn't bother me."

"Well, I'm like a personal heater, so I can help keep you warm."

Realizing how close I am to him, I inch away, but I am sure he can still hear my heart beating.

"What gives you the idea that you are staying here?"

He smiles and his eyes spark to life, "I'm technically your soul, and I think as your soul, I should stay close to you."

He crawls into my bed and gets under the covers.

"Umm, no... just no." I rush over to my bed and grab his ankle and pull him out of it. "You will not be sleeping here."

He narrows his eyes, "You have two choices, Alex, either let me sleep here with you or I will go for some food."

I snarl and let go of his ankle as if it's disgusting. I keep forgetting that he is still a Lucifen and needs to eat humans.

Mother, what were you thinking!

"How often do you need to hunt?" I spit the question at him.

He shrugs, "It depends... sometimes I can go without it for weeks, and other times I need to eat every other day."

I can't help it but I snarl again, "So, no matter what, you'll be hunting, so why should I let you stay here?"

He stands up, "If you let me stay here without complaining, I will let you pick the human." He sticks out his hand.

"If you want to stay here that bad, I get to pick them and I'll only pick humans with black hearts, but Jennifer gets to try and change it first, and if they stay black, you may have them. And the twins have to do the same... and they have to stay in a different apartment." I stick out my hand.

He shakes his head, "The twins won't go for that, I can't control them like that. This deal is only for me. But I will stay in your spare room."

"Same floor apartment. You aren't staying in mine," I snarl.

"Okay, see you later... I'll go hunting." He waves goodbye and heads for the window.

Can I kill him? Would that kill me too?

"Okay!" I scream at his back. "Fine, we have a deal!"

I stick my hand out again. He turns around with a huge smile on his face and takes my hand.

"We have a deal, Alex." He pulls me into him so fast, I don't have enough time to stop it. "Now, you better pick a human quickly because I am quite hungry," he says, licking his lips while looking at mine.

I can see the hunger in his eyes, but I have a feeling that the hunger isn't just for human flesh, but for me as well.

My lips curl and snarl as a warning to him and myself.

What have I done?

www.ingramcontent.com/pod-product-compliance
Lightning Source LLC
Chambersburg PA
CBHW060413180626
46817CB00007B/2561